The Zurich Numbers

The Zurich Numbers

Bill Granger

CROWN PUBLISHERS, INC.
NEW YORK

Published by Crown Publishers, Inc.,
One Park Avenue, New York, New York 10016
and simultaneously in Canada
by General Publishing Company Limited
Manufactured in the United States of America
Library of Congress Cataloging in Publication Data
Granger, Bill.
The Zurich numbers.
I. Title.
PS3557.R256Z45   1984   813'.54   84-7785
ISBN 0-517-55446-1
Book design by Jane Treuhaft
10 9 8 7 6 5 4 3 2 1
First Edition

This is for Aaron Priest.

Investigations conducted over the past decade by the Federal Bureau of Investigation, the principal domestic counterespionage agency of the United States, show that immigrants, illegal aliens, resident aliens, and visitors to this country from Eastern Bloc nations have been used as intelligence agents.

It is a working assumption of U.S. intelligence forces, including the Central Intelligence Agency, that all members of the Soviet Union's press contingent in the United States are intelligence agents to a greater or lesser extent and that they are controlled by the Soviet Committee for State Security (the KGB).

Since the assassination attempt against Pope John Paul II, the public has become aware of what the intelligence agencies have known for some time—that the Bulgarian Secret Service is an active *agence provocateur* of the Soviet Union.

The National Security Agency, headquartered at Fort George G. Meade in Maryland, has become one of the most powerful intelligence forces in the world, rivaling both its sister agency, the CIA, and the true Opposition, the KGB and, to a lesser extent, the military-dominated GRU.

Though there are some direct flights of LOT, the Polish airline, between Warsaw and the United States, many emigrants from Poland find their way to the United States through the "window" of Vienna, the easternmost free city in continental Europe.

The largest Polish-derived population outside of Warsaw is concentrated in Chicago.

Finally, the recruitment of journalists as espionage agents has been routine practice by all governments for more than 140 years.

Shall we submit?
Are we but slaves?

➤   ➤   ➤

I am the slave of duty.

—W. S. GILBERT

The
Zurich
Numbers

1

Chicago

"I don't think we need a pistol," Mikhail Korsoff said, getting out of the white Oldsmobile on the driver's side and automatically pushing down the lock as he closed the door. "Lock it. This is a bad neighborhood."

The Bulgarian pushed the lock and closed his door. He shrugged as though agreeing with Korsoff, straightening the lines of his gray coat around his large body. His shirt collar was too tight; his face looked pained, bloated.

They crossed the street, hands in overcoat pockets, shoulders hunched against the damp breeze. A late morning sky was hangover gray; the light was pinched and mean.

They climbed the stone stairs past the broken stone lion and knocked on the door. They didn't talk while they waited. Korsoff was going to talk when the door opened. The Bulgarian's English was limited.

The door opened on a chain. They saw part of a face in shadows. Korsoff was surprised and showed it; he hadn't expected a black man.

"What you want?"

"My name is George Klemper," Korsoff said. "You have a woman who works here. Name of . . ." He consulted a sheet of paper. "Name of Mary Krakowski."

"I don't know what you talkin' 'bout."

Korsoff frowned. "You better know."

The black face did not change, only the eyes darkened.

"I'm with Immigration and Naturalization."

"That right?"

"You got a Mary Krakowski work here?"

"Wait a minute." The door closed. They stood in the damp cold, on the stone steps, staring at each other. The Bulgarian wrapped his fingers around the .22 MIK pistol in his pocket.

The door opened on the chain again. A white face on an old woman appeared.

"What do you want?"

"Klemper," Korsoff began. He produced a badge and identity card and spoke more words.

"What do you want?" the old woman said.

"Ask you about one of your employees."

"Is something wrong?"

"This is routine," Korsoff said. He tried a smile and didn't get it right. "Can we ask you a few questions?"

"Let me see that identification again," the old woman said. She stared at the card for a moment and decided. She closed the door, removed the chain, and opened it. She wore a blue print robe and slippers. Her hair was sparse and gray, her eyes steel.

She led them into an old-fashioned room to the right of the door. The room was dark and had the look of a museum about it. The two men stood and she waved them with a single gesture to chairs. They sat down. Both removed their felt hats and held them by the brim. The Bulgarian still had not spoken. Korsoff did not understand why he was necessary for the trip, but control in New York had said the Bulgarian was to be included on everything.

"What's this about?"

"You're Melvina Devereaux?"

"And what's this about?"

"To ask about the woman you employ."

"She's perfectly legal—"

"A green card. Did she have a green card?"

"A green card?"

"A work permit. A green card. Did she have one?"

"Let me think." Her forefinger tapped her jawline.

"Did she show it to you?"

"Yes," Melvina lied. She never thought to ask for it.

Korsoff hadn't expected that. The lie made him nervous. "All right. Tell me something. Do you live here alone?"

"Why is that germane?"

Korsoff blinked, scanned the word "germane" in memory, could not find it. He said, "Pardon?" The accent was light but lingering.

"I said why do you want to know that?"

"As you know, your son works for the government. It is always important when you, when someone like you, employs an alien, even with working papers, from a foreign government. A communist government."

"I don't know what you're talking about."

"I mean your son, Mrs. Devereaux."

Her eyes narrowed suddenly, shifting from one face to the other. "I have never married. I have no son."

The two men glanced at each other, then at the woman.

"That is not our information," Korsoff said at last.

The Bulgarian stuck his right hand back in his coat pocket. He felt the cold pistol. He wrapped his fingers around it. He looked around the room but the black man was not visible.

"The government is interested in what, exactly? In me? In Mary Krakowski? Or in what, exactly?"

"In Mr. Devereaux. And you, madam. You are of the same family."

"I don't know what you're talking about," the old woman said, her eyes reflecting her words. "Would you mind showing me your identification again?"

"Where is the black?" the Bulgarian said in an accent so thick that pretense was dropped. He stood up.

"Oh," she said, smiling. She rose as well from a red

3

chair. "In the back, I think. I asked him to call the police."

"Police?" Korsoff began. His eyes widened. Was the old woman insane?

"Polizei," the Bulgarian repeated. He decided to kill this old woman. He removed the pistol from his pocket. Korsoff saw the gesture in time. He stood in front of the Bulgarian and stared at him. The Bulgarian, giving ground, took a step back and then, reluctantly, put the pistol away. Did the old woman see it? But Korsoff could only think to get out now.

"Madam," he began, offering apologies. Have to run along. Another time. But there was nothing to say.

They opened the door. She was behind them. Down the stone steps, past the broken lion. Korsoff almost ran across the street. Police. He unlocked his car door, slid in, reached across for the button. The Bulgarian got in, slammed the door even as Korsoff pulled away.

"She knew," the Bulgarian said.

"Why did you take out your pistol? I told you—"

"She knew," the Bulgarian said. "Do you think he has contacted her?"

"I don't know. But she knows now, if she didn't know. She knows."

"I should have killed her."

"And the black? And then who else? This won't solve your problem," Korsoff said. "You have to find him first."

"We will," the Bulgarian said. "He can't be invisible forever. We will."

2

New York City

When Devereaux's mail arrived at the post office in Front Royal, Virginia, it was restamped and sent on to his new address, P.O. Box 971, Fort Meade, Maryland.

Fort George G. Meade, an Army post between Baltimore and Washington off the Beltway, also houses the central offices of the National Security Agency. The NSA, because it ostensibly serves the various intelligence services even when it dominates them, also acts as postmaster in cases such as Devereaux's.

The mail was rerouted in large envelopes to an address on Fourteenth Street in Washington that houses the offices of R Section, an intelligence agency listed officially in the annual federal budget as "the agricultural estimate and crop information service" of the Department of Agriculture. The description of R Section in the budget has elements of truth. Devereaux's mail was removed from the envelope provided by NSA, placed in a new (though identical) envelope provided by R Section, and sent to a final destination on West 88th Street in New York City.

Because of all the routine security concerning the mail, it was nearly too late when Devereaux received the letter.

His mail was stuffed in the battered brass box in the marble lobby of the eight-story building where he had lived for nearly four months.

The lobby was cold, even though heat banged up the radiator pipes near the elevator. The floor was a checkerboard of broken black-and-white tile. On the marble walls were two spray-painted legends: Fuck Puerto Rican Porkies and Cobra

Black A. Stones. The graffiti had been scrubbed but the pale outline of the words was clearly visible.

Late in a fall afternoon he opened the outer door and held it ajar with his foot for light while he unlocked his mailbox. He grabbed the two manila envelopes, closed the box, climbed three steps to the security inner door, turned the key, and entered the foyer, crossing the checkerboard tiles to the ancient Otis elevator to the left of the entrance.

The elevator's steel door had been vandalized and did not shut properly. Graffiti was scratched on the inside of the door, including a crude representation of what someone named Penny liked to do with men.

Devereaux, the trained observer, had taught himself in the last months to see none of this. His life had become internal, as though he were in solitary, in darkness, existing by not resisting the horror of the endless dark. He was a child again on Chicago streets, immune to ugliness because he was part of it, adopting a sort of dream that became more real than real stones, bricks, smells, and shouts in the world that pressed him in.

On the fourth floor, he pushed against another steel door and trudged down the darkened corridor. The lights were broken or removed or the electricity was out; it was always like this, always dark, and no one had complained for years.

He fumbled the key into the top lock of the steel door to his apartment. Then he opened the bottom lock. The door swung open on a narrow foyer that led into a narrow dining room that opened onto a wider living room. The walls had once been white and now were gray. Radiators hissed heat into the rooms. The light switches on the walls bore the smudge marks of previous occupants. Who were they? What had they been and what had they been changed into? How many had been processed through this place? Devereaux always thought of the questions as he added his smudges to the others and flicked on all the lights.

There was a bedroom that he rarely used. He would sit in the living room and doze in front of the television set. Usually, he slept on the couch. The living room was littered with books, some still in bookstore bags, some opened with broken spines to keep the place, some waiting in patient piles on the plastic coffee table. Sometimes he read all day and all night until the next dawn when he could finally sleep. He felt like the child he had been in this place: a prisoner who had escaped quietly, not resisting the world, merely waiting for his mind to replace the world by reading of other worlds. Oddly, he felt most content rereading the books that had first given him escape. On a gray afternoon, a Sunday, he had begun again David Copperfield:

I am born.

He smiled now, coldly, acknowledging his momentary self-pity. He put the manila envelopes down on the plastic coffee table next to the lumpy couch with the orange slipcover. He went into the kitchen and opened an elderly General Electric refrigerator. It contained six eggs, two cartons of Tropicana Premium Pack orange juice, an unopened package of German black bread, a jar of Vita herring in wine sauce, and a liter bottle of Finlandia vodka. He stared for a moment and then reached for the vodka. He touched the bottle, almost removed it, and then slid it back on the shelf. He took out a carton of orange juice, poured some into a glass, and replaced the carton in the refrigerator. He took the glass into the living room and put it down on the coffee table. He took off his raincoat and threw it on a chair. He sat down and contemplated the manila envelopes and the books waiting for him. He tried not to resist in his mind; it was evening and another night in the cell, waiting for another morning, waiting for another night, enduring because he did not resist.

It had been a year since Helsinki. They had wrapped him in security so tight that there was no breathing room, no room to stretch his arms, no light to see beyond the limited horizon of four walls. R Section called it "reprocessing." He understood the procedure; he accepted it simply because nothing else could be done. No. He had accepted it because of her.

The Opposition had marked him and Rita Macklin for elimina-

7

tion after the Helsinki matter. *They had made themselves easy targets. Both thought they could escape their old lives and pool a new one together. How naïve. If he had not fallen in love with her, he would not have been so stupid. That's how he explained it to himself now. When they left their old lives, they left their old protections. They went to live together in the house on the mountain outside Front Royal. The idyll ended one afternoon in winter when two Bulgarian assassins stalked them up the trail and Devereaux killed them from ambush. He and Rita had buried the assassins and destroyed their car and fled back to their old lives, but they had only stayed their executions for a little while. They could never survive alone, even alone together. Reluctantly, docilely, like slaves locking their own manacles to the oars, they returned to what they had been. Only now they were apart. It had to be so.*

He picked up the glass of orange juice and sipped it. Hanley had contacted him that morning, in the lounge of LaGuardia Airport. Hanley was his control, ostensibly in charge of "reprocessing," though all the nitty-gritty was handled by a section at NSA. Hanley had been on his way through New York; the meeting place was for his convenience. It didn't matter; Devereaux only had time to kill.

"They tell me two months," Hanley had said cheerfully. "Not too much longer."

"No probes by the Opposition?"

"No," Hanley had said. "You're safely dead and buried."

"And Rita?"

"Nothing. No contact. I handled it myself."

"You're certain."

"It's been nearly a year."

"Is she all right?"

Hanley had glanced at him curiously. "I just said so."

Devereaux had said, "I meant . . ." He paused.

"I know. That, I don't know. She's safe. No probes. No leaks. They've given up on both of you. As long as you're back, you're safe."

"It's good to be back," Devereaux had said.

"Sarcasm," Hanley had identified.

He frowned to think of the meeting with Hanley. Not because it had gone badly but because Devereaux had been so eager to talk to his control. The solitary was getting to him; he hated that weakness in him. He picked up the glass of orange juice and took another swallow.

Devereaux was in early middle age and felt it sometimes when he awoke on the lumpy couch and felt his joints make noises as he stretched and felt the muscles in his broad back bunch up before he took a morning shower to loosen them. His body did not show signs of failing; aches and pains had no counterparts in a sagging paunch or softened chest. Only his face seemed older than his body, crosshatched with lines on his forehead and at the corners of his eyes. His gray, arctic eyes were a match for his gray hair thatched with tundra brown; but these manifestations of age were merely a bad guess by some chromosome—his hair had turned gray at twenty-two. His shoulders were deceptively large, his hands were large and calm; his fingers were flat, his fingernails broad. Everything about his appearance was deceptive: he would seem small in one light, then emerge larger than he was in another. He rarely spoke, especially now, in a neighborhood of strangers. He had lived among strangers all his life.

He tore open the first manila envelope.

Inside were three pieces of mail. One envelope was addressed in an elegant hand, blue ink on blue paper. He knew that writing. It chilled him.

He held the envelope a moment and then got up and went into the kitchen and dropped it, unopened, into the garbage can next to the sink. He opened the refrigerator and took out the bottle of vodka and brought it into the living room. He sat down on the couch, opened the vodka, and splashed some into the remains of the orange juice.

The second envelope was from American Express Company. He opened it and glanced at his bill—no charges—and at brochures advertising leather jackets. He read the brochures and put them down on the table. The third envelope contained a bill from Consolidated Edison Company of New York, along with a chatty newsletter explaining rate hikes.

Devereaux opened the second manila envelope. Two more bills. He dropped them on the table. What did he expect? A letter from Rita Macklin? How are you, I am fine? She didn't even know where he was. She'd never know about him again, after "reprocessing," after the new existence was grafted onto his identity.

He got up and went to the window and looked down on the darkened street. Three days earlier, it had snowed a little. The street was dirty with snow and ripped plastic bags of garbage at the curbs.

Sometimes, at night, he walked alone down Broadway all the way to Columbus Circle and then south of the park to the shabby heart of midtown on the West Side. He would settle into a seedy Irish bar off Eighth Avenue, watch the hookers work the bright, shabby streets around the bar, and drink until numbness returned and he did not think of Rita Macklin with pain. In the morning, sometimes, he ran for miles along the winding paths in Central Park, around the reservoir, running without the pleasure of the earnest joggers with their Sony Walkmans glued to their ears. Running just to run until exhaustion silenced his mind. He always thought of her when he ran but the thought faded after a while. In a little while he would not think of her at all.

Rita Macklin was a journalist. The first time he met her, in Florida, he had used her to pry a secret involving Soviets in Asia out of a half-mad old priest. He had used her and fallen for her and left her. But not the second time; the second time they had crossed paths by accident and he realized it really was a second chance. He had taken it. She had betrayed her life as a reporter for him, for what he had to do in Helsinki. And so someone on the Committee for State Security decided that he must die and so must the woman because she was certainly an agent as well.

He had made the deal with Hanley first, then repeated it to the masters of "reprocessing" at NSA: save her and he would be theirs. They wanted him back bad enough to accept.

Rita Macklin returned to her job at the magazine in Washington after a leave and now moved through the world of journalism there with a ghostly cynicism that her colleagues mistook for normal skepticism. She knew what she had been, what she had agreed to, what she had become, all because of him, because she had loved him. The price for her safety was compromise, the same price exacted from him.

The KGB watched her in Washington still, less because of her value than because she might lead them to the agent code-named November. That is what Hanley knew and did not tell Devereaux. She didn't even know where he was. The KGB would grow tired of her in time; Hanley assumed they would tire of waiting for Devereaux as well.

"You are a reluctant agent," Hanley had said once.

"Yes." There was no need to lie.

"But a reluctant November is still probably worth using."

All trace of his old life vanished. The General Services Administration, the government purchasing agency, bought his cabin and the land on the mountain outside Front Royal, Virginia, and gave Devereaux a certified check for it which was deposited in an account in the Schweizerische Kreditanstalt, a Zurich bank. The land was turned over to the U.S. Developmental Research Office, a cover organization of R Section. Devereaux didn't even know the morning when three yellow Caterpillar bulldozers rumbled up the single-track dirt road that led to the cabin and demolished it before lunchtime. That afternoon, Devereaux's name was deleted inside Tinkertoy, the R Section computer. A new existence was created before evening. His only remaining link with what he had been was the mail, the bills, the catalogs that still trickled in to the Front Royal post office. They would stop after a time; in the meantime, they were permitted to continue along their way to him simply because there was no reason to stop them.

Devereaux finished the glass of vodka and orange juice and considered another. But he put the cap back on the bottle of vodka and returned it to the refrigerator. He glanced at the alarm clock on the refrigerator: it was only six. The evening yawned in front of him.

Goddammit. He stood next to the garbage can, reached

into it, and took out the blue envelope and tore it open. It was dated three weeks before. He read it quickly the first time, to be rid of it; but it compelled a second reading.

Dear Red,

I am not well but I would not have bothered you about that. I don't care what you are or what you do, as I told you that time, but now you are involving me and I don't care for that at all. Besides, Red, you do have an obligation to visit a sick old lady.

M.

He read the letter a third time without expression. The blue paper, blue envelope; it never changed. Her name and address still imprinted on the top. Same address after all these years. She bought the paper each Christmas as a gift for herself in the main store of Marshall Field & Company on State Street in the Loop. The boy had accompanied her on these expeditions; each Christmastime, they ate luncheon under the great tree inside the store. Devereaux, the child, had hated the tradition, hated traipsing behind the old woman as she made her self-appointed rounds, hated the sentimentality of the season she tried to impart to him. He knew what he was, even as a child; he had no wish then to pretend to be something else.

The neighborhood had turned black and mean. She lived at the edge of the ghetto. Melvina. Great-aunt Melvina. An old lady when she took him in; he had been her good deed. It was either accept it or spend life at the Audy Home for Delinquents or the farm at St. Charles while the state decided if it was worthwhile to try him for manslaughter. He had killed a child on the streets because the child had decided to kill him; the choice had seemed simple to Devereaux at the time.

Melvina had taken him in and manipulated the law to have him, to possess him.

"You don't have a choice, do you?" Hanley had said.

Damn her. He dropped the letter in the garbage can. He had no obligation to her. He did not want to see her.

But now you are involving me.

The chill of the commonplace words settled into him. He

went back into the living room and looked out the window at the yellow-lit street. A wirehaired terrier pulled a reluctant owner along the curb across the way, straining casually at his leash. No others.

What had involved her?

Damn her. She was a person of vast silences, just as he was. A woman of enigmatic lapses into communication. What had involved her that she stated it so smugly?

The terrier stopped and squatted. The owner—a man in gray coat and gray scarf and gray hat—moved behind the dog with a dustpan. Devereaux watched the man clean up behind his dog, which was already straining to investigate a plastic garbage bag.

He should call Hanley. Why didn't Hanley intercept the mail? Damn them all.

➤   ➤   ➤

FORTY-FIVE MINUTES LATER, he climbed into the back of a yellow cab snatched from the stream of yellow cabs surging north along Broadway. "LaGuardia," he said and settled back into the greasy vinyl seat. A brown leather overnight bag rested on his lap. He wore a blue trenchcoat and black turtleneck sweater. In the bag were a few toiletry articles as well as a false-bottom case (made by NSA technicians and secure against airport X-ray devices) that contained the .357 Colt Python pistol.

He hadn't called Hanley after all.

No one would know. He'd slip in and out. Just a few days before, everything had been wiped away, not only records but memory. Days to remind Devereaux of what he had once been so that he could endure the future being fashioned for him.

"So where ya from? Ya from outta town?"

Devereaux blinked but didn't answer. The cab crossed 92nd Street, made the ascent up the East Side to the Triborough Bridge, and dashed across the somnolent grid of Queens to the airport.

Where was he from that he could admit to anymore?

He had not spoken to Melvina for a month after she had removed him from the Audy Home, after she had taken him to her house on Ellis Avenue, after she had given him a room of his own. Not for a month. Did he want more milk? Would he take a bath now? He obeyed silently.

"You'll outgrow that," Melvina had warned him without impatience, her voice lazy with threat. "I can outwait you. I have more patience. You'll break down before I do."

3 ____
Zurich

Gray Zurich, solemn as church, lay under the storm that had blown north from the mountains in the morning, picking up the damp winds from the Zurichsee south of the city. Bitter snow howled against the great clock tower of St. Peter's on the half-frozen Limmat River, which straggled north through the heart of the old town. Blue streetcars in tandem came grinding around the Bahnhofplatz in front of the central train station, the Hauptbahnhof, and turned down the mall-like Bahnhofstrasse that paralleled the river and descended three-quarters of a mile down to the frozen harbor of the Zurichsee.

The rich shop windows along the Bahnhofstrasse displayed Swiss watches and jewels and furs and leather goods; the windows were warm with lights, strung like jewels in the half-light of the stormy morning. Along the mall, the Zurichers strolled as though it might be summer, considering this window and that, this trinket and that, their faces bloated and gray, their eyes watering in the wind, their thick bodies wrapped in heavy wool against the cold. Few bent their heads to the heel of the wind.

No winter intruded inside the elegant, old-fashioned

first-class-passenger restaurant on the east side of the Hauptbahnhof. Beyond the dining room, the train station concourse was bustling and gay with travelers and shoppers emerging from the underground shopping center beneath the Bahnhofplatz. The electrified Swiss trains pulled in and out of the station with the precision of Japanese clockworks. All was as it had been, and it had always been as it was: five hundred years of peace, centuries of smug old-fashioned liberalism that saw the city provide sanctuary for capitalist and communist, conspired to make it seem that the ancient city was not so much a work of man as a monument of God's.

This was a sentiment that Felix Krueger had thought to share from time to time with those who were not as awed by Zurich as he was. But then perhaps they would not understand that Felix Krueger meant no blasphemy.

It was nine minutes to twelve by the clocks of the train station (which were always exact) and nine minutes to twelve by the hands of the glittering gold Rolex strapped by golden bands to Felix Krueger's freckled left wrist.

Felix Krueger, as massive and peaceful beneath the storm as the city, sat in his accustomed booth in the balcony above the first-class dining room and contemplated his plate of sausages and potatoes. Though the balcony was intended merely as a small cocktail lounge, an exception had long been made for Herr Felix Krueger. He was a man accustomed to acts of exception.

The thick-waisted waitress poured him a second glass of Zuricher Lowenbrau beer—he had consumed the first waiting for the meal—and he took a sip of the amber beverage a moment before tasting the food. He was a man of slow, deliberate actions, savoring the moments of his life as though each were prized equally.

Felix Krueger was not a fat man but was heavy in the German-Swiss way. His body was large, his shoulders rounded and powerful, his belly slightly gone to paunch. His eyebrows were reddish brown and thick, his cheeks were heavy without being jowly. His small calm eyes were as blue

15

as the Zurichsee in summer. He had very small hands for a large man and very small ears for such a large face. He combed the remains of his reddish brown hair flat and straight back from his long forehead, resigning himself proudly to approaching baldness. In winter and summer he was pale in appearance, despite a robust presence, and the dark blue suit he usually wore emphasized the fragile coloring of his skin. Freckles on the bridge of his nose attested to the fact that he sunburned too easily.

Felix Krueger picked up his knife and fork and cut carefully into the thick, blood-red sausage on his plate and pushed a piece into a puddle of horseradish at the side of the potatoes; slowly, a priest making offering, he raised the sausage to his thick, liverish lips and swallowed it.

Though he was a deliberate man in all things, he was more deliberate this morning because he was quite aware that his actions were being observed by a man he knew very well. They always played this game and Krueger never tired of it.

The Soviet courier was watching him. The Soviet courier always waited before the meeting. Who would follow him, Felix Krueger, in his own city, in his own country? So Krueger had laughed once at Rimsky. But Rimsky had no humor. None of them did.

Rimsky wore a dark leather coat trimmed with fox fur at the collar and a felt hat that emphasized his winter-red ears and ferret eyes. He had been sitting alone at a table in the first-class dining room since 11:30. No one had followed Herr Krueger, Rimsky had decided. Now he trudged up the stairs to the balcony and went to the booth and sat down across from the large reddish-haired man.

"There are fourteen this time, Herr Krueger," Rimsky began in precise, accented German.

"Not good morning or good afternoon? No amenities, no civilities?" Herr Felix Krueger paused with a bit of sausage on his fork, his knife held in his right hand like a weapon, his blue eyes twinkling.

"Meetings should be brief in public places," Rimsky said.

16

He pulled a small white envelope from the recesses of his leather coat and handed it across the table. He expected Krueger to take it. But Krueger popped the bit of sausage in his mouth and showed no inclination to drop knife or fork from his hands.

"Guten Morgen, Herr Rimsky," Felix Krueger said elaborately, smiling broadly, his teeth still moving to tear apart the sausage as he spoke.

Rimsky could not frown any deeper than the perpetual frown he wore for these meetings. He would not be made a fool by this man. "They are all from Poland this time."

Krueger chewed for a moment, swallowed, and then sighed. He put down the knife and fork and reached for the white envelope. "A mixed bag?"

"Nine men, five women."

"The usual terms?"

"Three years for the men, two for the women. Three are teachers. The women, I mean."

"Teachers do not frighten me," Krueger said. "The greater their intelligence, the easier to explain the situation to them."

"You mean to intimidate them."

Krueger was surprised; his eyes widened; he smiled. "Yes. That's one way to put it, Herr Rimsky. They see all the possibilities and realize they have no choice. The more intelligent they are, the more docile they become. The stupid ones, they can be problems. Like animals, some of them. The ferret, trapped, fights knowing it must die but knowing it must fight to death as well."

"You won't have problems with these. They were carefully screened."

"Yes." He weighed the envelope in one beefy hand. He slipped it into the inside pocket of his suit coat.

"You don't want to examine the list?"

"You can tell me what I need to know," Krueger said.

"One of them is Wanda Wyczniewski. Only twenty-one."

"A teacher."

"Yes."

"A husband? Child?"

"No. Unmarried."

Felix Krueger smiled. "Are you bringing me a virgin?"

Rimsky did not speak for a moment.

"A joke, Herr Rimsky."

"I see."

"You are so serious about this business. You never see the aspects of it that are . . . ludicrous."

"Do you think it is a joke?"

For the first time, Felix Krueger frowned. Rimsky was a dull man. A man without perceptions, without humor, without horizons. He saw so little. It made him a good workhorse, Krueger presumed, but a dull table companion. Krueger picked up his knife and fork and cut into a small boiled potato.

Because Krueger did not speak, Rimsky felt his rebuke had hit solidly. He went on: "Her father is forty-two, he was a professor at Warsaw University, he was disgraced. She wants to take him out of Poland. She will trade two years of her life for that. Frankly, the Polish government wants to be rid of her father more than she. He was one of the intellectual apologists for Solidarity."

"The father could be exported without—"

"He won't leave. The daughter understands. She will become . . . what would you say? Hostage. She will be hostage to us to force her father to leave. For his own sake."

"Interesting. There are so many motivations for them to . . . accept your conditions. I am fascinated by the variety of thought processes. Aren't you, Herr Rimsky?"

"No," Rimsky said honestly.

"No. I suppose not. You are as docile as a horse, do you know that?"

Rimsky frowned.

"A horse such as they had when I was a child, to plow the same row on the same mountain terrace spring after spring, without understanding anything of what he is part of, save that it is ritual."

"Are you speaking of philosophy now?"

Felix Krueger sighed again, massively, at the stupidity around him. "They are numbers to you, Rimsky, more than they are to me."

"You give them the numbers."

"Yes. And the guarantees without which this arrangement could not work for you. For your masters. I am the honest broker in this but you think I am interested only in numbers."

"Yes," Rimsky said. "The numbers in your accounts; the numbers in your bankbook."

"Numbers are order, Rimsky. I am a man of order. But don't suppose an accountant has no soul because he lives in a world of numbers."

"Capital," said Rimsky. "It is numbers because capitalism is a cold thing."

Felix Krueger had been in a good mood all morning. He had taken the funicular down to the square in front of the central train station. He had browsed among the shops beneath the Bahnhofplatz. He had even shared a glass of beer and a colorful story with the old drunks who stood around the beer bar on the train station concourse. He had felt the good feeling of approaching winter in his good gray native city and now the good feeling had trickled away with the dull, stupidly certain pronouncements of the Soviet courier. It was being replaced by irritation bordering on anger.

"No, Herr Rimsky." Slowly, as precisely as if he were chewing a sausage. "Capitalism is like an Italian church, all murals and candles and statues of the saints, marble arches and gargoyles in the ceiling. That is capital; that is capitalism. For you, for what you are, all is gray, the same, dull, each day folding into each day to come like a box collapsing itself into another box. Without my numbers, there is no order to things. But I do not worship numbers; you do. Order is the end to people like you; it is only my means."

Rimsky blinked, still frowning.

Krueger put down his fork and knife. The courier did not understand. He would never understand. Not the complexities of someone like this Wanda whatever-her-name-was, using her freedom to make someone she loved do something he did not want to do. Slavery to slavery, all for love. He longed to point out the absurdity of it but a man as narrow as Rimsky would never understand.

So. Business. "The papers are in order," Krueger said.

"As usual."

"Here is a receipt." Krueger removed a slip of paper from his pocket, wrote in a number, and signed it. "When does the shipment arrive?"

"In two weeks."

"The train from Vienna?"

"Yes."

"I will be the host for the lunch, as always. Is the schoolteacher very pretty?"

"Do you want to learn something?" Rimsky said coldly.

"I do not involve myself." Irritation flamed the back of his thick neck. "I observe, I am interested."

"I did not intend to insult you."

"Yes, I think you did."

A moment of silence. Then Rimsky said, "In six days, we want you to survey a group in Prague. A really large shipment. Thirty in the group."

"It will make it difficult to get back by the twenty-eighth—"

"We can arrange for you to fly back from Prague."

It was intolerable. Felix Krueger permitted emotion to play on his heavy features for the first time. His small, calm eyes became agitated; his left hand began to tremble. Of course Rimsky had meant it, meant to mock him.

"I do not fly in airplanes, Herr Rimsky," Felix Krueger said slowly in a warning voice. "You know that."

"I forgot, I apologize, Herr—"

"No. You do not apologize to me. I told you . . ." He seemed to choke on his words. "I do not want mention of this matter again and you mention it again. I do not wish to do business with you again."

Rimsky paled.

"You tell your control that he must send another courier. Another who is not . . ." Again, he made a choking noise. He thought of the airplane, the walls pressed in, strapped to his seat, the plane banking into clouds, fleeing earth, toy mountains below, the peculiar sickening smell of oxygen blowing dryly into the cabin, climbing through clouds, winds banging against the plane, this way and that, the warning lights flicking on overhead . . .

His face was covered with sudden sweat. He stared through Rimsky, seeing only his own vision, unable to step out of the horror his mind conjured.

"No offense, I meant no offense, I apologize," Rimsky was saying, the voice finally penetrating.

Felix Krueger blinked, the vision left him, his hands were trembling against the white tablecloth.

"You have spoiled my sausages," Krueger said, heavy as a church bell tolling.

Absurd. But Rimsky was more shaken than the large man in the opposite booth. Krueger was important to the Committee for State Security, more important than Rimsky; Krueger's demands were always small and businesslike; there was no reason to offend him. Control would not be pleased with Rimsky. There were worse assignments than this. Yet something in the superior manner of the fat Swiss always offended Rimsky and forced him to the edge of cruelty in dealing with him. Now he had gone too far.

"Herr Krueger. If it is possible for me to apologize. I could speak to my control, I could arrange for this woman who interests you . . ."

"You are a fool, Rimsky. I spoke to you of her merely to see her more clearly. If I were as limited as you, she would be a number. I would transport her from column A to column B and think nothing about her. Once in a while, I wish to see what these creatures are, to see if they are flesh and blood. It is curiosity, a quality of intellect you do not share because your intellect is so blunted by your stupidity." The words goosestepped over Rimsky's self-esteem. The smaller man shook with concealed rage; but it remained concealed.

"You may pay for my lunch. I will be in Prague in six days."

"Again, I apologize—"

"Perhaps I will accept it," said Felix Krueger, wiping his thick lips with the linen napkin and dropping it on the plate of congealed grease and sausage and potato remains. "These fourteen—" He tapped his breast pocket. "Is there one for Paris, a replacement for the Pole who was deported?"

"Yes."

"Then isolate him from the others at the lunch. My remarks are for those going to the United States. I will speak privately with this other one. What about Gemp?"

Gemp had been placed in a Paris cell three months before, working at the Institut Pasteur as a maintenance man. He had foolishly allowed himself to be taunted into a fight with two Portuguese in a brasserie on the Quai Voltaire one night, with the result that all three had been arrested by the Paris police and deported after a hearing. The time spent in preparing Gemp for his assignment at the Institut Pasteur had been wasted; now a new man was ready to fill the spot.

"Gemp? I don't know. He was taken care of, I suppose."

"You are still accountable for him. The replacement will cost you full value."

"We understand the terms, Herr Krueger," Rimsky said.

"So the manifest for the twenty-eighth is fourteen full-cargo charges? Agreed?"

Rimsky nodded.

Business as usual. Gemp or Wanda Wyczniewski or any of the others were shipments—precious shipments to be sure, marked "handle with care" and "fragile," but shipments of

22

goods nonetheless. Felix Krueger was a businessman in Zurich, an accountant and sometime banker and guarantor of insurance policies; he was a shrewd man of shrewd bargains with an eye for details whose books were always in balance. He dealt honestly; even the human cargo he dealt in had to admit to that. Someone who did not understand his business might think he bought and sold human beings on a perpetual international market that showed no signs of abating; Felix Krueger would have explained that a man who provides a service that benefits all, even those in temporary disadvantage, is merely a good man of business.

Felix Krueger was not a monster. Not in his own eyes. He had an aged father in Bern whom he visited every other Sunday and to whom he showed honor and respect; he had never married but he had enjoyed the company of beautiful women and was a witty and sometimes charming companion to them. He was a middle-aged man of vigorous health with middle-age mores and middle-age values. He was not a monster at all. The human cargo from Poland and Czechoslovakia and Hungary could trust Felix Krueger and therefore could trust the bargaining faith of the monstrous regimes they fled.

At the Grossmunster on Sunday morning, in the cold splendor of that Protestant edifice without icon or color, Felix Krueger prayed Sunday morning to God and felt certain that God would not judge him more harshly than He judged all men.

These thoughts soothed him and he was not angry with Rimsky anymore.

"The Prague shipments? For America?"

"Not all. Six are to be diverted to Montreal before overseas manifests are signed."

Krueger nodded. "If there is a separate lading for them, the usual fee is one percent."

"Yes. I was told that was acceptable."

Krueger opened a little leather notebook and consulted a sheet. "The license for shipment 239 expires in three weeks. Is everything satisfactory?"

"The bond sheets will be returned. There were no problems."

"I think I remember that shipment," Krueger said, staring at the notebook. "There were two sisters?"

Rimsky smiled with the sincerity of a servant. "You have a good memory. They were quite useful. In fact, we have induced one of them to continue . . . her employment voluntarily."

"Really?" Krueger's eyes widened. "Does that happen often?"

Rimsky felt he had said too much. But the need to ingratiate himself with Krueger was greater than discretion. "Sometimes. Not often. Sometimes."

"Remarkable sisters. So alike, so different. I wished I had known them better. I wonder which one it was."

Rimsky did not speak.

"All right. Business is concluded, Herr Rimsky. I shall expect to be met at Prague Central the morning of the twenty-eighth."

"I'll be there," Rimsky said.

"And now the bill." Krueger raised one freckled hand slightly and the waitress at the far end of the balcony came forward with the bill on a small plastic tray. She handed it to Krueger but the large man smiled.

"Not for me today, Fraulein. My associate insists on paying for my little meal."

The heavyset waitress turned. Rimsky flushed in that moment and nearly spoke and then reached into the pocket of his jacket for his wallet. He had stepped once today against Felix Krueger; it was best not to do it twice. He took the bill and added it and reached for the francs in his wallet; when he looked up again, Felix Krueger was already at the stairs, beginning his descent. The humiliation, Rimsky was sure, was intended.

4

Chicago

Nearly eleven. The plane had been twenty minutes late out of LaGuardia, as usual, and fifteen minutes late into Chicago. Devereaux had watched the descent out of his window, lazy as a cat. The city was broad and flat and crisscrossed with jeweled street lights. The American Airlines flight had banked north of O'Hare, fluttered down like a dove long accustomed to the miracle of flight. The wheels screeched on 19 R and the 727 lumbered across the tarmac to the central terminal building. He had not been in the city for more than twenty years. Not since he left the University of Chicago for the teaching job at Columbia University in Manhattan. A life ago, when he thought he had begun another life.

1962. The new professor emerging from the library at Columbia, down the steps, books in hand, tieless, his sportcoat flapping unbuttoned in the light autumn breeze. And a small man with a bowtie waited for him at the bottom of the steps. Wilson. Mr. Wilson wanted to buy him a beer; Mr. Wilson was from the government; Mr. Wilson was interested in his record, his familiarity with Asian studies and the languages of that continent. Had he ever intended to do fieldwork there? Yes, Devereaux had replied; when there was time enough and money enough. Perhaps, said Wilson, that could be arranged.

During all those years Devereaux spoke three times to Melvina, always at her insistence.

What are you doing now, Red, now that you've left Columbia? Up to no good again? In the business of heroin? Are you a dope dealer? Why do you go to Vietnam and Laos? How can you afford to go? I'm just an old woman, Red. I've made you the project of my life.

Did she understand what he was now, what he had become after that meeting with the man in a bowtie on an autumn afternoon in New York?

Perhaps. It was her favorite word for saying nothing. Devereaux unconsciously mimicked it all the times he had nothing to say. Which was nearly all the time.

Melvina, at least, was truly part of the past, unlike Rita Macklin. Melvina had remained untouched by all he had become. Until the letter on blue paper.

He walked stiffly along the corridor under indiscriminate bright lights, with throngs of cowboys in Stetsons and Indians in saris and California girls in white jeans and silk blouses and drug dealers in maroon hats with feathers in the bands: flotsam of the jetstream. It was like an Eastern bazaar selling escape, movement.

Five minutes later, he passed through the arrival door to the covered street and waved to a yellow cab first in the line, parked fifty feet away. The cab bolted forward like a horse through a fence opening. He grabbed the door; it was stuck. He pulled and the thin driver reached over, smacked the door with his hand, and it opened.

"Forty-six oh one Ellis Avenue," Devereaux said, sliding into the backseat of the elderly Checker Corporation car.

He remembered the address so easily. He hadn't said it for twenty years. Engraved in memory along with all the other bits of the past that were useless to him and to the Section and were not in danger of being erased.

The Pakistani driver turned in his seat and stared at Devereaux. After a moment, he spoke, his shining brown eyes unblinking. "No, I cannot." His voice twittered like a bird. "Bad. Very bad, sir. It is a neighborhood for the blacks. Perhaps you have the wrong address, sir."

Devereaux stared through him. "No."

"Then I cannot go there," said the Pakistani. "I do not go to the South Side at night. Very bad, sir."

"You'll be safe," Devereaux said in a slow voice, still staring through the Pakistani. He did not feel part of the conversation. He was thinking of the house, thinking of the old woman still, of the strange message she had sent to him. "I'm not black."

"No, sir, you are not. All the more danger."

"There's no danger from me," Devereaux said.

The Pakistani smiled then. Logic. In the half-darkness of the cab, his face was illuminated by the brightness of his smile. His eyes glittered. "Sir, if I may? What do you want there, sir? It is a very bad place if you do not know it. Should I wait for you? You cannot get a taxi from that place at this late hour."

"You can't get back here from there," Devereaux said.

The Pakistani nodded as though he understood and then thought better of it. He smiled. "I do not understand, sir."

"Neither do I."

"Sir? Are you a police officer?"

"Yes," Devereaux agreed. The driver wanted an explanation that soothed him.

"Oh, sir. I see, sir. I do not want to be robbed, sir. Or hurt."

"No." Gently.

"Then, sir, as you say, I will take you." The Pakistani banged down the meter arm. "I cannot wait for you there, sir, do you understand?"

"Yes."

"Will there be any trouble?"

"No. Nothing at all."

The Pakistani pulled away from the curb as suddenly as a thought. The old heavy cab bucked into the light stream of traffic, the driver leaning on his horn around a Continental bus, pushing past the last terminal building and onto the Kennedy Expressway heading southeast to the heart of the city. Bungalows along the expressway embankments, overpasses—the urban sprawl continued from Queens. Devereaux closed his eyes but saw the old house too clearly. He blinked them

27

open and felt tired. The Hancock Center with its blinding ribbon of white neon on the 101st floor poked over the urban horizon and then the full crown of downtown all the way to the Sears building at the south end of the Loop. The expressway skirted the edge of downtown and then plunged south into the Dan Ryan. Through the heart of the South Side ghetto, brightened by orange anticrime lights and crowned by high-rise colonies of housing projects.

Why rush a reluctant homecoming? He could stay downtown, see Melvina tomorrow. Not even see her. He could have called. He could have called from Manhattan in the first place.

Perhaps it pleased him to return so late at night, wake the old woman from a sound sleep, bang on the door . . .

The taxi pulled off the Dan Ryan at 47th Street and plunged east through the still glittering ghetto heart. The cold streets were alive with hookers and cops and pimps and drunks and, in vacant lots, with winos congregated around fire barrels. Dirty snow waited in bundles of ice at the curbs, like garbage that wouldn't be picked up until spring.

"Do you know where Ellis Avenue is, sir? All the street signs are gone."

Did he know? "Turn here." St. Ambrose Church on the corner, dark as a forgotten faith. Did he know?

"Down there. By the corner."

The Pakistani hit the brakes too hard on the dark side street. Even the orange lamps failed to penetrate this darkness. Devereaux pulled a bill out of his pocket and dropped it on the front seat. "Keep the change." He reached for the bag beside him. The door was stuck again. He hit it with the heel of his palm. It squeaked open.

He climbed out. His knees ached stiffly. He stood for a moment, bag in hand, on the silent, cold street. He stared up at the house of his childhood, his reluctant refuge.

"Sir?"

Devereaux glanced in at the driver.

"I have changed my mind, sir. I will wait for you if you wish, sir. I can take you downtown when you are finished."

"No," Devereaux said.

"Is this a place of prostitution?"

Devereaux stared.

"This is no place for white men such as us."

"Then go away." Quietly.

"It is very bad here, sir. There are murders waiting here."

"Yes," he said. He saw it then, as he had lived it, some thirty years ago, his shirt covered with bloodstains. Unrepentant. Silent in the back of the squad car. *Ya killed him, ya little fucker, ya killed him and he mighta had it comin', but you know what you done, kid? You even care what you done? Ya killed him.*

No. He didn't care.

Devereaux opened the iron gate that led to the broken concrete walk to the three-story redstone house. The Pakistani decided: the cab ground into gear, pitched forward. Gone.

This had been an elegant house, an elegant neighborhood of homes. But that was in a time before even his time. Decayed now, locked into the grid of the ghetto, broken. The remains of one stone lion next to the broken cement stairs. There had been two lions guarding these stairs.

He rang the bell and then, when there was no answer, knocked at the oak door at the top of the stairs. He felt afraid, he realized, but not of physical danger. What he feared was more terrible. The lights of the cab winked away down the street, around a corner. He rang the bell again. He rang it a third time.

An overhead light flicked on. Someone observed him through a sheet of plexiglass set in the door. Then a voice:

"Who zat?"

Devereaux did not speak.

"What you want?"

29

Still he could not speak. If the cab had remained, he would have fled. This was too frightening.

The door opened a crack, secured by two chains. He did not remember the chains.

A black face peered at him.

"Who you?"

"I want to see Melvina."

"Who?"

Devereaux didn't speak.

"Who you?"

"I told you who I want to see."

"She ain't here. Too late."

"Where is she?"

"You got business?"

"I don't remember you."

"Who you to remember me, man?"

"Where is she?"

Then, behind the door, the iron voice, sure and upright. Unchanged. "Who is it, Peter?" Clear as an iron bell.

"White dude."

"What does he want?"

"He don't say nothin'."

"Who is it?" Imperious, the empress Melvina to her court.

Devereaux would not answer.

"He don't say nothin'," Peter repeated unnecessarily, marveling at this strange specimen.

"Why doesn't he answer?"

Peter turned. "I dunno. He stand here, he don't speak. Gotta bag."

Silence.

"Then that must be Red, Peter. You can open the door."

"You sure, miz?"

"Open the door, Peter."

The black face disappeared. The door closed, chains dropped, and the door opened again slowly. Devereaux took a step inside. He was standing in the carpeted foyer at the center of the townhouse. Above him, the same glass chandelier dimly lit the foyer; the light had always been too dim.

She stood on the stair. She had a pistol in her hand.

"Is that you, Red?"

Devereaux looked at her. Older, certainly. She gripped the pistol with both hands. Her hands had blue veins. She had once held the bannister like a boulevardier holding his walking stick; he supposed she used the bannister now as a crutch. Except the pistol, glittering in the dim light, did not waver in her grip.

Old and frail, he thought. An almost indetectable quaver in her iron voice. A mere symptom of age, like the pain in his joints in the morning. She wore a blue print robe and her thin face was barely visible in the shadows cast by the dim light. Pale and stern still, with a pronounced chin and sharp, large gray eyes. Her hair was streaked with gray.

"You finally came," she said. It was a rebuke. He was not on time. As though he had been expected after all these years, all these silences.

She lowered the pistol to her side. With her right hand, she gripped the bannister. Devereaux stood, bag in hand, waiting.

"What happened?" he said finally.

"You came here. You took your time."

"The mail gets slower."

"Everything is slower. Even me. I suppose you came to see if I had died. Or become senile."

"No. I wasn't curious about you."

She smiled. "Promise you won't come to my funeral. I couldn't bear it."

"I promise I won't come to your funeral." He was rooted to the spot in the hall, aware of the black man called Peter closing the big oak door behind him, unable to move either away from her or toward her, transfixed by Melvina descending. Still the frozen, mute child.

"Red," she said. She kissed him on the cheek. Her lips

31

were dry. She stood back from him. "You're older. Much older than I expected."

"You haven't changed," he said, not meaning it as a compliment to age.

"Do you still drink, Red?"

"Yes."

"I have some scotch. You know I like my scotch."

He knew everything about her.

"Peter, will you get the scotch? We can sit in the front room, Red. And ice, Peter? Do you want soda?"

Devereaux did not answer. He pushed the door to the front room. Unchanged. A museum room, musty and neat. There should have been velvet ropes around the chairs. He entered and she turned on a lamp behind him. Peter came to the door. "You shouldn't be drinking at night, miz."

"I drink when I like, Peter." Iron.

The black frowned.

"Don't be such a worrier, Peter. This is an occasion. Red has come to visit me."

Devereaux turned, sat down in a blue chair, stared at her. That touch of arrogance in her voice. She had ruled the world all her life. Melvina never married, not because she was not a pretty woman or because the young men had not loved her, but because no man had measured up to that smile, that arrogance in the curl of her lip, and been able to overcome it. Certainly not a boy taken from reform school. All the men eventually ran away. Even the boy. Perhaps that was their loss.

They sat across from each other at the coffee table in the front room. Devereaux picked up the bottle of Laphroiag and poured himself a second glass and pretended not to feel guilt. She watched everything and rarely said anything. Everything he did in front of Melvina provoked this strange feeling in him. It was as though his smallest act testified against the coolness of his words. He tasted the scotch. The smoky liquid made him want to shiver with comfort, a dog shivering at rest in front of the home fire. The house was cold, furnished with old things that had been precious. Perhaps they still were. The radiators clanged up steam heat from the oil boiler in the basement. As always.

Everything reminded him of something past. He knew it would. He had not wanted a remembrance of the past. Until when, exactly? Perhaps when his past was stripped from him while he waited in the building on West 88th Street. One last look, Devereaux, before fading. The old woman, the old house. Even Rita Macklin.

The past wasn't so much, was it? Cartons of old clothes in shopping bags in a dead man's room in a men's hotel. Absolutely worthless when the life that accumulated all that rubbish was extinguished.

"I've been ill," Melvina said, puncturing his reverie. "As I said in the note."

He stared at her, gray eyes cast upon gray eyes. A family trait, she said once; gray eyes make us appear wiser than we are.

Somewhere in the vast silence of the house, Peter lurked. From the street came a shout and a girl's laughter, and from farther away a car backfired. Or perhaps it was the report of a gun. Devereaux smiled at the memory of the Pakistani's concerned face.

"Cancer," she said.

Still, he waited.

"Oh, thank God you won't make a great fuss about it. I'm so tired of sympathy, the sad looks people give you."

The smile remained. "People never gave you sympathy, Melvina. If you wanted it, you took it from them."

In the half-light of the room, she chuckled. "I suppose you're right, Red. You were a clever boy. I saw that in you. Even in your room at the Audy Home. You were worth my while."

"I'm glad, Melvina."

"No, you're an ungrateful child. But I do receive sympathy, Red, even if you choose not to believe it. Say cancer to people, they will be concerned. They're so afraid of everything but especially that. It's going to happen to them. One out of four, or is it three? They see me and they see themselves, a cancer eating away at them."

"What people, Melvina? Your neighbors?"

"Red. They're all black. I don't have any friends here."

"Except Peter."

"He's an employee."

"Did you save him as well? Stray dogs from the Anticruelty Society, stray children from the Audy Home. Where did the black come from, Melvina? Recruited by Sergeant Gottlieb down at Area Two?"

"Sergeant Gottlieb died three years ago, Red."

He said nothing.

"Are you sorry?"

"No."

"Good, Red. Never give in. Even to me. It would be out of character."

"He was a bastard."

"And you became . . . what? A saint among your fellow men? Little brother of the poor?"

"Who sympathizes with your cancer, Melvina?"

"Monsignor O'Neill, for one. He's still alive. I'm sure you remember him. He remembers you in his prayers."

"I feel his presence nightly when I lay me down to sleep."

She ignored him. "He sees me when he can. He gives me Communion, he hears my confession. He sits with me and we talk about the old days. He's a great comfort."

"And he sympathizes with your cancer."

"My fears."

"You're not afraid, Melvina. Not at this late stage of life."

Again, she smiled but he could not see the turn of her lips in the half-darkness. "Yes, Red, in a way I am not afraid, but Monsignor O'Neill, for all his faith, is. He sympathizes with my final agony. He prepares me, Red. For the end."

"Because he can't prepare himself."

"Perhaps."

Silence. In the great house, a clock ticked unseen.

Devereaux sipped the smoky liquid again, tasted the sweetness. He did not want to speak to her but he could not stop himself. In all the years of his silences, he had felt that words were deceptions, tools of his trade; or that words were self-betrayals. And now he resisted the urge to speak to Hanley and Melvina and anyone who would still affirm his existence. He felt as pathetic as a drunkard in an afternoon saloon, trying out a bag of stories on strangers to momentarily halt the march of silences.

"How does he do it?"

"What?"

"Prepare you for the end?"

"Prayers, Red. That's obvious, isn't it? He tells me what I shall see when I shall see that day."

"How clever of him."

She leaned into the light; he could see her face clearly. She smiled a thin, pretty, and wicked smile, the smile of an arrogant woman who appreciated the young men with their gifts of charm. All the young men had left her, without rejection, save him. Perhaps Melvina had understood Red would go away from her long before he had left that morning, without a note or word of parting, carrying his single suitcase and ticket for the United flight to New York City. For a life away from her. Long ago. She tracked him, of course; it wouldn't ever end on his terms, only hers. She had mailed a note to him (blue stationery in a blue envelope in his mailbox) at the ratty apartment he had occupied on 111th Street twenty-five years ago:

My brave little man, going off into the world alone.

He thought he hadn't hated her until he saw that note and saw that she had imprisoned him as a child for his own good; still a prison, though a polite and brittle glass prison, a prison of manners and civility and enough money to buy him out of the trouble he wanted. Buy everything after taking away the one thing beyond purchase.

She said, "Monsignor O'Neill is a fool, I suppose, but an

old fool, which excuses everything. When you are old, as I am, you make do with what you have."

"Like Peter."

"Peter is a colored man. It's wise, I thought, to have someone of that color to look after my interests, given the time."

"You didn't have to live here."

"That would not have suited me, Red. You were always too willing to accept the world as you found it. That's why you fought so hard against it."

"I don't fight anymore."

"That would make me sad, Red, if I believed it."

Another silence. She leaned back into shadows. She waited but he would not speak.

"I think I know what you are. Rather, what it is that you do."

He still said nothing.

"I was mystified for quite a long time. But I'm sure I know now."

"As Monsignor O'Neill is certain."

"My knowledge is more mundane."

"The truth shall make you free."

"Yes. Exactly. I have always had the sense of my own freedom."

"Because you disregard the freedom of others."

"You, Red? You were a child. You weren't free. You were doing the best you could not to be free. I did the best for you, Red. You refuse to admit it, even now. When I'm dying. That woman never cared if you lived or died. She might have cried for you but she wouldn't have saved you."

"Dear Melvina."

"No love, Red? Even at this late date? No pity?"

Silence.

The clock struck one. The song of Westminister chimed and then the single bell tolled.

"What involves you, Melvina?"

She seemed startled, confused. She leaned into the light

36

again. Her gray eyes watched him sitting coolly on the blue chair. "You mean my letter to you." Disappointed. "Too bad. I thought you meant more. But the matter intrigues me. It's good for an old woman who is dying to be interested in something beyond the Last Judgment. The Last Judgment is too weighty a baggage to carry around every day, don't you think?"

"I don't know."

"You never were cursed with faith, were you?"

"No."

"You were such a terrorist. Your survival counted before all others. I think that made you more afraid to die than me. Like your father."

"Did he survive?"

"No. Your mother saw to that." A flash of malice like a thin knife waved in half-darkness, the cutting edge turned toward the victim. "Neither will you. Survive, I mean. But the thought of all that energy spent on staving off the inevitable tires me. How futile, Red, don't you ever see that?"

This was stupid, he thought. He put down the drink. Had he returned for old home week? Tours down memory lane? Something had happened, it had made Melvina write to him. "What involved you, Melvina?" The voice was cold, remorseless.

"You sound so strange."

Silence. He could endure silence, not words. Not even if he needed them.

"Something happened."

"What?"

"I haven't been able to keep the house as I wished. I employ a woman. An immigrant. Named Mary Krakowski."

He leaned forward, did not touch the glass, waited.

"Your eyes, Red. So old. You've aged."

Merely survived, he thought. He said nothing.

"She lives in a room in an apartment in Hyde Park. I never thought to ask her. You know, about working papers. I assumed."

"How did she contact you?"

"Peter put a note in the Hyde Park Co-op. I needed a cleaning lady once a week. I thought I'd get a colored woman. I was surprised."

"When was this?"

"About a year ago."

About the time of Helsinki.

"She's been here two years. Once she said to me she wanted to work for me. After. I said, 'After what?' She didn't say. Not for a couple of weeks. I thought it was some waiting time for naturalization or something. Then, out of the blue one day, she said she had a bond. A bond. She doesn't speak English well but she knew that word. I said, 'Like a bond-woman?' Yes, she said. I couldn't believe it. I told her I couldn't believe it. I said there was no such thing in this country. I think she was a little drunk when she told me. She worked in the kitchen that morning, singing to herself while she worked. Sad songs. Polish songs. I didn't understand the words, only the way she was singing them. I think she was that. Is that. Some sort of bondwoman."

"Bond to whom?"

"I don't know. She lives with others. Immigrants. She has a friend, Teresa Kolaki. Teresa worked here for Mary one day when Mary was ill. I asked Teresa what the bond was that Mary talked about. She seemed afraid."

"Why does this involve me?"

"I don't know. Two months ago. Two men came. From Immigration."

"How do you know?"

"They showed me identification. They were foreign. Accents, I mean."

Devereaux felt perfectly still, perfectly cold: this was why he had come. His hands were resting on his thighs. He stared at the form in the half-darkness. He did not speak.

"They asked me about Mary. Then. Red. They said you worked for the government. They said they were concerned because . . ."

He waited.

"You don't make it easy."

"What?"

"I don't know what's happening. I'm tired, Red. I want to go to bed. You can stay up. You can sleep in your old room."

"Tell me."

"No." The coquette again. "In the morning, when I'm refreshed. I didn't expect you."

"I didn't expect myself."

"Does it feel like a homecoming, Red?"

"This wasn't home."

She smiled. "Good, Red. Never give in, not even when I'm old and dying."

"What cancer are you dying from?"

"Oh. I'm not sure. Perhaps I'm not dying yet. But it pleases Monsignor O'Neill to think he finally has something interesting to say to me."

Devereaux smiled.

"I'm wicked, I know."

"Yes."

"Red."

He waited.

"One of the men had a gun. I saw it. The other man blocked me from seeing it but I saw it, just for a moment. I think they meant to kill me."

"They asked about me? And your cleaning woman?"

"Yes. A bondwoman. Do you think there's still such a thing as slavery?"

"Yes."

"Good. So do I. To own people."

"You owned me."

"You were a hostage, Red. To your own bad deeds. I didn't demand payment when you freed yourself, did I?"

Silence.

She rose. She put the glass on the side table. "I'm so tired."

"The men. Are you going to tell me about them?"

"In the morning. I'm worried about Mary. I'm rather fond of her. I know she drinks. I saw vodka in her purse."

"You went through her purse?"

"Of course."

"Are you going to save her?"

"I don't know. I'm eighty-five and terribly tired. Perhaps I really am ill. I feel too old to save anyone. You were lucky to reach me in my prime."

"Jean Brodie," Devereaux said.

"You could have done much worse," Melvina said with a smile that was almost a secret. "Mary drinks. She reminds me of your mother. I wanted to help your mother."

"You wanted to help yourself."

"The world is such a wicked place, Red. It has always been so. It has never disappointed me. You never disappointed me. But slavery? I don't expect that. Not in this age. My God, it is hard to grow old, not because the end of days has come but because nothing has changed, nothing at all. Life was mean when I was a child and grows meaner still. What a stupid thing for life to do."

"What about the two men?"

"Yes. That interests me too. To see what you want to tell me about them. In the morning, Red, when I'm not so tired. I have a lot of things to tell you."

He waited.

"That poor woman. I did love your mother, you know."

"Are you talking about her? Or about your cleaning woman?"

"Your mother is dead, Red. The living concern me."

God. He wanted to kill her. He sat very still.

"Why does this involve me?" he asked.

"But you know it does already, don't you?" Smiling, swaying slightly, moving to the hall, gripping the bannister. "In the morning, Red. When I'm not so tired. There's time in the morning."

5

Washington, D.C.

Frankfurter and Gleason circled the apartment building in Bethesda slowly, passing along the front on Old Georgetown Road, down to the turn into an unmarked lane, behind the building (through the parking lot), around a second lane, back on Old Georgetown Road. It was their ninth pass in the last two hours. They parked on the unmarked lane. It was just after eight; the darkness in the semirural section was palpable. No wind, no night sounds.

"You wanna turn on the radio?"

Frankfurter belched an answer.

"Is that yes or no?"

"No, I don't want the fucking radio on. Fucking radio drives me crazy. I hate shit like this, you know? I hate shit like this."

Gleason knew.

"She's been in there three hours. Don't she go out?"

"She doesn't get a phone call, she doesn't go out. She doesn't look that bad a broad. Maybe she's a lesbian."

"So? Lesbians go out, don't they?"

"I don't know. You can't tell about lesbians. My daughter brought this girl home from Smith. Over last Christmas. Nice girl. Nice tush. You know."

"Jesus."

"Hey, I don't mean that. You can't help but noticing these things. Nice girl. Very polite. Please and thank you and mother, may I. You know. One day I'm driving down to the Seven-Eleven with Tammi—"

"Tammi your daughter?"

41

"Yeah. I thought you knew. I thought I mentioned it."

"No. You never mentioned it."

"Tammi and me, I don't know, we're getting some more stuffing or something. I think it was Christmas Day in fact. I think the Seven-Eleven was the only thing open, so we're talking and out of a blue Tammi says, 'You know, Beth is a lesbian.' Just like that. I nearly went off the fucking road. I mean, why the hell would she tell me something like that?"

"Maybe she was trying to tell you something."

Gleason turned to Frankfurter and rested his left arm on the steering wheel. "What the hell is that supposed to mean?"

"It means what it says. Maybe she was trying to tell you something."

"You mean Tammi is trying to tell me that she's a fag too? Is that what you're saying?"

"It happens. Kids go through stages."

"You've got your mind in the fucking gutter, you know that?"

"You asked me, I told you."

"I didn't ask you. I was telling you that you can't tell about these things."

"And I was agreeing with you."

Silence.

Gleason turned on the radio.

"Aw, why'd you turn that fucking thing on?"

"Because I want it on. You mind?"

"I mind. I already told you I mind."

"Too fucking bad."

"This is a goofy idea, you know."

"What?"

"Watching this broad. If our customer didn't contact her all the months we had him stashed in that flat in New York, he isn't going to contact her now. I think he just got stir crazy, decided to take off for a few days."

"Maybe he got lucky in that Irish bar on Eighth."

"Jesus H. Christ. What a freak show, huh? I had two weeks' duty up there, I was going out of my mind. There was this one bimbo goes in there every night for a J & B and Coke. You know, shine broad. But a blond wig. And she's got the miniest miniskirt. I mean, you can see her snatch when she walks. Boots. They all got boots. You think fashions would change."

"Whatever turns you on."

"When I was with DEA, we'd do some shit on Broadway. This is ten years ago. Same fashions. Why the hell he'd go down there, to get looped?"

"Just sat in the bar, two, three nights a week, watching the freak show passing by. Couple of babes hit on him, he ignored them. And a guy hit on him. Same thing. This guy is not interested in sex."

"That isn't what got him into this wringer in the first place. He put it all on the line for this broad. I mean, she's a good-looking broad but a broad is a broad; they all look the same upside down."

"He's lucky Uncle wanted to save his ass. She is too."

"Yeah." Frankfurter turned the radio off. It was all right.

Gleason said, "I'm thinking about it. You figure the Red Machine is off his case?"

"Sure. We haven't had a peep for months. Nothing in the spaghetti on the radio either. Nothing. They were watching her for a couple of months but now she's clean. I figure they never were much interested in hitting this Macklin broad at all. I think they were just on our customer's case. A case of a real hard-on for the guy. What'd he do? They lost two agents in three years because of him, not counting the hits that went down. And that business in Florida that blew up in their faces. And Helsinki last year. You can see from the Red Machine's point of view, this guy is a problem. He doesn't play the game."

"He doesn't follow the rules," agreed Gleason.

"Right. He's a fucking intelligence operative, not fucking James Bond. He keeps sticking his neck out, naturally they're gonna chop it off. We're supposed to gather intelligence, not knock off each other."

"Uh-oh."

Frankfurter reached for the "Record" button on the built-in tape. Over the radio speaker, they heard a telephone ringing. It was the line to Rita Macklin's apartment. It rang five times.

RITA: Hello?

VOICE: Hello? Rita?

RITA: Yes. Is this Tom?

TOM: Yeah. Listen, I wanted to see if you wanted to go down to Sharko's. I just found out Teddy Brown's band is booked back there starting tonight.

RITA: You always call up at eight o'clock on Thursday night for a date?

TOM: Listen, I just found out. We go down tomorrow night, we won't get in the place. You're a big girl.

RITA: A big girl getting an early night in. I'm flying up to Boston on the shuttle tomorrow.

TOM: Shit. Too bad. 'Nother time?

RITA: Give me a day or two notice, okay?

TOM: Sure. I figured you'd rather I call you than not call you just because it was something that was happening now. I mean, this is the twentieth goddam century.

RITA: Are you mad at something?

TOM: Just you.

RITA: Good. I thought it might be something important.

(Click.)

Frankfurter switched off the tape. "Sassy bitch, huh?"

"Well, the guy's an asshole too, calling her up for a date the same night he wants to take her out."

"Listen, she's been around the track. We're not talking about high school."

"Yeah."

Silence.

"You know, she's making an early night of it. Soon as we see the lights go out, we can head over to Wisconsin, get a hamburger or something," said Frankfurter.

"How about a beer?"

44

"A beer, okay. Let's go off now. Nothing is happening tonight."

"What if he comes?"

"He isn't going to come. He comes, then we turn on the super set, pick up the bedroom bug, listen to our honey tussling with him."

"Or snoring."

"Or snoring."

> > >

MALENKOV TURNED OFF THE TAPE when he heard her snores. He picked up the black phone which was swept daily for taps and dialed a number in Arlington, Virginia. The phone rang three times. The conversation was in Russian, in the accent of Moscow.

"Yes."

"Asleep. I shut down the recorder. I looked out the window a little while ago, and the two watchers from NSA have gone. I don't know if they'll be back tonight."

"What else?"

"She's going to Boston tomorrow. There was one conversation with a 'Tom' regarding a date at a place called Sharko's. It is in Georgetown, on M Street."

"Did you recognize the voice?"

"Yes. There was a conversation four weeks ago. He dated her. I looked up the relevant data. It was filed by Adamovich at three hundred eighty-seven."

"What else?"

"Boston. Perhaps that is where he has been kept."

"We have also received information about an apartment in New York City but it's still very vague. They have begun construction of a new file for him but we have not penetrated. The woman seems the best chance. Adamovich will be at your post in the morning. Follow her to Boston. Report at 18:30, use frequency 102.44."

"At this number?"

45

"Yes."

Malenkov replaced the receiver. He turned on the receiver but not the tape.

He listened for a moment to Rita Macklin snoring. It made him tired. He stretched, rose, and began to unbutton his shirt.

6

Chicago

Devereaux watched her for a long time before he spoke. She was aware that he watched her but there was nothing she could do about it. Once she smiled at him; he did not smile at her. He watched her as a cat watches a curious thing. Yes, she thought: exactly like a cat watches.

He stood in the doorway to the kitchen. From there he could see both the dining room and the foyer that led to the front room. The downstairs windows were barred against break-ins. The ugly tips of the bars were sharpened to impale any felon stupid enough to vault them or try to squeeze between the bars and the window. The windows permitted thin sunlight to cloud the rooms; a pattern of the bars was made on the lace of the dining room table.

Mary Krakowski was on her knees in the kitchen, scrubbing the white tiles.

She was thirty-four. Her hair was dyed red. She had large, cloudless blue eyes so common to Poles; her cheeks were red with exertion and that made her pretty. She would be heavier as she grew older; her waistline was thick. But her youth carried her extra fifteen pounds now. She wore a cotton housecoat over her skirt and sweater. She had taken off her nylons when she changed into the housecoat and she would put them on again when she left the house.

The man in the house excited her because John Stolmac had told her that someday a man might come to this house. John had described the man. He would have gray hair and gray eyes and a worn face. He would be so tall and weigh so much. When he came to the house, Mary Krakowski was to tell John. Depending on what happened, she might not work for Miss Devereaux again.

John Stolmac had told her these things almost a year ago. She had nearly forgotten them. Then this morning she saw the man John had described, sitting at the kitchen table with Melvina, drinking coffee.

She had become so excited that she blushed.

The man noticed this but said nothing. The man noticed everything. It made her feel strange to be watched so closely. She scrubbed the tiles harder. She thought she had a pretty face. She had smiled at him and even flirted with him but he had not responded to her.

She was finished with the floor. She dropped the scrub brush into the pail of water and got up from the floor and went to the doorway with the pail on her way to the bathroom. She looked boldly at him and then turned her cloudless blue eyes away. "Excuse me, mister," she said in a thick accent.

Devereaux, coffee cup in hand, stepped aside and let her pass to the bathroom, where she dumped the pail of water into the toilet and pulled the chain to flush it. Melvina, who had a Betamax machine in her bedroom so that she could watch old movies at night, had never updated the bathroom. The tub (there was no shower) sat on cast-iron lion's paws.

Mary Krakowski came out of the bathroom. He was still watching her. It unsettled her. She thought about the small bottle of vodka in her purse. But her purse was upstairs in the changing room, and he would notice her leaving to go upstairs and might even follow her. He was bold, as bold as the men who stood on War Memorial Square and eyed the women in the evening as they promenaded. Long ago, when she had been young.

"You are visit?"

"Yes," Devereaux said.

She tried the smile again.

"You live?"

"New York."

"New York? I see New York in airport only. Then go on plane to Chicago. John wait for me, take me to this place."

"Here?"

"No. Where I live."

"Who is John?"

"John. Also old country."

"Melvina says you work at the university."

"Yes. Clean at night, four nights, work here one day. Once I work five nights but no more."

"Where do you work?"

"Building. Is Randall Hall?"

"Randall?"

"Ya. Big building. We clean."

Devereaux stared at her silently for a moment. Mary Krakowski felt compelled somehow to stand very still. What had she said to him?

John might be angry. She should have said nothing. When John was angry, he could hurt her. John was very strong, very mean at times. He could be gentle as well; he understood Mary, he could get money for Mary to buy vodka. Sometimes, he drank with Mary. But when he was angry, he hurt her. Afterward, Mary always felt ashamed, somehow dirty, somehow of no worth.

"Family? You have a family here?"

"Not here," she said.

"In Poland," Devereaux said.

For a moment, her eyes reflected hurt. She squinted and her eyes misted, as though summer rain fell while the sun shone in another part of the fields. "Yes. My son. He is ten."

"Are you going to get him out?"

"Hard, mister. Always too hard. Many times I apply, I have to . . ." But then, what should she tell him? Who was he that John had warned her to watch for him? "Polonia," she said. "Much trouble."

"Does he stay with family?"

"No family, mister. We are alone. The orphan place—"

"How could you leave him?" Without mercy or pity or even judgment; asked in the tone of a man asking about a bus trip or the place to purchase a newspaper.

How could he know how hard it was? American. "Soon," she said with sudden fierceness. "Soon I have Karol with me."

"How can you be sure?"

Her hands trembled. Was this a threat? Who was this man? All those months. The contract was nearly fulfilled. Why did he come here and ask questions?

"Do you have a contract?"

Panic welled in her. She staggered back a step. She looked from left to right but there was no one except her and this man in the old house.

"Who were the two men who came here two months ago?"

She blinked, confused.

Devereaux stared and then asked another question. "You have a contract. With whom?"

"Contract. For work. Always need for permit. To come to United States. Cannot work if there is no guarantee for work. I have. I have green card."

"What did you promise to do?"

"What you mean? Clean."

"No." Quietly. Coldly. She was too afraid, too guarded. He played a hunch. "What did you promise to get Karol out of Poland?"

"Mary, Mother of God." She dropped the pail on the carpet and was not aware of it. She took another step back. She covered her breasts with her right hand and arm. She felt very afraid.

"Sit down, Mary. In the kitchen." Flat and cold and

49

without sympathy, a voice without resonance, depth, life. A dead voice sailing on a dead sea.

He took a step forward. His mother had made the gesture in the same way, hand across her breasts, the eternally threatened woman, the universal victim, the slave. Slave of what master?

Devereaux had never accepted the gesture. Not from his mother, dimly remembered. Not from Mary Krakowski.

She sat down. She folded her arms on the table in front of her. Her head was bent, her eyes cast down. Devereaux noticed her nails were cut short, for work.

"I have papers, mister."

"I don't care about your papers, Mary."

"What you want?"

"What do you do in the Randall Building?"

"Clean."

"What else?"

"Clean. Only this."

"Who were the two men who came to this house two months ago? They asked about you. They asked about me."

"I not know."

"They were from Immigration they said."

"I have green card."

"I don't care about that."

"I have all papers. Papers, green card, legal."

"And a contract."

"Contract for work. Need this."

"Contract to get Karol out of Poland. When is it fulfilled?"

"Three—" She cut herself off.

"When does Karol come to you?"

"Why you ask this?"

"When does Karol get out of Poland?"

"Mister, who you?"

"A man you shouldn't lie to. I know everything about you, Mary."

Tears. "God. Mother of God."

"How many live with John?"

"Six."

"Counting you?"

"Yes."

"What's John's name?"

"John Stolmac."

"That's not Polish."

"Hungarian man. Immigrant too but citizen now. He foreman, Universal Janitorial Service. We work for him."

"You have a contract with John?"

"Yes. I tell you this, mister. Need guarantee to work in United States. To get green card. No can come without this thing."

"What about the other contract?"

"What contract?"

"Mary, stop bullshitting me." The words were delivered lean, harsh. He was standing over her. He leaned close to her face. "You better start telling me the goddam truth."

"I know I immigrant. No speak English too good but not dumb Polack, not to you, mister."

"Mary, tell me about the contract."

"Mister." Teary eyes again. She touched his hand. Look at me, mister, I'm flesh and blood. I'm so close to being all right. All the nights I cried, the nights John beat me, the nights John made me . . . Mister, please don't do this to me.

"Mister, I'm afraid."

"Don't be afraid of anyone but me." No mercy, not a drop of kindness.

He waited. She removed her hand. She stared at the table in front of her. "No tell John this."

"I won't tell," Devereaux lied.

"Contract. All have contract. Contract to work, then after two years, we free."

"Free of what?"

"Three weeks Karol come. That is contract."

"They let your kid out if you work for them?"

"Contract," she repeated.

"What do you do for them?"

"Work. Only work."

"What do you do for them?"

"Who are you, mister?"

"The man you came to spy on," Devereaux said. "Now I want to know about it."

"Mister. I work only. No spy." Very quickly.

She understood, he thought. He got up and went to the cupboard and took down a bottle of vodka. He poured two glasses. He dropped ice cubes in the glasses. He gave one to Mary.

She didn't know what to do.

"Drink, Mary."

"I work, never drink—"

"You've got a bottle of vodka in your purse."

"Mister, you—"

"Drink, Mary."

Just like his mother. She couldn't sip it fast enough. Down the hatch. Salute. Here's looking at you. Mud in your eye. How about another? I just need a little drop, I'm not feeling well today. Hair of the dog. Morning after.

Color returned to Mary's face.

Devereaux poured again.

She knew he was watching her, judging her. "American," she said after the second glass was empty. "You can say anything, do anything. You don't know. You get drunk, you no get drunk, all the same to you. What you think to be Polack? What you think my son in Polonia, my Karol, I tell you things, I no see Karol no more. What you think?"

"I think you have a problem," he said.

"You American, so cold. You have son? You never see someone again? You have anyone you love so much you not see if you do something? My son, mister. My Karol. You man no has someone?"

"No." Devereaux put down his glass. "No. There's no one."

52

"My son, Karol. Three weeks, mister. Karol come, it is finished. You leave me alone. Okay, mister?"

"I want to help you."

"No. You no help dumb Polack."

"When Karol comes. In three weeks. Then you can tell me."

"Why I tell you?"

"Mary, I want you to understand what I'm telling you, all right? If I say something you don't understand, you stop me. All right?" His voice surged lazily, a river in flood, casually destroying.

She waited. Nodded.

"I don't want to harm you. I won't. I won't harm your son when he comes. When you are together, I will get you away from John Stolmac. And I want you to tell me everything. About the contract, everything. The government will take care of you, relocate you."

"What you mean, relocate?"

"Move you to another state where you won't be harmed. Not by John, not by anyone. The government will get you a new name, get you a job. Do you understand?"

"Why you do this?"

"Because we want to know about the contract."

"I don't know."

"Listen, Mary. Look at me." Gray eyes, arctic fields. "That's the good part. The bad part is if you don't tell me when Karol comes. Then we arrest you and question you. You'll tell us anyway, the nice way or the not-so-nice way. You think everything is different here than in Poland and you're right. Except when we want to know something, we'll find out, the same as they find out in Poland. Do you understand?"

"Yes."

"So if you don't help us after Karol comes, we arrest you and we find out what we want to know. Then we throw you in prison for ten or fifteen years. You're a spy, Mary, a goddam spy. I know you are but I don't care about that. Uncle Sam doesn't care. We can give you everything nice, a nice home, a nice place for Karol to grow up in. Or we can put you in prison and take Karol and put him in an orphanage and—"

She bit her knuckle. "Please, I do this thing you say."

"I know, Mary."

He poured another glass of vodka for her. She drank it without hesitation.

"Mary. John wanted you to tell him about me, didn't he?"

Mary stared in silence at him. It was an answer.

"Are you going to tell him, Mary?"

"No," she said.

"That's right. You're not going to tell him anything. Not about this talk, not about what will happen in three weeks, after Karol comes."

"Why trust you, mister?"

"Why trust John? Or the Polish government? Or the people you spy for?"

Mary considered his questions. But she said nothing further to him.

7

Vienna

Morning. The air in the railway carriage smelled stale. Some of the passengers still snored in restless sleep; some were wide awake, huddled over cigarette embers, staring straight ahead. Two borders had been crossed during the long night and there were the usual delays as guards searched the train and collectors examined tickets and customs agents shuffled through passports and visas. All of it slow and usual and routine and slightly unnerving. Even those who had nothing to hide acted as though they had secrets.

The child saw all this, savored the experiences. He was not afraid; he had no secrets. He had slept at one point, reluctantly, but was awakened by dawn light streaming through the dirt-splattered window he leaned against.

"Here," he said softly. "We are here."

The priest next to him scarcely heard him. The priest made a face and yawned and stretched. His bones felt old. He touched his waxy collar and seemed satisfied with the prim gesture.

"Only the beginning of our journey, Karol," the priest said. "We go to the airport in the afternoon. First we fly to Frankfurt and then to America."

"And how long is the airplane flight?"

"Only an hour, I think, to Frankfurt. And then eight hours to Chicago."

Karol closed his eyes to see his mother better. "She will be there?"

"Of course. You asked me a hundred times."

A hundred times were not times enough. Karol opened his eyes. For a long time, they had been on the edge of a great city. Gardens dressed brown for approaching winter; houses with green shutters and red tile roofs; streets and walks; cars waiting for the train to pass; morning workers walking up hills to morning factories.

And now the train slowed as it rolled across a tangle of tracks and slid along the platform, under a vaulted iron ceiling, into West Bahnhof of Vienna. As almost an anticlimax, the long journey down Central Europe from Warsaw was over. The train shuddered, doors were flung open. The aisles, empty a moment before, suddenly were filled with people struggling to carry their bags down the narrow corridor to the exits at either end of the car. A man in a cap with a fierce mustache was handing bags through the window to a second man on the platform. Everyone had waited so patiently so long, but now the journey was over and it seemed as though everyone had a sudden appointment that had to be kept immediately. Blasts of cold air blew refreshingly into the stuffy, stale, overheated compartments of the train. Karol smiled and shivered. He felt cold, a little afraid, happy.

Karol Krakowski lifted up his plastic imitation-leather bag and threw the strap over his shoulder and stood. "Ready," he said and the priest absently patted him on the head. The two of them joined the surging river of people in the aisle and pushed along to the exit.

The sight on the platform was wonderful to Karol.

The platform was filled with life. Passengers tramped along toward the station entrances, lugging too many bags, pausing now and then to readjust their grips. The platform was crowded with baggage trains pulled by electric carts, with hotel hustlers waving enigmatic signs ("Mr. Vladost" and "Regency Group" and "Austro-Hungarian Tour") at the advancing river of passengers.

Inside the terminal, all was dirt and noise and long lines. People shuffled through their Polish currency, waiting in a snakeline in front of the currency exchange. Men with sallow faces and unshaven chins stood at high tables in the station bar, drinking in solitary silence, waiting out the cold morning with steins of Gosser beer.

Karol Krakowski looked here and there, trying to see everything, filling his eye and mind with the circus of colors around him. He had never seen anything like it before.

The dream had been building for two years. But in the last week, the fantasy of what would happen began. He had been taken out of the state orphanage eight days ago. A man who did not speak to him took him to an apartment building in a part of the city where he had never been before.

The apartment contained two bedrooms in which two policemen took turns sleeping. The policemen wore plain clothes but showed him their badges. They gave him papers to sign, papers he did not understand. One of the policemen was always in the apartment with him. He stayed there four days. One of the policemen was named Stanislaus and he told

Karol he had a little boy just his age and hoped to see the child on his next leave, after the assignment was finished. He gave Karol candy when the other policeman was not around.

Their instructions to Karol were simple.

A priest named Thaddeus Wojniak would take him by train to Vienna. He was to obey the priest in everything. After they arrived in Vienna, they would go to the airport and take a plane.

To where? Karol had asked, though he was certain he knew the answer.

"You know where." Stanislaus had laughed and tousled Karol's dark hair. "In a couple of days, little one, you are going to be very, very happy."

So, though they did not say it, he knew he was going to see his mother at last.

She had promised him they would let him go to her in two years and had shown him how to count the time they must be apart on a calendar he kept on the wall behind his bed in the state orphanage on the outskirts of Warsaw.

Two years was a long time, immense as eternity. Day by day, he marked off the two years with neat *X*s across the numbers of the days.

He marked from January until June and then through that long Polish summer, the first of two summers away from her. Marked the days off into fall and down to bleak winter when it was dark all the time, and then up the long slope to spring again. The people who ran the orphanage knew he was not an orphan. He told them of his mother. He told the other children. Some of the other children were driven mad by his boasting that he was not a real orphan. Sometimes, after lights out in the dormitories, there were dreadful fights. *Admit it! You're an orphan the same as we are! You don't have a mother!* But he would not admit it.

*X*s filled the leaves of the calendar now. He thought of all the *X*s across the stretch of weeks, across all the pages past, and it was as though he had accomplished some great feat simply by keeping to his task, marking off the days, as his mother wanted him to do. *Remember me.* But how could he ever forget her?

Some days would be so pleasant that Karol nearly forgot to mark the X at night. And once, when he was sick with a high fever, he neglected his nightly task for four days, which made it more pleasurable to fill in the days when he recovered. Most days were simply days, neither good nor bad, days endured.

His mother's letters came sparingly. She would send articles of clothing with them, and he would show the letters to some of the other children to prove that his mother was alive. Karol became very solitary in those two years in the orphanage; he was not an orphan.

He was just ten. He had been just eight when she left him.

"My darling," she wrote to him. "I love you very much and pray for you every night. Do you pray for me? I am going to make you so happy when we see each other again. I have money saved, we will have toys, we will have our own place together and never be apart again. I did this for you, for your future, and you will understand that someday. We are working hard here and the work is good because when I work hard I can forget, just for a moment, that you are not with me. I think of you all the time, most of all at night. I know you are a brave man and that you are marking off the days until we see each other again. I miss you very much. Be my brave man, Karol. In a little while, we will be together again."

He saved her letters. On Sundays he would sit alone in the dormitory, on his bed, and read all the letters from the first to the latest. Then he would take down his calendar and go through the pages of the months marked off, from the first to the latest.

Karol's own letters to her were brief. He did not write very well when he was only eight years old.

"Dear Mother: I love you and miss you. Please come to see me. It is lonely here. I love you."

He did not think his letters caused her pain. He was

aware only of his own pain at first. How could she have left him? He didn't understand what future she always talked of. He didn't want a future. He wanted her.

On some days Karol hated her, hated her memory, hated her for letting him be so alone. On some days, very bad days, he would forget her features. He would remember parts of her: her eyes but not the curve of her lips when she smiled at him. When he forgot her, he would be frightened and take out the little photograph of her and remember her again. He never forgot her odor; it was the smell of his mother, basic, without parallel in the world.

Stanislaus gave him a new hat to replace his cap. He gave him a clean new coat. "You can't meet your mother in old clothes," he said. On the last night in the apartment, the policemen gave him his instructions for the journey: Karol was to speak to no one, he was only to obey the priest. Their voices were stern, even Stanislaus's. If he had not learned to be brave in two years alone he might have cried. It was the first time they had mentioned his mother.

The following day, Father Thaddeus Wojniak came to the apartment. The child was taken to the rectory of Our Lady of Sorrows, where he stayed another day. Father Wojniak said he was an official with the Catholic Relief Society of Poland. He said that the society cooperated at times with the government in reuniting families broken by immigration or economic circumstances.

The next morning Father Wojniak took the child to Warsaw Station, where they waited for the express train to Vienna to be made up. The station was cold. The priest had bought him a cup of milky coffee and he drank it for breakfast. When the express train was ready, the gates were opened and the priest and the child boarded the train and sat in the open first-class compartment. The priest explained the difference between first class and second class to the boy; he was fascinated. He had never been on a train in his life, nor a plane.

Traffic clogged the streets around Vienna's West Bahnhof, which is in a neighborhood about one and a half miles south of the great Ring Road that encircles the old city.

Red Viennese streetcars ground noisily against the metal tracks outside the station, then screeched into the thick of rumbling traffic like enraged birds. The noises were terrifying and comforting; all life surged around them on the steps of the station. Karol, feeling frustrated from his long imprisonment on the train, ran down the steps ahead of the priest to the park in front of the station.

The priest knew the way. They took one of the streetcars and, after a long ride to the Ring Road, got out and walked across the wooded park, past the official-looking buildings, into the heart of the old city. Karol filled his eyes with what he saw. Women with bags bulging with food and so many cars that they could not all fit into the streets; it was wonderful.

Karol and the priest walked hand in hand down the pedestrian malls fashioned out of streets deemed too narrow to have motor traffic on them. Past shop windows with cream cakes and rich, inventive pastries in a dozen shapes, past store window after store window laden with a thousand trinkets. At times, the child paused and stared at one item or another, but the priest would tug his hand and Karol would follow along reluctantly.

Father Wojniak treated the boy to a rich lunch of heavy cream cake and hot chocolate in a little café just down the square from St. Stefan's Cathedral.

"We have two hours to wait," Father Wojniak said after the meal, while he idled over coffee and stared out the window of the shop at the bright, cold morning light.

Karol said nothing. He carefully ran the edge of his fork across the plate to pick up the last few crumbs of cake. He tasted them.

The priest stared at the child. "Would you like to see the inside of St. Stefan's? It is just down the street. It is one of the greatest churches in the world," the priest said in a proprietary way.

Karol said nothing. He licked at the fork.

"Well?" A tone of annoyance crept into the old man's voice.

Karol stopped licking his fork and put it down. He stared at the priest. No, he thought, he did not want to see the church. He did not like churches. His mother had taken him to church when he was younger, before she went away. His mother had prayed intensely at mass. His mother had taught him all his prayers. At the orphanage, the children were not encouraged to attend mass. He did not do so.

But the priest wanted him to say something.

"Yes," Karol said. "I would like to see the church."

"And we can pray to the success of our long journey, which is only half over."

"Yes," Karol said. It was what the priest wanted.

Once, a long time ago, perhaps a year ago, he had prayed with the same fervor as his mother. In his prayers he asked that his mother be sent back to him. The prayers were not answered and Karol felt it was not because he did not pray hard enough but because no one heard him. He stopped praying.

"Do you want to pray, Father?"

"Of course," Father Wojniak said. There was a note of irritation again. He had gray hair and a gut that swelled beneath his black overcoat. His arms were thin. To Karol, he did not seem unkind or even kind, merely indifferent, as though the child were merely an extra piece of luggage he was required to carry on a long trip that might have been easier undertaken without the extra bag.

"I'll pray for my mother," Karol said. It was what they always wanted to hear.

The priest paid the check and the two of them rose and claimed their bags at the front of the café. They walked out into the bright sunshine.

Stefansplatz is the square in front of the cathedral. It is a pedestrian zone, but on occasion delivery trucks or taxis use the square to make an illegal shortcut from one tangle of

61

vehicle-bearing streets to another. It is not done often, just often enough.

Karol ran into the square, transfixed suddenly by a squadron of gray pigeons rising and dancing in formation across the winter-hard sky. Karol stopped, whirled to see them better, and made himself dizzy following the dance of the birds.

Father Wojniak was behind him. He said something. Karol heard the priest but did not answer. There was the moment of beauty to consider. He was free as the birds were free, whirling in patterns against the cold, cloudless sky.

A taxi dropped off a fare from the airport at the side entrance of the Am Stefansplatz Hotel, directly in front of the main entrance of the cathedral.

The driver turned to look at the square after glancing behind him at the departing passenger, a woman with blond hair and quite extraordinary legs. His Mercedes shot ahead, and for a moment he was blinded by the light dazzling off the windows of a shop opposite the cathedral set at an angle to the hotel itself.

The taxi struck Karol Krakowski 125 feet north of the church entrance. The driver stopped immediately. The child, still clutching his bag, slipped beneath the left front wheel of the diesel Mercedes-Benz 190. Two tons of steel and rubber rolled across Karol's chest.

The red-and-white ambulance came six minutes later, its siren wailing the sad cry that is already like mourning. Father Wojniak, his hands splattered with blood, was on his knees beside the still form of the boy. He said prayers for the dead and raised his hand in benediction. Blood still trickled, faintly, from the boy's nose and mouth. But he was beyond pain.

The people around the child and priest were still. A woman at the edge of the crowd cried silently. The old man was a priest but no one in the crowd understood his words because he prayed in Polish.

62

Karol's imitation-leather bag lay beside his body. His pale, dead left hand was still wrapped around the handle of the bag. Articles of his clothing were scattered on the square. A piece of paper that had escaped from the partially opened bag was caught by the wind, fluttered up, and danced with the pigeons on the cold breeze. It was a page from a calendar in which all the days had been marked out with rows of neat *X*s.

8

Zurich

Felix Krueger lived on Frohburgstrasse on a hill that rose above the university hospital on the east bank of the Limmat River. The house was made of gray stone and was hidden in summer by extensive bushes that grew down to the public walkway. It was shaded by oaks and evergreens.

From a large window on the second floor of the house, Felix Krueger looked down from time to time on the spires of the old city, on the towers of St. Peter's and Grossmunster and Frau Munster, on the buildings of the old town that filled all the streets down to the Quaibrucke and the Zurichsee beyond. He never failed to enjoy the view. He thought it very sad and a little strange that people who visited Switzerland did not find the beauty he found in Zurich, in the solidness of it, in the patient quaintness of its manner.

A gray sea sky sent clouds scudding in like raiders low against the towers of the city. Felix Krueger, hands in his dark trousers, his large belly pressed against the wainscoting beneath the large window, stared at the gathering storm as he tried to concentrate on the words of the agent who had come to his house ten minutes before. He frowned as he turned reluctantly away from the cityscape at the window and stared at Rimsky, the Soviet agent.

Rimsky had finished his recitation some moments before and waited awkwardly, fur cap in hand, for Krueger to speak.

"Despite all you have said and explained, the child is dead," Felix Krueger said. "And that cannot be altered; that, Rimsky, is not satisfactory."

"It was not our fault. I have told you three times—"

"He was in your care."

"The priest—"

"I don't care who you used for a courier; he was in your care." Not said quietly. The words were punched like buttons on a machine. Each word was separate, short, clipped, final.

"We need to . . . have a plan."

"I am the guarantor of the arrangement. It is my reputation, Herr Rimsky, not yours. In fact, your reputation makes my job necessary to your people. And now I find I cannot guarantee anything."

"It was an accident."

"I don't care. What have you told the boy's mother?"

"That there is a delay—"

"Mein Gott." Krueger pulled his large, freckled hands from his pockets and rested his thumbs under his suspenders at the waistline. It was Saturday; he was tired from the long journey back from Prague as well as from the stupid delays at the Czech-German border. But he must be alert now, he must think of what to do.

Krueger frowned. "You lie to her, Herr Rimsky. The Russian mind is truly amazing to me. Your instinct is to lie, always, even when the truth would serve you better. For what purpose did you lie? You only create suspicion in her that will turn against you. I do not understand you Russians, I admit it. You lie out of such ingrained habit that you cannot even understand the truth when it confronts you."

Rimsky would gladly have killed him with the light Uzi automatic pistol with wire stock and a ten-shot clip that he carried in a holster over his right breast. But he did not move. He said nothing. He stared at Krueger with large, hate-filled black eyes.

"The boy is dead. It's too bad. You have to tell the mother the truth immediately and arrange for her to return to Poland—"

"We had decided to tell her the boy was sick and that we would fly her back to—"

"Stupid, Rimsky. Stupid. It is such a palpable lie. And what is to assure that the word will not come out of Poland eventually? What will you do, kill the mother?"

"We're not barbarians."

"Do you not think a double-cross like that would get out? To the very people we are dealing with? The truth, Rimsky, however unpleasant it is to you. Or your masters."

"This is something we will decide."

"No. It is something I will decide, Herr Rimsky. Something that involves me and my reputation and our whole . . . arrangement. What about the priest?"

Rimsky was startled. "What about him? He has returned to Warsaw."

"Send him to Chicago. To the woman. She's a Catholic?"

"Yes."

"She'll believe a priest." Felix Krueger frowned. "Have him tell the truth."

"But what if she doesn't believe him?"

"Who will she believe better? You?"

Rimsky frowned. He could remove the pistol so easily, begin firing, watch the blood spread across the pompous well-fed Swiss gut. "But if she does not believe the priest?"

"What then?" Felix Krueger's voice was mocking. His face was flushed, his freckles stood out on the bridge of his nose. His large eyes seemed to protrude from their sockets. He seemed to fill the room as a full autumn moon might fill a countryside sky.

"We can take care of her."

"What a foolish thing to say. How many are in the cell run by John Stolmac in Chicago? How many?"

"Six women now—"

"Yes. Six. What will you do to Mary Krakowski? Kill her?"

Rimsky said nothing. He pursed his lips as though under strain. It was exactly what would be done to Mary Krakowski if the woman did not believe the messenger, if she would not return to Poland.

"There. You answer the question," Krueger said, smiling. "Then what will you do with the others, Herr Rimsky, after you kill the boy's mother? Kill one of them and the guarantee, the whole arrangement, is broken for all of them. Do you think they will trust you anymore? Do you think they will work for you anymore?"

"But they will fear us."

"It is better, I think, to arrange that Mary Krakowski is given her American citizenship before you even think to bring her back to Poland. Give her the papers you've prepared, give her the bonus money. It is a guarantee for her that she can return to America if she chooses."

Rimsky said, "Is that what you suggest?"

"It is more than a suggestion. Our arrangement can't survive without trust. Their trust. The priest will speak to her. One of your agents will give the priest her papers—"

"You know it is difficult to arrange . . . citizenship on such short notice. There is the problem with altering their computers and—"

"I don't want to hear details. I'm a businessman, I don't believe in miracles. Just hard work. And deadlines. We need action now and you have wasted time already."

"This must be approved at the highest level."

"Have it done then. Now." Felix Krueger took a step into the center of the room and stared at Rimsky. The Soviet was the same height as Krueger but not as large. "The Numbers exists as a network only because of a trust, and I'm the center of the trust. They trust in me." He pounded one thick finger against his chest several times for emphasis. "Without me, there is nothing."

> ➤ ➤ ➤

IT WAS DONE. But not as Felix Krueger wished it to be done. The priest named Thaddeus Wojniak left for the United States on a flight connecting through Vienna and Frankfurt and arrived in Chicago thirty-nine hours after Felix Krueger's conversation with Rimsky in Zurich. The priest had been under no orders to the Polish Security Police, but the Church cooperated with the government in matters that were not political; this was one of those matters. So the bishop had told a reluctant Thaddeus Wojniak.

The priest looked brittle coming out of the connecting tunnel to the plane at O'Hare Airport shortly after nine o'clock Monday night. He trudged with the others through customs and immigration, enduring the lines, his face drawn and chalky. He had seen the dead child in dreams during the last four nights.

He knew Chicago. He had visited the city many times to raise money for the Catholic Relief Society of Poland. This visit would not be pleasant. And there were delicate matters to be dealt with.

The cab took him down into the South Side, to the address on Kenwood Avenue he had given the driver. He trudged up the stone steps to the entry level of the three-story building. He had papers for Mary Krakowski; he had instructions from his bishop, relayed to the Church through the office of the primate, Cardinal Glemp. Why was this matter so important to all of them? Father Wojniak felt himself involved in something more than a mission of mercy.

The priest pressed the button of the mailbox marked "Stolmac."

He felt tired and sorry for himself. He felt a continuous pain at the memory of a child running across a square, so happy. He will rest now with God, his Father, and the angels and the other saints. So he would tell Karol's mother. But would he believe it when he said those things?

John Stolmac buzzed the outer door, then waited at the door of his second-floor apartment. He was a large man with thick black hair and fierce brown eyes and a black mustache that curled beneath his long, large nose. His skin was very white.

"Father," he said. "I was told." He opened the door wide. He wore a black suit and tie. Perhaps in honor of a priest visiting their home; perhaps already in mourning.

"Have you told her anything?"

"No," John Stolmac said. They spoke in Polish, in half-whispers. The apartment, built along a corridor that stretched from kitchen to front room, was in shadows. "Are you tired? Would you like coffee, beer?"

"No. Better to tell her. First."

He stepped into the hallway. John Stolmac took his bag. Along the corridor were closed bedroom doors.

A door opened now. Father Wojniak saw a young, pretty woman in sweater and skirt, with long brown hair. She wore no makeup. She stared at the priest for a long time with resentment in her eyes. She was a smart one, the priest thought suddenly; she knows.

John Stolmac said to her, "Teresa. Father, this is Teresa Kolaki. She is Mary's friend. Teresa. Get Mary, please."

The woman stared at the two men for a moment longer and then turned, closing the door behind her. A moment passed in awkward silence. Then a heavier woman with dyed red hair opened the bedroom door. Teresa was behind her. Mary Krakowski was pale despite her heavy makeup. Her eyes were red. She was already in mourning, Father Wojniak thought. She only wants me to say it.

He took a step toward her and held out his shaking hands.

There. No words passed. It was as though she realized the message in that moment.

Karol.

68

She fell to the floor without another sound, unconscious for a moment to all the pain that would follow.

9
Chicago

They had spoken four times in two weeks. No one else knew they made contact. The calls were never made from the house where he stayed nor to headquarters or Hanley's apartment. There was a longstanding arrangement for special calls, calls that would not be tapped by anyone.

Always at four in the morning. The simple arrangement was called "Red Sky" because of a poetic streak in Hanley that defied analysis:

Red sky at morning, sailors take warning.

Devereaux had made the initial call after speaking with Mary Krakowski that first morning in Melvina's kitchen. The system was initiated always by the agent, never by control. The phone rang in Hanley's office; a clear voice said:

"Red Sky."

Thereafter, every fourth day, Hanley waited by a telephone in an all-night Huddle House restaurant three blocks from his apartment in northwest Washington. The early morning was the easiest time to lose tails (or spot them in the first place); it was the time of day when even agents slept, when the world of security was at its most unguarded.

"There is something," Hanley said.

Devereaux waited. He was in a telephone booth in an all-night Walgreen's drugstore nearly a mile from the block where Melvina had lived for more than forty years.

Hanley's voice did not sound sleepy, though he had not slept much since the first call from Devereaux. This was not supposed to be happening. Security at NSA had promised a thorough cleansing for Devereaux and Rita Macklin; the KGB would not continue on their trail simply because Devereaux would cease to exist, and mere revenge for Macklin's minor role in the Helsinki business would not be enough to risk a hit on U.S. territory. That's what the spookmasters at NSA had assured Hanley.

But now two foreign agents had visited Melvina trying to get a line on Devereaux. And a Polish alien who spoke vaguely about "guarantees" and her "contract" had been placed in Melvina's house to spy on Devereaux as well.

"The women contract with Universal Janitorial, a national chain headquartered in Roanoke, Virginia. But it works on a franchise basis. The franchise in Chicago is Excell Importers, Inc., which is a very odd name for a very odd business. They contract to bring in immigrant labor—Mexican, Colombian, Venezuelan, Pakistani, et cetera—for low-paying domestic and factory jobs. They are both recruiter and employer."

"Is it legal?"

"Seemingly so. Something like that is never strictly legal but this is legal. Anyway, they have the contract for special cleanup projects at various places, including the Department of Special Mathematics at the University of Chicago."

"What's special?"

"A government contract, of course."

"To do what?"

"Research," Hanley said in a dry, never-give-it-away voice.

Devereaux waited. Hanley had something. Something more. The phone booth was nothing more than a plastic divider in a line of similar booths along a wall in the back of the store. At the all-night drug counter, a tired man in a white smock was grinding something in a glass bowl with a glass pestle, while a large, fat man with heavy black skin like coal oil waited patiently. The air was stuffy. The store was

70

crowded with sale items jumbled on shelves, stuck on boxes in aisles, advertised on tired cardboard signs hanging in strings across the ceiling.

"Research contracted by NSA a year ago. Actually part of a fairly broad, theoretical, interservice, interdisciplinary—"

"Cut the crap, Hanley," Devereaux said.

Hanley smiled at his end of the line. "It's about developing new cryptography, both software and hardware. The project is ongoing, split between a dozen universities and think tanks coast to coast."

"So is any part of it critical?"

"You mean, for the Opposition to make probes?"

Devereaux waited.

"Perhaps. We don't know. We get on the receiving end at the Section. NSA doles out little secrets from time to time to its sister services and we are grateful for each new coding machine or computer sending device."

"And you can't ask NSA because I'm supposed to be under its tender loving care."

"Which, apparently, is not quite as good care as it should have been."

"What about security?"

"What do you mean?"

"Security. At this project, others like it."

"You mean, actual theft? Well, it happened two years ago in Palo Alto. A member of the Polish Secret Service was dealing with one of the cryptographers at a private firm. The cryptographer said he sold out because he needed money to buy a second car for his wife. FBI broke that one. But they still don't know the extent of the damage. These things get very involved."

"So the Opposition would keep plugging away, year after year, hoping to burrow in, every now and then stumbling across a bit of good luck."

"Yes," Hanley said in his quiet, dull voice. "Exactly as we do."

"Does this Excell Importers . . . do they have other contracts?"

"No, not in this area. For all we know, Excell could be legitimate."

"Something isn't though."

"You keep suggesting that a bunch of immigrant cleaning ladies who barely speak English are being used as spies by the Opposition. It's ludicrous, isn't it?"

"Yes. Just as silly as that traitor in California needing money to buy a second car."

"But they wouldn't know what they were looking for."

"At least now we know there's something worth looking for. Mary Krakowski is a spy, Hanley. Maybe an unwilling agent, maybe even stupid, but she knows. She knows when I talk to her."

"Will she . . . has she given you away?"

"I don't think so. It was a risk. I had to make her more afraid of me than of them. She doesn't want any trouble." He closed his eyes for a moment. He saw her, clearly, saw the pain in her face, saw her greedily drink down the tumbler of vodka he gave her.

"The child was supposed to be out. But she said there was a delay."

"What happened?"

"Hell, Hanley, how can I know that? I'm waiting for the boy the same as Mary. I can use him as leverage. Once she's got him, she won't be afraid of the other side. We can put pressure on her."

"What a dirty business," Hanley said.

Devereaux waited.

"How many of these people are they using?" Hanley went on.

"I don't know. But it's my ass, Hanley. You and the Section and the geniuses at the Puzzle Factory were supposed to give me a new face. How come they're still looking for the old one?"

"We never thought about covering the trail out there.

You hadn't seen your great-aunt in twenty years. I nearly forgot she existed—"

"No, Hanley. You *did* forget. And before I could figure out what was going on, I walked into it. I might as well see it through now. About Mary, I mean. Then you're going to have to help me out of here," Devereaux said. His voice was tired, not because of the hour but because a sort of fatal tiredness had overwhelmed him in the last few days. He didn't want to keep at it. Survival, which is all that had counted for him in his years as an active intelligence agent in the field, seemed about to slip out of his hand. And he didn't care.

➤   ➤   ➤

DAWN BROKE AS THE WOMAN NAMED Teresa Kolaki slipped along the alley. Her head was covered by a red babushka. A dark coat of no particular color wrapped her slim body. She wore boots against the cold, although her legs were bare.

Every few hundred feet she stopped and glanced behind her. Nothing changed, nothing moved. Once she was frightened by a large gray rat that leaped from the top of an open garbage can across her path. She nearly cried out. Her face drained of color. The rat paused, looked at her with gentle understanding on its mean, pinched face, and then scampered on, down a gangway strewn with garbage between two brick apartment buildings.

Her hands were cold. Her fingers were pinched red from raw, wet north winds. She carried a large brown parcel tied with white twine against her chest as she ran along the alley.

Teresa Kolaki turned into a gangway marked 4601. She pushed against an iron gate into a small backyard bare of grass or trees. She climbed five gray painted wooden steps to the back door of the three-story townhouse. For the first time, she hesitated; if she had stopped to think, to reconsider, at Stolmac's apartment in the black minutes before dawn, she could not have done this thing. Not even for Mary.

She bit her lip and knocked hard at the door and then

looked around her. A dog barked joylessly from a yard up the alley.

She waited a moment and then knocked again.

A bolt was drawn from behind the door. She saw the door open a crack.

Thank God, she thought. It was the same man Mary had described to her. A man from the government. A man who said he would do something.

"Mary told me. You are the man," Teresa said. Her light voice was accented but clear; unlike Mary, she had studied English for two years at school.

"Who are you?"

"Teresa Kolaki."

He opened the door wide. She hesitated a moment and then, chin down, walked in. "It is about Mary," she said. Her brown eyes were wide. There was terror in them.

She put the parcel down on the bare kitchen table. She turned. She considered him shrewdly a moment. He closed the door behind him but his eyes did not leave her. Was he strong? Was he to be trusted? Sometimes men seemed strong and broke so easily. "Also about me." She decided by rushing into the words. "A bad thing has happened."

Devereaux went to a pot on the stove. He took down a glass and poured Teresa some coffee.

"Sugar?"

"Yes."

He mixed it and gave it to her. "Sit down." Quietly.

Devereaux sat down across from her at the table. He waited. Teresa sipped the scalding coffee. "I did not know you are up."

He waited. It was only small talk. She wanted to feel sure. But she would have to make up her mind without help. It was the only way.

"John does not know I am here."

Still he waited. What could he offer her to reassure her? Nothing. Words were not real promises; they carried no guarantees.

"They killed Mary's son."

She put down the glass of coffee and stared at it, her hand still around it. Anger had been banked in her by the long, cold night of fear, of listening to Mary's tears. Her eyelids flickered a moment as though she had become lost in a trance and was trying to break it, or trying to awaken from a dream by force of will.

When she spoke again, her voice was filled with ashes, leaden. "They sent a man they say was a priest last night to tell Mary her son is dead. The priest says it was an accident. He says that Karol was run over by a car. He showed Mary a picture from the Vienna paper. He said he was a priest. I don't know what he was. They promise Mary it was an accident and they want to take her home now. Mary tells me, in the night, that she does not believe this man is a priest. She says they kill her son and now they will kill her. She has a contract. Here."

She snapped the twine with sure, strong fingers. She opened the parcel. Papers. And a letter from someone who wrote in a childish hand. He examined the papers slowly.

Something had been wrong from the beginning, from the moment he got Melvina's strange letter. He was still targeted by the other side. Perhaps Rita was being watched as well and would be dealt with after they were sure Devereaux was dead. Rita Macklin was still of use to them if she could lead them to Devereaux. They were like bulldogs. They had held on so long they had forgotten why they bit in the first place. Devereaux was to be killed. There was no change in the plan from the day two Bulgarian assassins walked up a mountain trail in Virginia and were ambushed and killed.

Part of what was wrong was Mary Krakowski, the reluctant agent. And now this one. They were all agents, all seemingly reluctant, all closemouthed. Teresa wanted to change the terms of her deal; she wanted assurances not just from them but from Devereaux. What did she want him to say?

I am a dead man, Teresa. I can't save my own life. I can't save the life of a woman I love. And what can I do for you?

"This is a contract," she said in a stubborn voice.

Devereaux picked up the document. A legal paper, in German. Devereaux picked through it; he had studied German a long time ago and the words came back to him, slowly. A contract between the American-Polish Export Agency and Excell Importers, Inc., of Chicago, as well as Universal Janitorial Service. All involving one slightly sad alcoholic woman named Mary Krakowski.

He read slowly, unconcerned that Teresa Kolaki sat impatiently across from him. The kitchen filled with gray light. The house was quiet. A clock ticked on the second landing.

There was a bond in the amount of 500,000 Swiss francs. A guarantee bond of performance. At the end of two years, a period of indenture to Excell Importers would be ended and, as an inducement (on a second sheet of paper), the signature of one Felix Krueger guaranteed passage of a Polish minor, Karol Krakowski, from Warsaw, Poland, to Chicago, Illinois, United States of America. To be effected four days ago.

"You see, mister?"

Devereaux put down the paper. For a long moment, he stared across the table at Teresa Kolaki. She was afraid but not the way Mary Krakowski had been afraid, a woman on the edge of panic that was kept down only by doses of alcohol at regular intervals. Perhaps Teresa's fear was mitigated by the stubborn cast to her chin or the clear brown eyes that did not leave his face. Then he saw what it was: her hands, strong, with long fingers and broken nails, extended like a spider's web over the bits of paper on the table. "You see," she said, "I have brought you what you wanted. Brought you proof. What will you do for me now? What will you do for any of us?"

"Do you have a contract as well?"

Again, she hesitated, but her eyes did not leave his face. She bit her lip. The warmth of the room, the utter silence of the house around her, both assured her and frightened her. Who was this strange, solitary man sitting alone in a kitchen at six in the morning as though he had always expected Mary

76

or Teresa to come to him, waiting as a cat waits beneath a tree for its victim to make a mistake?

"Yes," she said.

"For how long?"

"Two years."

"You work with Mary."

"Yes."

"At the university."

"Yes."

"You live with her and John Stolmac."

"Yes."

"Who have they promised you?"

"What?"

"Who will be released when your time is up?"

Her hands trembled but she kept her eyes on him as though she would be lost if she turned her gaze away.

"My son. Stefan."

"And now that Karol is dead, you're afraid."

"Yes."

He waited.

"My God," she said. "I am sick with grief for him. Do you understand? I don't want to be here. I want the contract to end, I want Stefan . . ."

She had started to cry but there were no tears. Only her eyes shone wetly. She wiped her hand across her eyes. He made no move. He watched her.

"What do you do for them?"

"Work."

"What kind of work?"

He knew, she thought. He knows everything.

Devereaux spoke again, flatly, without warmth or feeling. "You can't tell me part anymore. None of you. You have to tell me everything."

"They would kill me."

"No. I don't think so. Why did you come here if you thought that?"

"What can you do?"

Devereaux let the ghost of a smile turn at the corners of his lips. She wanted leverage. She wanted an American side if that could serve her; but she didn't want to close the door on the other side either, not until she got Stefan out safely.

"What do you want me to do?"

"What I said," Teresa said. "I said I want Stefan."

"Perhaps I can do that."

"How?"

"I don't know. I have to know why I'll do it."

She understood but she wouldn't acknowledge it. "We are just dumb Polish cleaning—"

"Cut it out, Teresa. You're a schoolteacher. You speak at least one foreign language. Don't waste my time. If you came here, you came here for a reason."

"What can you do for Stefan?"

"What can you do for me?"

"What do you want?"

"The university. How do you arrange it?"

She kept her eyes on him. She hated him as much as John Stolmac. All men were the same when they had power over women. "In the trash. I don't know what to look for, no one does. They want many things. Anything from a computer, on computer paper. Also notes, handwritten notes. They are very careless. And nobody sees a cleaning woman. No one."

"They have security."

"Guards? One is a boy, nothing; he flirts with us. I think Tanya is in love with him. But we let Tanya and the boy go into one of the laboratories together. They make love." Teresa made a face. "I know it is hard for Tanya but she should not be so easy. She wants to be married. To an American. So her brother can come more easily."

"Everyone at Excell has someone back in the old country."

"Yes."

"That's their hold on you. But why do you expect they will honor the contracts?"

"Always in the past. Until—"

"Until Karol was killed. And you think they did it."

"They want to take Mary back. Tonight. They give her drugs. Last night. She is sick, holding her stomach." She closed her eyes. She couldn't describe the horror of that long night with Mary, half mad with grief, drugged, sleeping and dreaming and calling out Karol's name over and over.

"What is the guarantee?"

"Mr. Krueger."

"Felix Krueger. The name on the guarantee. Who is he?"

"A rich gentleman. A businessman. In Zurich. He promised us."

"What?"

"You see, he says that he has no interest in this." Teresa frowned. Her English was good but the concept that Felix Krueger had explained was subtle. She had understood it when the Polish interpreter had repeated the words but now she was not certain she could explain it.

"Mr. Krueger says that we are numbers. We are only numbers on a sheet of paper. He says we are an account to him. And because we mean nothing to him, we can trust him. He says it is all business. We want something, they want something, and Mr. Krueger makes money by helping to everyone to get what they want." She realized her grammar had slipped; again, characteristically, she bit her lip. But she saw that Devereaux understood.

And so did the woman who had been standing at the door behind them. "My God, Red, just as I said it. Slavery."

Teresa turned, startled.

Devereaux glanced at his great-aunt with lazy eyes. "This doesn't concern you, Melvina."

"This is my house, Red; everything concerns me here." Cold.

"You don't want to be involved in this business."

"I am involved, Red. You didn't even know about it until I wrote to you."

And that was perfectly true.

Devereaux placed the tips of his fingers together in an

attitude of prayer and leaned back in the wooden captain's chair.

"I can help you," he began. It was the first lie. He stopped, stared at Teresa. Her eyes questioned him and then believed him. He proceeded to the second lie. "You won't be harmed. Not by us. Not by them."

He stopped again. She wanted to believe him, that was working for him.

The third lie was easier. "I know what to do but I need you to give me full information. Not now but when you can arrange to meet me. Away from this house. I want to keep these contracts—"

"No. I have to bring them back with me."

"Then we'll make a copy. There must be a goddam copy machine in this ghetto."

"Then what?"

Then what? He paused, considered a fourth lie, and decided it might work. "I need a description of Stefan—where he lives, where he goes to school, everything. We have people in Poland."

"You can get him out?"

"Yes." The lies were very easy now.

"Oh, my God—"

"It's too late for Mary."

"But they will kill her."

"Probably not. In fact, I'm sure they won't harm her." The next lie. They all were underpinned with Teresa's belief; believing made his lies so plausible. And his manner was calm, gentle even. He was a strong man, she thought. He could do these things.

Perhaps Melvina, who should have known better, believed him as well. "How will you do it, Red?"

"This doesn't concern you."

"Red. This poor woman. And Mary—"

"Mary's child is dead. He was killed. Intentionally or not. I think not. And Mary has to go back to Poland. And

80

Teresa has to go back to the apartment and be quiet and say nothing until I see her again."

"But it's slavery, Red."

"Yes. In a way."

"But she's a slave."

"Yes. I suppose."

"My God. You can't permit this—"

"I can't do anything about it. Not right now." He looked at Teresa. Did she understand that?

Teresa, as though answering, nodded almost imperceptibly.

"Let's go, Teresa—"

"I won't permit you to let—"

"Be quiet, Melvina." Sharply, the crack of an ice field. "This doesn't concern you anymore."

"I am not a slave."

They both looked at her. It was so fierce a pronouncement that it startled them.

She looked from one to the other. "I am not a slave."

"You are, dear," Melvina said in her icy, patronizing voice. "You are a bondwoman. You traded your freedom for . . . for what?"

"You cannot understand anything," she said. What did they know, playing with her, even using her, arguing over her in this great kitchen of a great house? Did she seem like a stupid animal to them? Her hand brushed at her sweater. She felt they were examining her. "My husband was Michael Kolaki. He is a great man, intelligent, very handsome. He has trouble at the university because . . . this was at the beginning of Solidarity. He joins the workers, he argues with me about the cause. And I am afraid. Of him and for him. And one day he is run down in a street by a car, just like Karol. But this is no accident, surely. And I am a widow now and I cannot teach at the school, and one day I meet a man who tells me there is a chance still. If I do this one thing, hard thing, then there is a chance for me. In America. Do you know what that

81

means to me? My life is over and I am twenty-three years old and then a man tells me, no, there is still a new life if you want it. My husband's brother is Stefan, he lives in Chicago, he can take care of me, of my little Stefan, after . . . after this is over for me. I want to go to America because there are many jobs here. Not too hard for Polish immigrants but too hard for you." She looked at him sharply. "But if I can get visa, Stefan cannot get visa. Always the same. So this man in Polonia, for the government, he tells me what I must do. A little thing. I don't trust them. But he tells me of Mr. Krueger, and when Mr. Krueger speaks to us he gives us many names. Write to them, says Mr. Krueger. I am a man of business, I do not break my word, he says. And it is so. A contract. He gives a contract. Two years I work, I do for them, then Stefan is free. It is so; it is written down."

"Until Karol was killed," Devereaux said.

"My God," Melvina said. "Red, this is monstrous. This is horrible."

Devereaux said nothing. He saw all the horror of it from the moment Teresa decided to believe he could save her, save Stefan. He saw the horror was just beginning for Teresa. And for himself.

10

Washington, D.C.

Across the street, the FBI watchers stood at the window. The 250-mm. lens attached to the black body of the Nikon on a tripod focused sharply on the figure turning into the grounds of the Soviet Embassy. Once Malenkov half turned to speak to the Red Army guard near the door and that is the picture the camera caught—a man in shadows, his face large and rubbery, his eyes hidden beneath dark brows. He might have been one of a hundred such men who slipped into the embassy every week. Malenkov knew he was watched; the watchers knew that he knew; it was all part of the game, piecing together this bit of information with a thousand random bits of other information, hoping that it all would mean something.

Four minutes later Malenkov entered the bare, fluorescent-lit room in the second subbasement of the embassy and sat down at a plastic-topped table. The room contained two chairs. The walls were smooth white plaster. No windows or photographs adorned them. Even the light switch was outside the room.

The Soviets believed that the room was totally shielded from even the most sophisticated listening device trained on the building. The FBI had given up trying to penetrate the lower floors of the embassy. Shieldings of lead along with layers of white noise between the walls and the earth outside—the earth had no worms or other insects, the grass did not grow well—defeated the agency's best efforts.

Six blocks from the embassy, a recording machine automatically started up inside a small office in a six-story building that contained quarters for dentists and not very successful lawyers. The machine was programmed to record the moment any sound was detected inside the safe room in the subbasement of the Soviet Embassy. The machine, the people who tended it, and the office were all part of Synetronics, Inc., a dummy corporation owned by the National Security Agency.

This was the translated transcript (the conversation was in Russian, Standard Moscow dialect) delivered twelve hours after the conversation to Assistant Director of Security Operations Henry L. Craypool inside the NSA complex at Fort George G. Meade, Maryland:

MALENKOV: Nothing except routine. Here. (Sounds of paper rustling.) The two from NSA took an unauthorized lunch at 6:00 P.M. yesterday. I suspect they missed the telephone call.

83

OTHER: Was it of interest?

MALENKOV: I don't know. Here. (More paper rustling.) Something's up. She asked for a week's vacation yesterday, it was granted. Now she tells her caller—this "Tom"—that she has an assignment in Paris, she'll be gone for two weeks.

OTHER: (Laugh.) You don't understand. Women always lie. It is probably nothing. She doesn't wish to see this one. This is the one who always calls at the last moment?

MALENKOV: Yes. I suppose you're right. But where would she go on vacation? She hasn't taken time for a year. Since Helsinki. She knows the risks, as long as November is undergoing reprocessing.

OTHER: Umm.

MALENKOV: If I may, Major?

OTHER: Of course.

MALENKOV: Korsoff is in Chicago. I'd like him to go back to that old woman again. Without the Bulgarian this time. Talk to her alone, out of the house, away from the blackie.

OTHER: She rarely leaves the house. Korsoff says she is a sort of invalid.

MALENKOV: We wait for her. It would be no less frustrating than waiting for Rita to make contact with November. It is nearly a year.

OTHER: Patience. I realize you call her "Rita" now. I understand. One becomes intimate after a while with the subject. You hear her every day. You see her in the building. You hear her make love, wash, you hear her sing. She is like a wife to you. I think you're becoming jealous of "Tom."

MALENKOV: I am frustrated, Major. The separation has been total. Eleven months now. KGB looks foolish.

OTHER: To whom?

MALENKOV: The Americans. We made a contract, a commitment. To take out one of their agents. And we haven't done it.

OTHER: But we've forced them into a neutral position. They can't use him because it will expose him. They know we're still waiting.

MALENKOV: They guess it. Put up the pressure, Major. Tell Korsoff to get the woman alone. She must have had some contact.

OTHER: It was useless before. They are not a close family, apparently.

MALENKOV: He's close to no one. (Pause.) I don't think I understand him, even now. I've read all the profiles, the operations he took part in. What is his motivation? He chafes under

84

command. His best work is brilliant but idiosyncratic. It is as though he courts disaster—from us, from his masters. Why?

OTHER: I had a theory once.

MALENKOV: (Garbled.)

OTHER: Well. I think he is bored.

MALENKOV: Bored?

OTHER: It would explain some things.

MALENKOV: No. I can't accept it, with all respect, Major.

OTHER: Her motivation is obvious.

MALENKOV: That she loves him? Yes. I suppose. Remember the recording?

OTHER: Yes. It was affecting. I've never seen her but when she cried that night. It was—

MALENKOV: January. Right after Helsinki. Affecting. As you said. She even said his name in sleep. She woke up, quite afraid. She had a nightmare.

OTHER: She saw him kill two men. The Bulgarians. The Americans knocked down that house, leveled the ground so the bodies wouldn't be found. Sometimes I think they are barbarians. Perhaps I've been here too long. Tanya watches television all night. Her English is proficient. I wish it wasn't. She fills her mind with such trash, I can't get her to read a book anymore.

MALENKOV: Forbid—

OTHER: (Laughs.) Dear Malenkov. This is America. Children are not forbidden. Even the Second Secretary has problems. His son threatens to run away if he can't have a motorcycle. Remember what happened the other time? I tell you, this country is the serpent.

MALENKOV: We need to put on pressure. I feel something is happening.

OTHER: Why?

MALENKOV: The old woman. In Chicago. She must be a key. She knew what Korsoff was. She wasn't so stupid. I saw the report but I talked to Korsoff as well. He had an instinct about her. I think we should try Chicago again.

OTHER: (Sigh.) All right. Anything to shift this away from Washington for a while. I wish the new man would simply drop this—

MALENKOV: I know. Bureaucrats. They've made an execution order in some subagency of the Third Directorate and no one has gotten around to rescinding it. So it falls to you and me, Major, to carry on, spend our lives if need be, for something that may not even be so important.

OTHER: Well. We're both in service. That is what it means to us, eh?

MALENKOV: (Garbled.)

(Sound of chairs scraping. Footsteps. A door closes. Ten seconds of silence. The tape ends.)

➤ ➤ ➤

"DO YOU ALWAYS EAT HERE?" Mrs. Neumann said. Her plain face was merry with mischief.

"Yes," Hanley replied. His face was dour, his nearly bald head glittered under the harsh lamp hanging over the table from the tin ceiling.

"Wonderful. I didn't think official Washington still permitted such places."

"The owner is talking about selling. Someone wants the land for an office building. They raised his taxes again." Hanley mournfully bit into the cheeseburger.

The little bar and grill on Fourteenth Street was a relic. Land costs had risen to drive out other, similiar enterprises that had once littered this section of official Washington. The Greek immigrant named Sianis who owned the bar and grill still resisted all blandishments to sell and move on. He had a mysterious belief that he would certainly fail in the same enterprise if he had to locate it in any other building, on any other street. The bar section was dark, filled with the nodding presence of regular customers drinking their lunches. On a back wall, the television set was turned on but the sound was turned off. Photographs filled a second wall. Yellowed clippings from the old Washington *Star* and the old *News* and even the *Herald* were preserved in dime-store frames along with photographs of families, weddings, old-timers. None of the photos carried identification; they were more icons for Sianis, warding off evil spirits and rapacious landlords. Hanley had taken a solitary lunch here for nearly thirty years.

His lunch menu was always the same: one cheeseburger well done with a raw onion, and one perfect martini straight up in a chilled glass.

Lydia Neumann's company here was not usual. She was a large woman with spiky hair and a raspy voice and a plain way of speaking. She was also director of computer analysis of R Section. Hanley had invited her to lunch out of desperation; nothing that he wanted to say could be said in the Section. Nothing could compromise the situation. He had worked this way, secretly, with Neumann before, during the business in Paris. He knew she would help, could be trusted.

Hanley was second man in the Section, chief of operations, a dry and punctilious bureaucrat who had survived changes of administration and policy for three decades simply because he knew where the bodies were buried. But now a buried body had returned to life.

"Devereaux," he said to Lydia Neumann now, putting down the remains of his burger. He picked up the martini and sipped it.

Lydia Neumann thoughtfully spooned her chili. "It isn't spicy enough."

"Are you a gourmet?" Hanley's pinched face matched his flat, pinched Nebraska voice.

Mrs. Neumann smiled. "Spice, Hanley, is the spice of life." She took a small bottle of Tabasco sauce and shook it into the chili. "That's better," she said.

"Devereaux," he repeated.

"Our November man. Is he still an unperson?"

"No. Not quite. Not quite anything. Except we have problems. I need your help."

"But we couldn't talk in the Section."

"No."

"I see." She did. She put down her spoon and waited.

"Three weeks ago he dropped out. He was in an apartment in New York. The Puzzle Factory uses it, places like it, for stashing ghosts until a new identity is made for them."

"And he wouldn't stay dead."

"It's more complicated than that."

"You've talked to him."

"Yes."

"You haven't told anyone."

"No."

"Why are you telling me?"

"Because I need help. A special sort of job, getting around without anyone knowing that you're getting around."

"Damn you, Hanley. I have four years to go before pension—"

"It isn't like that," Hanley said. It was a lie. It was exactly like that. "Nine weeks ago, two men visited his great-aunt. She lives in Chicago. She raised him."

"Really? I never thought of November as having been a child."

"Everyone is a child once."

"Even you, Hanley?"

He ignored the needling. "Melvina Devereaux."

"I like that name."

"The two men identified themselves as Immigration and Naturalization. They weren't. Opposition."

"So they're still after him."

"Stubborn bastards. But that isn't the real problem. He's stumbled by chance on an operation by the other side."

"In Chicago?"

"Part of it is there. But it must be very large. There is a lot at stake; a lot of people are involved. Very low level but the effort expended is enormous. What I can't understand is how an operation this big has been going on and not a word of it. At least, that's what makes me curious. Makes November curious."

"He's still November then? I thought we were getting rid of the old nomenclature."

"He's nothing, Mrs. Neumann. Neither fish nor fowl. He isn't even assigned back to us by the Director of Central Intelligence. He's in the incapable hands of the people at the Puzzle Factory. Except they've fucked up and now this other matter. I'm in the middle."

"What about him?"

"November. Yes. I suppose he's in the middle as well. There's a flight tonight. Czech Airlines. To Prague. A woman is going to be put on the plane. She's drugged; her name is Mary Krakowski—"

"And she's part of this . . . what is this thing you find so 'curious'?"

"Part of a scavenger sort of operation. Polish immigrants, others, they work for a dummy company; it's an espionage operation. In this case, going through certain laboratories, computer rooms, at the University of Chicago. A cryptography project, sections of it all over the country."

"They steal garbage."

"How did you know?"

"Because nobody sees the cleaning women, right?"

"How did you know?"

"I'm a woman, Hanley. I see what you don't see."

"I don't believe in the myth of female superiority."

Lydia Neumann smiled. "Neither do I. Not as a myth at least. He wants you to stop the flight?"

"Yes. For starters."

"He's got a scenario planned?"

"I doubt it. He says Rita Macklin is in danger."

"Is she?"

"He made contact yesterday, again this morning early, and then later in the morning—"

"He should use Sprint. Or MCI."

Hanley didn't even respond to the sally. He was staring at a point on the table, frustrated, trying to see his way out of a problem that seemed more complicated in the last twenty-four hours. "I put a casual watcher on her. Yesterday. He reported this morning. The woman is in a fishbowl. There are at least two, possibly four men monitoring her at her apartment. I don't even think they're aware of each other. And he checked the roof. He says there's listening equipment inside, outside, everywhere. His beeper went crazy; it was like walking into a uranium mine. So what the hell is going on? Who's spying on whom? Why are they wasting all this time, all these people?"

"Because they have them. A bureaucrat like you ought to understand that." She sipped her soda. "The question is: Who are they? And is this Macklin lady in danger?"

"I don't know. I don't know anything. Except there is something wrong with this espionage business in Chicago. It's a clumsy arrangement. It had to have broken apart before now. Someone has to know about it."

"You want me to tickle FBI?"

There. Hanley nodded glumly.

"And if they don't laugh, tickle the Competition?" The Competition usually referred to "Langley," slang for the Central Intelligence Agency.

"They'll find out."

"How long can you keep it secret?"

"It depends on their safeguards, how deep the file is buried. The deeper you go, the more you run the risk of tripping alarms. Can you do it?"

"I can do anything," Lydia Neumann said. "I am woman."

Hanley stared at her.

She smiled again. "Poor old Hanley." She patted his hand in a motherly way. "I can do it, but what are you going to do? Stop the flight?"

"I told him I would."

"But you're not going to do it."

"No."

"He's dangling out there."

"It's his own fault."

"*Not this time*," Lydia Neumann said. "It's the goddam Puzzle Factory. Why do you suppose they blew the assignment?"

"I don't know. Maybe they wanted him hit. But they took their sweet time about it. Who are all those people waiting around for Rita Macklin to make contact? I mean, the opposition simply doesn't know where Devereaux is. For now,

90

at least. But he's probed one of their operations. Somebody is going to tell them. Soon."

"And they won't need to hang around Rita Macklin's door anymore. Which means what?"

"They kill her. Or they don't kill her."

Mrs. Neumann nodded. "And they kill November."

"And we are in the middle of uncovering some operation that is too fantastic. There has to be something wrong with it."

"How do they induce the immigrants to—"

"He said it's a form of bondage. They want relatives out—"

"My God, Hanley. That's so crude."

"I know. There's nothing sophisticated in any of this. I don't like it."

"All right. I'll work my computer magic and maybe I'll get through and maybe I won't. But what if they know about this . . . Soviet operation in Chicago? What if they know about it? I'll use the names you give me, times, places. What if I get a matchup?"

"If you get a glimmer, let it go. Just tell me," Hanley said.

"But what do we do then?"

"You mean if it turns out one of our sister services already knows about this operation?"

"Yes."

"It's a possibility I don't want to think about," Hanley said.

11

Chicago

"You got a piece?"

"I don't carry no guns," said Peter.

Devereaux paused. "You better start."

"Why's zat?"

"Shit is going down."

"Zat right?"

"Melvina's in trouble. If you can't do the job, I've got to get someone who can."

"What kinda trouble? Trouble you bring?"

"Yes."

"What kinda trouble?"

"Who the fuck do you think those two guys were who came to the house nine weeks ago?"

"I don't know. I don't mess with white boys long's they don't mess with me. That's how I get along."

"If I want philosophy, I'll read Schopenhauer. They were agents."

"Immigration?"

"Come on, Peter. If I thought you were that dumb, I wouldn't be talking to you."

"Foreigners."

"Soviets. You know, the Big Red One."

"And you a spy."

"You don't want to know that. You want to know that those two men are going to come again. Or maybe different men. But all of it's going to be the same."

"I got a piece."

"I know."

"You know, why you ask me?"

92

seat with the driver. The car prowled across 51st Street and wound down through a little park to 47th Street and then to the drive along the lake.

"Karol," she said in a small, weak voice.

"Be quiet, woman," John Stolmac said. He was upset. Teresa had been acting strangely. He grabbed Mary's arm above the elbow and squeezed it brutally, so that despite the drugs and alcohol Mary winced with pain. A whimper escaped her lips. She would be quiet.

John had terrified her from the first day because men had represented terror in her life. She was a woman who had learned to work around the brutal, unpredictable nature of these beasts. If John beat her, let him not beat her too badly. Let her endure.

That was exterior. Inside, Mary was all rage and anger. Even against the man in the kitchen of Melvina's house. He told Teresa he would help her but not Mary. Not Mary because Karol was dead. So cold a man, so brutal. He terrified Mary too; Mary had been too afraid to speak of him for fear of what he would have done to her. But what could he do to her now? She was dead, as dead as Karol, going back to a dead place, to live the life of death until sleep.

She was a slave. And no one would help her be free.

"Are you all right?" The man who said he was a priest stared at her.

"All right," she mumbled. John let go of her arm. It felt numb beneath the black coat. She had never understood what she was supposed to do to please John. Except for that . . .

John had showed her how to use the camera but she ruined rolls of film. So clumsy and slow. He had hit her. That was the first time. It had become easier after that. He had pinned her arms at the wrist with one giant hand and slapped her face until she cried. They were alone in the apartment. It was night, the others were working. John had grinned at her when she had said, "Please don't." The first time, it had seemed so easy not to be hurt. She did what he asked. She slipped to her knees, opened his pants, took it in her mouth. It was all he wanted. She was ashamed. John Stolmac said she wanted to be beaten but it was not true.

Once John struck Teresa, but Teresa had screamed at him, attacked and scratched him, and John had retreated, uttering threats. Mary knew Teresa felt contempt for her. They all did. They were right. It was because of her sins that God took Karol from her.

No more contract. She felt so tired, so tired.

She gazed sleepily out the side window at the glowing night city. The towers were full of bright yellow-lit windows. Snow lay crisp on the parkland along the lake, unmarked and glistening. The water steamed in the cold lake as though it were on fire.

"Mary."

She was outside the car. She turned. How had she gotten here?

The car had stopped at a light in Grant Park. She had opened the door somehow and just walked out, and now John Stolmac was calling her. He was so far away.

"Mary!"

What a strange feeling overcame her. She felt light. She was running across the snow. No, she was flying, leaving no trace of herself. She smiled at the beauty filling her. She could not hear John anymore. Karol was not far away; she could not see him but she felt him near her. She smelled him.

The park reached to Michigan Avenue, where the towers of the Loop began. The bare trees were stark in the lights of the street lamps, claws extending from the monstrous trunks.

Like a night in Warsaw, years ago, the cold all around stinging young cheeks red, the laughter coming from the café, and Mary dancing across the snowy street.

Karol.

John Stolmac was running across the snow but he would never catch her. She turned and looked at him and wanted him dead. Die. Die right now. But he ran toward her.

Where is Karol?

Dead.

She saw his broken body in the newspaper photograph. That was Karol. All else is false. That is what is real. You killed Karol because of your sins.

And so Mary realized in that moment she desired to die because it would let her be with Karol always. God revealed to her there was no hell, only an abyss beyond life where souls warmed each other.

She crossed to the bridge over the Illinois Central Gulf commuter tracks that lay in a wide trench between the lakefront park and the Michigan Avenue traffic. Her side ached; perhaps she *had* been running, not flying. John was running behind her, shouting at her. She saw his footprints on the snow but not her own.

She must fly.

The 6:09 commuter train pulled slowly out of the Van Buren Street station heading south toward the suburbs. Because the engineer was accelerating the electric-powered train, there was no way he could have stopped in time, even if he had seen the woman vault the stonework of the bridge and fall in front of the engine. She struck the window, her body fell, she was impaled for a moment by the bumper guard; then, almost gently, her body slipped beneath the carriage of the train, crushed by the wheels. It was no one's fault. Everyone agreed on that later.

➤ ➤ ➤

IT WAS NOT SO DIFFICULT to escape at night. At midnight, Teresa Kolaki and the other women in the laboratory took a break to eat their sandwiches and drink Thermos bottles of coffee laced with milk and sugar.

Teresa simply walked out of the building. She picked up a shopping bag full of clothes and walked down the steps of the university building to Midway Plaisance, a wide street with a sunken park in the middle that stretched along the southern border of the university grounds.

A taxi stopped at her signal and she climbed inside.

"Forty-six zero one Ellis Avenue," she said gravely. She had never ridden in a taxi before.

The driver turned and looked at her. He was a small-faced, dark-skinned man with glittering eyes. "Are you certain? That is the neighborhood of the blacks."

She said nothing. She was terrified of herself, her boldness, of all that had happened to convince her that she had to save herself if she could not save Mary. She had to save Stefan. John Stolmac had returned home less than an hour after departing for the airport with Mary. He had seemed shaken. The priest was not with him. She had asked if Mary was all right.

"Dead," John had said, his eyes wide with horror. He had refused to say anything further.

So. It was true. They wanted to kill Mary.

Maybe they would kill all of them. The contracts were worthless now.

12

Fort Meade, Maryland

"Go ahead," said O'Brien. He was deputy operations chief.

Craypool cleared his throat. A device on one wall created a thin coating of white noise that rendered the room routinely bugproof. Room 7398-A in the main building of the Puzzle Factory complex on the Army post was always used for the most sensitive debriefings. O'Brien had commandeered it because what was to be said was not to be repeated.

"Gleason and Frankfurter finally got lucky."

"About time. Did you come down on them yet about the translation we taped out of the subbasement room at the embassy?"

"No, sir. I thought it was better to keep Gleason and

Frankfurter in the dark. They don't have to know why we know they were goofing off. It doesn't matter. They tumbled to being watched by Malenkov and his crew. Made a verbal report two hours ago."

"Jesus Christ. This will mess things up."

"Yes, sir. But I still have to do something about it. They want to start tapping Malenkov."

"Idiots. I thought we picked them because they were strictly peons."

"Peons get lucky too. Gleason even said that it now seemed likely the Russians were still after the R Section agent, using his girlfriend."

"Brilliant. These guys take smart pills, right?"

"Well, I sent them to Chicago. They ought to be arriving in an hour."

"Why? Because of what Malenkov said in the transcript translation?"

"Partially. Get them out of the way. If November is in Chicago visiting relatives, it's easier to let them hit him there. It makes our part less complicated."

"Because of the fuckup in Vienna? A fucking priest can't even watch one kid. Asshole. You deal with these people long enough, you begin to believe Polish jokes."

"Well, I couldn't figure out a way to direct them to Chicago. The Russians, I mean. Short of just telling them."

"Fuck. They're as bad as the Polacks. They fucked this up from the beginning when they sent those two hitters from Sofia to waste our man. Dumb. So you send Gleason and Frankfurter and what do they do?"

"See if he's there."

"Is he?"

"Probably. Remember, we weren't much interested until this fuckup of the Zurich operation. If he's sticking his nose in it, and I suppose he is, he hasn't talked to the Section yet. We've got Hanley tapped like a maple tree in spring and he isn't leaking a damned thing."

"All his phones, everything?"

"Sir, his apartment is like a stage set. I mean, we have opened him up. If November is contacting him, I don't know how he's doing it."

"I don't mind fucking up R Section. Strictly amateur night over there. But this other thing. I don't like November getting so close."

"November would have contacted—"

"Maybe, maybe not. He plays a lone hand more than I like. That's what gets him into trouble in the first place. How's this scenario? Malenkov takes out Devereaux; we help by spotting him, setting it up. Then if he kills the broad, we do a trap on him—get some smart guys for a change, will you?—and do this booga-booga about the Russians killing innocent journalists on our own shores."

"It might play. The other thing, it keeps attention away from Chicago."

"Okay. Morgan is on his way to Zurich tonight. We've got to keep the fat man calm, keep the Big Red Machine humming quietly to itself. And get rid of this fucking Section hand. Keep him here one more night. Morgan, I mean."

"And if they don't kill the broad, we let Malenkov keep rolling along as he is. He's been useful to us since we penetrated their secret room, you know that? He does better work than our guys do—Gleason and Frankfurter going out to take a crap when they should have stayed on the broad. Assholes. The quality of people you got to deal with."

"Yeah."

13

Chicago

Teresa Kolaki was drained. She finally fell asleep just before three in a second-floor bedroom in Melvina's house. She had been awake nearly two days. She had told them everything before she fell asleep.

The house was dark.

Peter sat on the couch with a .44 Smith & Wesson revolver on his lap. Devereaux stood at the window and watched. Two white men in a blue rental car were parked in the alley across the street. Two or three white men in a white rental car had been circling the house every ten or fifteen minutes since midnight. He wasn't sure either of them had seen Teresa Kolaki when she came to the house in a cab; he wasn't sure they hadn't.

"What are you going to do?" Melvina asked him in a brittle voice after she put Teresa in the bedroom and rejoined the two men in the front room of the silent house.

"I have to get out at four and make a call. I'll be gone in a few hours, Melvina."

"But why did you give Peter that gun?"

"Ask Peter."

"Peter? You won't tell me, will you? You're breaking parole."

Peter grinned. His teeth were bright in the darkness. "No big thing, Miz Devereaux."

He felt alive. He had been dead so long. Inside. Even here for the past four years. She meant well but she was hard to get along with too. Peter kept his head down, kept out of her way. White women like her were strange sometimes. And she was real old.

101

"You made him do it?"

"Be quiet, Melvina. If you want to go to bed, don't let me stop you."

"What is going to happen?"

Devereaux did not turn from the window to look at her. His voice was flat, without guile. "They've found me. The Opposition. I don't see I have much chance. Peter is going to protect you. He needs a piece in case they want to hurt you. Teresa is the complication. I didn't expect her so soon. They've killed Mary Krakowski."

God, she thought. As though she had lived her life in sanity and all had become madness at the end of it.

"Will you go to California, Melvina?"

"I'm an old woman."

"Yes. I thought you'd say that."

"Why California?"

"I know someone. For Teresa. It could be safer for her. For a while. While I make arrangements."

"Arrangements?"

"For my funeral. I've got a will to write out, a few things."

He was smiling at her.

"Don't say such things, even in jest," she protested.

"Melvina, I'm not kidding. Not now. They've been after me for a year. If they want me that badly, they'll have me. We'll trade a few volleys. They'll get me, we'll get one of theirs. It's a trade-off."

"Who are 'they'?"

"Just the other side. I told you."

"I won't let them kill you."

Devereaux turned then and stared at her. "Why, Melvina? Why does it make any difference?"

She walked across the darkened front room. She spoke across the years. "Because it does, Red. It matters to me, it always did. I loved you, even if you never saw it. I loved you. I love you now. I'd give up my life for you. Anyone's life. You matter, not me."

Devereaux didn't speak. He kept staring out the window.

For a moment, she thought she saw something in the hardness in his face, just a momentary thaw.

"I'm sorry, Melvina."

What did it mean? Had he ever said it before? Why now?

It didn't matter. He turned away from her, back to the window.

"Peter. You've got to get Teresa out of here. Before morning. I'll leave the car in the alley. Just dump it off at the O'Hare lot when you're done with it; they'll find it eventually."

"I ain't going nowhere."

"Tell him, Melvina."

"Peter," she began.

"There's a place in Los Angeles. She'll be safe. Stay with her two days, I'll have arrangements ready by then."

"I can't leave—"

"Melvina is going to have to take her chances today. Someone will be here before night, Melvina. Someone I knew a long time ago."

"Not you, Red."

"No. I'm dead. I have to go away from here."

"Like the cat we had. It went away when it was sick. You found it."

"I told you that. I never found it. I just knew it was dying, it had to die. You couldn't have stood not knowing." Devereaux's voice was low, even. "You always thought your projects had to be successes. But there aren't any. You just try. You tried, Melvina."

"No. I won't accept that."

He smiled thinly in the shadows. "You insist on there being more. But there isn't more, Melvina."

"What if they come—"

"Don't answer the door. Call the police. I'll send someone as soon as possible. He'll call you, he'll describe himself. Then he'll come. You can trust him."

"Who will it be?"

"I don't know. It's an arrangement I'll have to make. You'll be alone until then."

"I could call Monsignor O'Neill."

"Don't involve him. This isn't one of your games with him."

"All right, Red."

"I need money," Peter said.

"Give him money, Melvina."

"All right," the old woman said. "You? Do you need anything?"

He turned again away from the window. "I hated you for a long time. But that was over a long time ago too."

"I know. It broke my heart," she said.

He was silent a moment. "And mine."

"Poor little Red."

"Not anymore. I'll be all right. Until I work everything out. Then they can have me."

"No."

Her voice was so sharp they both stared at her. "Don't give up like that."

"I'm tired, Melvina. The odds catch up with you."

"No," she said. But could think of nothing more to say.

> > >

GLEASON WAS SNORING. Frankfurter could barely keep his eyes open. It was nearly four in the morning and they had been watching the house since midnight after a hasty flight out to Chicago from Washington.

Frankfurter nudged the other man.

Gleason farted in his sleep. The smell filled the car. This time, Frankfurter hit him sharply in the side.

"Jesus Christ," Gleason said, suddenly bolt upright.

"You're stinking up the car."

"Oh. Jesus Christ, you didn't have to do that. I didn't even know I was farting."

"Christ. I gotta open a window."

104

"It's freezing. We got the wrong clothes. How do people stand living out here?"

"I dunno. A fucking nigger neighborhood too. This gets weirder. The Polack broad drove up in the cab? Maybe they got a sex scene going on in the house."

"This is the most fucked-up assignment I ever been on. We tumble to that Russian in the apartment building in Bethesda, the guy is doing exactly what we're doing, and we want to move in on him and they send us out here. What the fuck is going on? You tell me."

"All I know is that I'm getting it right up to here. If our friend from Section walked out of that house right now, which wouldn't surprise me, I think I'd just blow the son of a bitch away."

"You know what I was dreaming about?"

"No."

"A hamburger."

"Where's the beef? Where's the beef?"

"That breaks me up. That old broad. That breaks me up. Where's the beef?"

"You're unfuckingbelievable, you know that? Dreaming about a hamburger."

"I was dreaming about eating it. Maybe that's why I farted."

"You farted because you ate that fucking awful food on the plane."

"I farted because I ate that fucking chili when we were coming out here. I like chili but it don't like me," Gleason said. "It's getting cold."

"I'll roll up the window. Just don't do that to me again. You gotta fart, get outta the car."

"I said I couldn't help it. I was sleeping, for Christ's sake."

Frankfurter did not notice Devereaux until he saw the pistol pointed at his head. It was between his eyes. He felt the steel against the skin of his skull.

Devereaux's face was very near. The muzzle of the .357 Colt Python short-barrel was nearer.

"There wasn't supposed to be anything like this," said Gleason. "Nobody said nothing about this."

"Who are you clowns?" Devereaux said.

"Same side, buddy."

"You know that, huh? You know me?"

"Yeah. We been looking for you."

"Is that right?"

"NSA," Gleason said.

"Is that right?"

"That is fucking right," Gleason said.

"Don't show me identification. I might kill you. I mean, thinking you might have a piece under your coat."

"Jesus Christ," Frankfurter said. He had two kids. He thought of them for a moment. "We are the government."

"So am I. So why are you tailing me?"

"We're—" Frankfurter began.

Devereaux broke his front teeth. He pushed the barrel of the pistol in his mouth. Frankfurter leaned away but he couldn't get the barrel out of his broken mouth. He knew he was bleeding.

"Tell me all about it, fatso, before I blow his fucking head off."

"We—"

Devereaux cocked the revolver.

"We're listening on this girl—"

"What girl?"

"Your fucking girlfriend, who—"

Devereaux's gray eyes glittered. The cat watched, smiled, prepared.

"I mean, we were watching her—"

"Put the bug on her."

"Sure."

"And what happened?"

"This afternoon. Yesterday, I mean. We tumbled. To one of the Opposition. He's living in the same fucking apart-

106

ment building, doing the same shit we been doing. Everybody tapping everybody else. It gets crazy." Gleason talked too fast.

"What happened?"

"We wanted to move on the guy but we got marching orders. That you might be out here. We were told—"

"What?"

"Watch you."

"I'm going to put a hole through his throat, and his brains are going all over your face," Devereaux said slowly.

"Jesus Christ," Gleason said. "We were fingering you."

"For who?"

"I swear to God I don't know. We just sit here, we tail you, we keep sending out reports in the clear, on the open line, like we were fucking newspaper reporters or something. I mean, nobody says finger someone. It's just the way they tell you the assignment. I mean, someone is targeted, you're just the guy selling the bullets. You know. I mean, it didn't mean anything—"

"And Rita? What about her?"

"She's okay. We were just watching her, trying to find out if you guys were getting kissy-kissy again."

"Nice."

Devereaux pulled the barrel out of Frankfurter's broken mouth. Frankfurter was crying but didn't realize it; the pain was too great.

"Get out of the car."

"What are you going to do?"

"Get out of the fucking car, assholes."

They climbed out.

"In front of the car. Walk down the street. That way. When I put on my turn signal, you turn. You got me?"

They walked down the deserted length of Ellis Avenue to 45th Street and turned right, toward the east, Devereaux following in the car.

At Greenwood Avenue, Devereaux stopped the car. He opened the door and got out.

"Nice night for a walk," he said.

Frankfurter turned. The moment of fear was past; he felt humiliated. "You're dead, asshole. Not today but you're walking around waiting to die."

"So's everyone," Devereaux said. He suddenly turned his pistol and aimed at a house across the blackened street. It was just after four; dawn was hours away. He fired once and the shot reverberated down the dark, quiet streets in the heart of the black ghetto. He fired again. Lights flicked on yellow in squares of windows. He slid back into the car. He drove away, east, his lights flashing brakes at the corner. Then he was gone. For a moment, in the silence in the middle of the street, Frankfurter turned to Gleason and said, "Why the fuck did he do that?"

In a moment, they knew.

A man leaned from a second-floor window with a .12-gauge pump-action shotgun and fired, destroying the windshield of a car behind the two men.

"Motherfuckers, shooting up my house, fucking honky—"

"Jesus Christ," Frankfurter cried, pulling his gun.

"Got your piece, motherfuckers? I got mine." Now the face at the window had some sort of handgun. More flashes of fire. And then, suddenly, more fire from other windows.

Lights from windows up and down the street.

"Call the poh-leese!" a thin female voice cried.

"Fuck the motherfucking poh-leese. Ahm all the poh-leese I needs!"

Frankfurter and Gleason started running east. At Lake Park the two men—out of breath, Gleason's mouth bleeding—turned south, dodging the early morning traffic, pointed to by people in windows and chased by packs of black dogs. One dog got lucky and bit deeply into the flesh of Gleason's thigh. He shot it. Nine minutes later two police cars cornered the frightened men at 47th Street. Cops tumbled out of the blue-and-whites, guns drawn.

"Freeze, freeze," one of the cops cried. Frankfurter and Gleason threw down their guns and threw up their hands.

Devereaux parked the rental Lincoln town car in a no-parking zone at 31st and State streets. He left the keys in the ignition and the door unlocked. He hailed a State Street bus at the corner and shortly after 4:30, he arrived in the empty, predawn Loop.

The Lincoln was stolen five minutes after he left it. It was never recovered, but the motor was found in a chop shop in Muncie, Indiana, ten months later.

Devereaux boarded a United Airlines flight at 5:45 A.M. He fell asleep before it taxied to the runway.

14

Washington, D.C.

Sixteen hours after Devereaux left Chicago, Rita Macklin turned the key in the lock of the front door of her apartment in Bethesda. They were waiting for her. Two of them.

Before she could speak—her hand was still on the key in the lock—the first one, seated in a straight chair next to the table she used as a desk, held up his four-color plastic identification card.

"That's not good enough," Rita Macklin said. She removed the key and dropped the chain in her purse. She closed the door behind her. She faced them. The second one sat on a ledge by the window that looked out over the parking lot behind the four-story apartment building. There was a grassy knoll beyond, decorated with sad young spruce trees naked for winter.

She was frightened. She glared at both of them. Her face was flushed, adrenaline surged through her. Her green eyes were shining. She wouldn't show them how frightened she was.

"Good enough?" said the one at the desk. "If you want a court order to search the premises, we can get you a court order. Honey, we can get you anything you want."

"How about a court order for breaking and entering? Is that a new clause in the Constitution?"

"Shit," said the second one at the window ledge. He was lanky and sallow. His clothes hung on him as though they were permanently wrinkled.

Rita Macklin caught her breath and pressed her back against the front door. She tried to breathe deeply. *Don't show anything.*

"Who are you guys?"

"From Uncle," the one at the table said. He was meanly handsome with black hair and Irish blue eyes. He tried a smile.

She thought: *This is about Devereaux. He's dead or they want to kill him and they're going to use me somehow to do it.*

She took a step into the room. She sat down suddenly in an armchair that hadn't been there six months before. The furniture was minimal. There would have been less except that her mother had visited during the summer and ordered this armchair because she said the place was too cold. "You live like a monk," her mother had said. Rita Macklin's dark red hair seemed to become redder as she waited for them. Her eyes were angry.

"My name is Morgan," the black-haired man began. "You know the arrangement so I won't bore you by repeating things you already know."

"No," she said. "Bore me. I may know something you don't know."

Morgan grinned easily. The cadaver at the window didn't.

"Okay, honey. Devereaux. Remember him? And you? Remember why Devereaux came back to Uncle? You were targeted, right? Uncle takes care of his own. And we watched over you in case the nasties forgot that you were under our protection."

"It was his arrangement, not mine."

"Is that right? You went along with it."

Her eyes never left his face. She didn't speak. She sat quietly. She still wore her light green coat, a striped wool scarf over her shoulders.

"Where's your boyfriend?"

She watched his eyes. He wasn't lying. He didn't know. Devereaux was gone.

She suddenly felt tired.

"Something wrong?" Morgan said.

"No. Funny. Ha-ha funny. You've lost him? I don't believe my government sometimes."

"Not funny. Wrong. Not funny."

"You've lost one of your spooks."

"We were pretty sure we knew where he went. We sent a couple of watchers after him. You could help us, tell us where he is now. Save yourself, save him, save us. Nobody wants grief."

"Fuck you."

"Shit," said the cadaver. "What a mouth on her. How'd you like me to wash it out with soap?"

Morgan ignored him. "We watched you. He contacted you?"

"If you watched me, you'd know."

"We weren't here twenty-four hours a day."

"Inefficient."

"Listen, honey."

"Why do you keep calling me 'honey'? Did you pick that up in a fag beauty shop?"

Morgan flushed. "I asked you a question."

"You mean by phone or in person? He said that he'd be put on ice for a while. I suppose you guys didn't run out of ice." She talked tough, afraid. Her slight overbite made the words seem tougher than she felt. "Your tap on my phone gone bad? I expect a degree of competence in my government's spook agencies. I expect your wiretaps to work."

"Nobody said anything about wiretaps. We watched you to protect you. You're still a target."

She knew that. He had told her that. She'd be safe, he said. She had told him she didn't give a damn about that, only about him. But it wasn't true and they both knew it. God, she didn't want to die. So he had left her. To save her. Save himself.

"You think you're so fucking smart," said the cadaver.

"No. Except I didn't lose him, did I? I'm not the one asking questions, am I?" Rita Macklin said. Dammit. She wasn't going to let them make her afraid. A couple of spooks. Nothing would hurt her now. He slipped the traces after all. Was he out there? Was he watching this place now? "When did he get out?"

"Get out? You think this was involuntary on his part?"

"I know it was. He didn't have a choice."

"He left you out there. You're the one in trouble now, honey."

"You're cute. I bet you wear lace panties."

"Shit," said the one at the window. He didn't move.

Morgan spread his hands in a gesture of sincerity. "We pulled the watchers off you yesterday. We knew where he was. He slipped them."

"So you don't know where he is."

"We know he's in trouble the longer he's out there. They've got hitters out there. They're going after him. After you. And you don't want us to help you. Help him. That leaves you holding it."

"Fine. You hold yours and I'll hold mine. I'm not one of your goddam spooks. I don't want you in here. Get out."

"Is that right? Tough, huh?"

"Tough, huh," she mimicked him.

"Fine." He was getting mad. She could see it in his eyes, in the way he shrugged now as though loosening his shoulder muscles. Did she want to make him mad?

112

Rita smiled.

"What if we go over to your editor someday, show him transcripts? What if we tell him about Helsinki?"

"He knows. He reads the papers."

"Not everything. You were working for us. A journalist. You were working for us."

"Not the first day."

"A journalist. What about your code of ethics?"

"Don't use words you don't know the meaning of."

"You won't be such a smart ass, honey, when we get through. Star reporter and loyal agent in Uncle's intelligence service. Give that to the New York *Times* and see what they do with it."

"I don't work for the *Times*."

"You won't work anyplace. This is not an idle threat."

She waited. What were they going to threaten her with that she hadn't lived with? She had helped Devereaux because there was nothing else to do. She loved him. Had loved him? It didn't matter. They weren't there when the two Bulgarians came up the mountain road that day, when she and Devereaux lay in a trench at the edge of the woods, when Devereaux fired that shotgun. She still heard it in her dreams. She saw their bloody faces. They had buried them on the mountain in the darkness.

"He slipped yesterday morning."

"Where?"

"What difference does that make?"

"Where was he?"

"Shit," said the one at the window. He got up. He walked across the room and stood in front of her. "Honey, why do you think we're going to put up with this shit?"

She stared up at him. "Because you look like you've been eating it all your life."

When he hit her she expected it, but not the pain. She vomited on herself and on him. He pushed her out of the chair. He kicked her then, hard, with the side of his shoe, across her ribs. She blacked out, just for a moment. She

113

opened her eyes and she was on the floor, on hands and knees. He pulled her red hair and she was upright, on her feet. "You want more of this shit, you want to talk to us?"

"Where is he, Miss Macklin?" said the other one. Morgan. He hadn't moved out of his straight chair.

"Tell me . . ." Her mouth was choked with phlegm and vomit. She shook herself away from the cadaver, went to the sink in the kitchenette off the living room. She took a glass from the drainboard, filled it with water, rinsed. She wiped her mouth on a paper towel. God, she was a mess. She turned, braced herself on the sink. "Tell me where he was. Maybe I can tell you where he's going." Softly.

Morgan smiled. The cadaver, his trousers flecked with vomit, did not move.

"Chicago. He tell you about Chicago?"

Once he had. Briefly. After he said a name in one of his horrible nightmares. He had told her so little.

"He told me about Chicago," she said. "Was he visiting his aunt?"

"Great-aunt."

"That's it." She considered the question carefully. "And he knew you were coming after him?"

"After him? We had him for eleven months. We were the babysitters for him, throw them off the trail. They picked up the trail again. We had a couple of watchers—"

"What?"

"Agents. Went to Chicago. To watch out for him."

"You tapped my phone, bugged this place. You know he didn't contact me."

"That was before. We didn't have anyone here after we pulled them off."

"He hasn't called me," she said. "That's the truth."

Morgan stared at her, deciding.

The cadaver said, "What do you think?"

"Rita," Morgan said. "We're Uncle. We don't hurt people. We want to help him. Give him a home, a new name."

"That's what he said."

"When?"

"The last time I saw him. Nearly a year ago."

"That the truth?"

"The truth."

"Don't forget. We've got shit on you."

"I haven't seen him." Dully, muted, the coda to the symphony, the soft restatement of themes.

> ➤ ➤ ➤

AFTER THEY LEFT, SHE CLOSED the door and chained it. Big deal. The chain, she realized again, was not very substantial; the door had a hollow core. Safety depends on the civility of others.

She shoved the armchair in front of the door. She got a bottle of Lestoil from the kitchen counter and paper towels and mopped the vomit from the rug. Then she took off her clothes and went into the bathroom and took a long shower. Standing under the shower, letting the water clean her, she thought of him. No past, no future for them, he said.

"Dev."

She had promised not to say his name. She couldn't control her dreams but she could control her waking life. She wouldn't let herself think of him.

In a towel, in the living room, she sat with a tumbler of Red Label on ice and let herself think of him.

Why had he slipped his traces, exposed himself, exposed her?

Hitters. Morgan had said they were still after him. They never gave up. And maybe they were after her as well. Kill her after she led them to Dev, after she was useless to them.

She leaned over, turned on the television. News, news, news. And an old movie, Richard Widmark and John Wayne.

She reached for the phone to call someone and let her hand rest on the mouthpiece. She had friends awake at midnight but what was she going to tell them? I'm afraid. Two spooks came and beat me up and said they were going to protect me.

She smiled, sipped the scotch.

But she wouldn't go into the bedroom. She wouldn't turn the lights off. She left the television set on.

She stretched. Her ribs ached.

She thought about him. Accidental lovers in the beginning. She wanted the old priest's secret in Florida and so did he. He said he worked for a wire service. He used her. He used her to get the secret. She trusted him, slept with him, loved him. And when she found out, when she hated him, he saved her life as casually as if this thing happened all the time to him. And then he said it was no good, that what he did stopped them from having a life together. Something like that. Words and words, all the clichés of loving and then parting. She wanted him so much.

She shivered. She got up, crossed to the bedroom, turned on the light, and took a white terrycloth robe from the closet and slipped it on.

She thought it was over. The nightmare part of the last year and all that went before. It was really over with him, with the whole strange world he existed in. She had decided to take a week of vacation, go back to Wisconsin and see her mother. Her mother wasn't getting any younger; Rita was all she had left.

Now she would wait. In case he needed her.

She curled up in the armchair that blocked the front door and wrapped her long fingers around the tumbler of scotch.

A year ago, by accident this time—real accident—she had crossed paths with him in Helsinki. Again he had used her but they both knew it from the beginning; no tricks, Rita, he had said. And when the business was over, he had resigned and she had taken leave from her job and they were going away, they were never going back. They were free.

Except people are never free, are they?

Two assassins. And then they realized they were safe only if he went back to the Section. Away from her. Drawing the trail away, back into the safety of the government service.

Nearly a year. She put down the glass.

Dev.

> ➤ ➤ ➤

THIN SUNLIGHT THROUGH THE WINDOWS, a cold cast to morning, frost drawn on the panes. Rita Macklin opened her eyes and shivered. She felt cold. She had fallen asleep in the chair in front of the door. She stretched, felt pain, remembered the men waiting for her. She got up, pulled a comforter from the couch, and sat again in the chair and wrapped the comforter around her.

She rubbed her eyes. An electric clock on the wall of the kitchenette read quarter past eight. She yawned and felt as tired as if she had not slept at all.

Then she heard the knock.

Him.

She got up quickly and pushed the armchair aside. She hesitated then.

The knock again.

But he wouldn't come here. They were watching the building, they had the phone tapped. He would know that.

She unhooked the chain and glanced through the peephole. She saw the distorted image of a woman waiting on the other side of the door.

She rehooked the chain and opened the door against it. "Yes?"

"My name is Elizabeth Redford," the other woman said. She was older than Rita, elegantly dressed, a tall woman with a certain bearing that comes more from style than clothing. "May I come in?"

Rita frowned, felt a little frowzy around the edges, shut the door, unhooked the chain, patted her hair, and then gave up and opened the door wide.

Damn. She was well dressed. Perfume. Rita shoved her hands in the pockets of her terrycloth robe in a tough-guy way and waited.

117

The woman wore a fur coat over her silk dress. She glanced around the apartment quickly, as though accustomed to sizing up things rapidly. She stared at Rita oddly for a moment and then stepped inside and closed the door behind her. Then she did a very strange thing. She placed her forefinger to her lips and winked.

Winked.

Rita blinked and stared back at her.

"Who are you?"

"I've tried to reach you. You were out," Elizabeth Redford said.

"I was out?"

Again she put her finger to her lips.

She reached in her purse and took out a piece of paper. Rita looked at it. It was from him. Tears blinded her a moment. She staggered. She felt the other woman's hand on hers.

The woman led Rita to the kitchenette and turned on the tap water and bent close to the sink. She looked under the kitchen cabinet, felt along the molding, and pulled out the bug. It was quite small. Elizabeth held it under the tap water for a moment and then threw it in the wastebasket next to the sink.

"I knew him a long time ago," Elizabeth whispered. "Before you met him. He explained to me what this was about. He could trust me, you see."

"I don't see." Rita paused. "Where is he? What's happened to him? Is he all right?"

"He thinks you're in trouble. Terrible trouble. So is he. He wants to see you. Now."

"But where is he? Is he hurt?"

"No. He's all right." She looked oddly at Rita.

"What trouble?" Rita felt afraid suddenly; for a year she had lived at the edge of fear, reliving the nightmare of that last moment on the mountain, trying to make herself believe that the horror of it would never happen again. And now it was happening.

The woman spoke in a low voice, close to the sound of the water running out of the tap. "Two men downstairs in a white Pontiac. I don't know if they have one car or two. They don't seem terribly undercover. Maybe they're just supposed to watch you. But we have to shake them."

"Who are you?"

The other woman frowned. "I told you. I knew him. I worked for the Section. A long time ago."

"But not anymore."

"Do I look like I work anymore?" Said a bit archly, with just some bitterness at the edge of the words. "In Ireland. Six, seven years ago. I owed him. He knew it. He always knows the use of leverage. Last night, Richard was out—my husband. He came to our house—"

"Where?"

"In Georgetown. He told me—"

"What? Where is he?"

"Here. In D.C."

"Those are spooks out there."

"I suppose so."

"Why would you do this?"

"He asked me."

"What are you, a Samaritan?"

"What do you want me to say? He asked me."

Said as simply as Rita would have said it. She understood and felt terrible suddenly. Did he use you too? Does he use everyone?

She could suddenly see him clearly, staring at her with gray eyes, answering: Yes. Sometimes.

"What am I supposed to do?"

Elizabeth stared at her almost wistfully for a moment. "You've got the fun part, I've got the hard part. I get you out of here, in my car, and I lose them. And you find him."

"You don't have to take that chance. I'll go alone."

"You couldn't lose them, Rita. I can." And Rita believed it.

> ➤ ➤ ➤

TWELVE MINUTES LATER THEY WERE in the Cadillac, pulling onto Old Georgetown Road, heading toward Wisconsin Avenue. The morning traffic noise was sealed out the moment they slammed the doors.

Rita looked behind them through the smoked rear window. The Pontiac dipped out of the parking lot. A second car followed but she couldn't see the make.

"Two of them," she said.

"At least," Elizabeth said. "A good tail, you need five cars. But not if you aren't too concerned about being followed yourself. Or fingering the person you're following."

"I don't understand," Rita said.

Elizabeth smiled. "I just know what it says in the Manual of Instructions."

"Were you married when—"

She glanced sharply at Rita and then back to the road. She turned right into Wisconsin. Bumper-to-bumper traffic, all the way down the sloping hill to the District line.

"No. My name was Campbell. I got out of the business after Ireland. I found out I wasn't strong enough for it. No one is, I think, it's just a game of pretense. Men live more in fantasy so they can stay at it longer. They see it as a game."

"He doesn't."

Elizabeth smiled, her eyes on the rear-view mirror. "Is that what you think?"

Damn her for pretending to know him better. Rita's face flushed. Rita had taken the time to put on earrings, not for herself, not for him; for this other woman.

"Why did he come to you?"

"He said he didn't have many old friends he could count on." She smiled still, a ghostly, sort of sad smile. "Poor Devereaux. He smiled when he told me that, about old

120

friends. It was a joke, like everything. But he meant it. He told me you were in trouble, that you both were in trouble. I said to him, 'Do you love her?' He said, 'Perhaps.'"

"Bastard," Rita said.

"I said, 'No, you can't get away with that. You have to tell me.' And he said, 'If I tell you, will it make you happy or sad? Will you help me better if I tell you?'"

Despite herself, despite the fear settling around her, Rita smiled at that. "Arrogant bastard."

"He is, isn't he? God, this is so serious and yet it seems fun to me. I told him that. 'You bastard, you think I'd be jealous?' He said, 'No.' Said it the way he says lies, with perfect insincerity. He doesn't even care if you know he's lying. Then he smiles. Damn heartbreaker. But that makes me a fool, doesn't it? Here I am."

Rita realized she wanted the other woman to tell her all about him, the way she saw him, what he said to her. But she bit her lip. She stared behind them again and saw the white Pontiac in the traffic stream.

"Why did he come here?"

"He said it was trouble. Nothing else. He said I didn't want to know too much. The good agent." She paused. "They'll probably pick me up. After."

"What will you do?"

"Tell them to call my husband. Richard is a commodities broker. He's been in Manhattan the last three days. He's worth four million at the moment if the sowbellies or whatever they are don't go bad. It's exciting in a way, I suppose, what Richard does." Softly. "I like him very much. I was saying, he's worth four million, which doesn't make him J. Paul Getty but does make him slightly more powerful than some GS-14 in a spook agency. I'm not worried."

"I've got to get money out of the bank."

"No. He said that's the first place they'd watch after we do our act. He said there's a bar and grill on Fourteenth Street." She gave her the address. "Be there by noon but come in through the alley entrance. On foot. He said to keep looking over your shoulder."

"Jesus," Rita said.

"Yes. It sounds bad, doesn't it?"

"How are we going to . . . to do our act?"

"There's a carwash on M in Georgetown. This'll be fun. A drive-through."

The Cadillac swayed into M Street, down another hill toward the river. The carwash loomed. Elizabeth wheeled the big vehicle right over the apron and pushed down the power button on the window.

She handed a black man a ten-dollar bill.

"You want a wax too?"

"I guess so."

"Wax is two dollars extra."

"All right."

He went to the wall, pushed two buttons, returned with change, and passed it through the window to Elizabeth Redford. She closed the window and guided the car to the track.

The car lurched forward, wheel hooked on the chain. The first brusher came and pounded at the hood, yellow brushes at the sides, the whole car suddenly coated with soapy water.

"The unpleasant part is about to follow," Elizabeth said.

"Damn," Rita said. "I'll be soaked."

"Not if you're fast enough. After the wax, the blower turns on to dry the car. They're either behind us or waiting out on the street. I'll bet the street. In any case, get out. There's a door to the left where the washboys have their warm room, keep the towels. I don't know what else is in there. Wait there. Be amusing, they don't often get female company."

Rita smiled.

"When I pull out, I'm pulling out fast. If he's on the street, he'll be right after me. If he's behind us, in the wash, all the better. He won't be able to see a thing until he gets clear of the dryer. Now!"

Rita pushed open the door. The dryer nearly knocked her off her feet. She ran around the front of the dripping Cadillac, her hair gone wild in the artificial wind. She pushed against the door and went inside.

Two black men were smoking cigarettes wrapped in yellow paper. "Say. Miss. You come in the wrong door."

"Say maybe the right door."

"Shit, Todd."

She ignored them. She waited at the door and watched through the glass. The Cadillac lurched past the men who were wiping it down and hit the street, bouncing on soft springs, turning into the line of traffic down the hill. She saw the Pontiac shoot across the apron after it. A moment later a second car, a black Ford, was after the first. She waited.

The two black men stared frankly at her but couldn't think of anything to say. Finally, Rita opened the door.

"Hey," said one of them. "You don't have to go already, do you?"

Rita walked into the wind tunnel again and out the entrance of the lot. It was just after nine. She crossed the alley behind the carwash, walked to the next street, turned and found herself in a cul-de-sac of shops. She entered the first one on the left.

A thin blond man wearing gold chains looked up from a woman with wet hair bent over a sink.

"Something?"

"I'd like to get my hair done," Rita Macklin said.

Blondie sniffed at that. Well, her hair did look a mess.

"I just went through a carwash," she said, smiling.

He wasn't buying light stuff today; maybe not any day. "Do you have an appointment?"

"No."

"I don't have anything open until ten-thirty," he said.

Rita sat down in a leather chair and picked up a copy of *House Beautiful*.

"I'll wait." She grinned.

15

Chicago

Malenkov lit a cigarette, puffed, threw it away, lit a second one, all in less than two minutes. He wasn't aware of it.

They hadn't told him enough. It was their fault and that asshole Major's, not his.

He was looking for November; it had nothing to do with some kind of goddam operation with Poles in Chicago. Now they told him. Why didn't they tell him in the first place? Bureaucrats.

It was snowing hard. Just after dark. A single light was on in the house on Ellis Avenue.

Was the Pole there? Teresa Kolaki? Missing a day. Every code red in the embassy was working overtime. The operation in Chicago—whatever in the hell it was—was penetrated, at risk. And it turned out that it was all November again, all over again, messing up their arrangements.

"I thought I was supposed to confine myself—"

"Orders are changed," the Major said on the phone. "Besides, you missed him."

"I'm one man, Mikhail Korsoff, and I can scarcely—"

"It doesn't matter."

"It does matter. Why did you think it was going to be so easy to find him? Did we have a finger on this?"

The Major said nothing to that. It must have been the truth. Whatever was supposed to have happened, didn't. It was a real mess all right. "At least see if you can get a line on him. See if Teresa is there in that house."

"And do what?" asked Malenkov.

Kill them. Both of them. No exception. No one would be in the house but them. It was assured.

So he had waited a few hours for night. Night would be better. He couldn't put it off any longer, though. He flicked his second cigarette into the snow. He pulled up his collar around his neck and ears. Snow flecked his brown hair. His eyes were wide, his face carved from granite.

He took the Uzi out of his pocket. He screwed a silencer into the barrel. He unsnapped the safety, removed the clip of ten cartridges, reinserted it with a snap.

He pushed open the gate past a snowy broken sculpture—what had it been before it was broken?—and climbed five steps. Direct, without subtlety. Always the best way. He felt the pistol in his coat, his hands around the wire stock.

He knocked. He waited. He knocked again.

The door opened on a chain.

A woman. An old woman. The one he would have to talk to. To find out what she knew about November. He considered the chain: thin, probably more for assurance than security. That was his experience with these chains. They made people behind the door feel better about opening it.

He hit the door hard and broke the chain, sending the old woman spinning back against the balustrade to a staircase leading upward.

She cried out. He turned, slammed the door, removed the weapon, snapped the safety, pointed it at her face.

"Where is Devereaux?"

She would have three seconds. He didn't want to prolong this. Kill her and then upstairs to search the house for Teresa. If he found her, he killed her. Back in the car in two minutes.

Two. Three.

The blast shattered his eardrum. For a moment, he stared at his silencer. What was wrong?

Then he turned and saw the dark man in the corner of the room. With a gun. Without a silencer. Blood tasted salty on his lips. He was conscious, he knew he was awake, but he had the strange feeling his face was gone. The second shot caught him in the ribs, exploded his heart. The third was unnecessary.

The man in the corner still had a half-eaten apple in his left hand. Melvina held the balustrade and stared at the blood-stained body crumpled at her feet. She looked at the swarthy Italian emerging into the light of the hall. He looked down at the dead man. "I figure Dev knows what he's saying." The voice was a half-whisper, very hoarse. "He wants me, he got me. See? You didn't think it was necessary I was here. Ain't you glad now I came here like he wanted?"

But Melvina, though she did not cry, could not speak.

16

Fort Meade, Maryland

O'Brien stared at Morgan. "You're pathetic."

Morgan said nothing.

"She was a fucking Girl Scout."

"Not the one driving."

"Elizabeth Campbell. Another amateur nighter. Where do we have her now?"

"We don't have her. What are we going to charge her with? Her old man has a pile."

"I'll shove his pile up his piles," O'Brien said. "Devereaux slipped, now this Macklin broad. You told me you made an impression on her."

"George hit her."

"'George hit her,'" O'Brien mimicked. "Great. He really got her attention."

"We'll find her."

"You couldn't find your ass with a flashlight and a map. And those two mental giants in Chicago. We just got them out of the fucking can. We had to make contact with the police superintendent, for Christ's sake. A couple of cowboys, shooting up the ghetto. The next thing you know, we'll start race riots in Detroit. Just to keep it interesting."

Morgan waited, his neck prickly with anger. At O'Brien, at himself.

"Go on. Go on to Zurich and see Fatso and put it on him and try to find out what the fuck is going on."

"Is this all related now?"

"Now it is. One goddam kid gets killed and now we got runaway spooks and the network is starting to break up. I don't believe it, I really don't. You know, before I didn't care much one way or the other if the Opposition wasted November or not. Easy come, easy go. We do our little disappearing act on him and it works or it doesn't. But in the last couple of weeks, I have developed a real antipathy toward that motherfucker, you know what I mean? I mean, this is more than putting a crimp in the line for R Section and those Mickey the Mopes over there. This is getting personal with me. You understand?"

Morgan thought: It's so fucking personal, why don't you take a piece and go after him, you asshole? He said nothing.

"The broad? I could care less. But I want you to lean on this Campbell broad. Do a midnight visit."

"I told you, her old man is a stockbroker—"

"Fine. Put the SEC on his case. Leak to the IRS. Put him through the hoops. I want you to lean on this Campbell broad, I want you to tell me how many pimples she's got on her ass before you're through with her—"

"And what about our friend in Switzerland?"

O'Brien flushed dangerously. "All right. This will hold. Devereaux's not going anywhere, wherever the fuck he is. Damage-control drill. Get our fat friend interested in the matter. From our perspective for a change."

17 _____

Washington, D.C.

Devereaux said, "Hello."

Rita Macklin turned, startled, saw him in the shadow of the back of a bakery, next to the bar and grill. It was just before noon. He stepped out of the shadow. He was eating a bagel. "Want a bite?"

"I'm starving."

He gave her half.

They ate the bagel quietly, a little apart, staring at each other in the bright morning light. Their breath puffed on the cold breeze.

"You been here long?"

"Half an hour or so. Securing the alley."

"Is it secure?"

"I suppose so."

"I got my hair done."

"Everything worked all right."

"How did they find you?"

"Melvina sent me a letter. They were at her house. I told you about her."

Rita nodded.

"I went there. Got involved in something. One of their operations." He smiled, almost gently, a smile for the season, warmth edged with cold. "I'm afraid I screwed them up."

Rita grinned suddenly. She dropped the remains of the bagel on the bricks of the alley. She grabbed him hard, and kissed him hard. For a long time. He held her just as hard. They didn't speak. They smelled each other, they felt their bodies beneath too many layers of clothing press at each other.

"God, I miss you."

"I love you, Rita."

Okay. They broke. Touched hands. Stood apart. Stared at each other.

"Want a story?"

"I'm on vacation."

"Okay. Get a freebie to California."

"Are you coming?"

"For a while," he said, still smiling at her. "I love you, babe."

"You have a funny way of showing it."

"I thought they'd let it go. The other side. I thought I could keep you out of it."

"Two goons from our side came last night and worked me over."

"I saw them go in."

"Why didn't you do something?"

"Save you, you mean? That wouldn't have worked. They weren't going to hurt you."

"The guy slapped me around."

"I'll challenge him to a duel," Devereaux said.

"Bastard."

"There's a woman. With a kid in Poland. She's safe now, a little while. I'm working on Hanley, trying to tie the loose pieces down. Before."

"Before what?"

"What have I been telling you?" He frowned. "Game's over, Rita. They won."

"Don't say that."

"All right. I won't say it."

"Dev. Hold me." Little girl. He wrapped his arms around her. She pressed her face against his chest. She felt so frightened.

"A Polish woman. She worked here for KGB. She was forced. It's complicated, big, sort of crude, a typical Russian operation. They have the sophistication of farts in a crowded theater."

Tears in her eyes but she smiled.

"It's a long story. I'll tell you on the way to California. Right now, we see the man."

"What man?"

"Shh. You'll see in a little bit," Devereaux said. Gently again. As gently as he had ever spoken to her, with an edge of sadness to his words, as though they were all precious, said for the last time.

> ➤ ➤ ➤

HANLEY AND MRS. NEUMANN LEFT SEPARATELY but met a block away from the Department of Agriculture building on Pennsylvania Avenue and continued along Fourteenth Street to the little bar and grill.

Hanley wore his brown fedora and brown overcoat. Mrs. Neumann said he looked like Fozzie bear in the Muppets in that overcoat. He was vaguely aware of the Muppets but had never seen their program.

He carried a briefcase. Carefully assembled contents.

"I think this is exciting, much more exciting than computer searches," Mrs. Neumann said as she took his arm. He couldn't remember the last time a woman had taken his arm. It felt strange.

"I don't like it."

"You don't like anything."

"Every name flagged in the NSA computer. Mrs. Krakowski, Teresa Kolaki. And Felix Krueger."

"And Melvina. Don't forget Melvina Devereaux."

After a moment, Mrs. Neumann said, "What do you suppose our part is in this?"

"You mean the Section?"

Mrs. Neumann frowned and gave Hanley's arm a squeeze. "Don't be parochial. I mean us, the big US."

"I don't know. I don't know that we have a part. I don't even know why I'm involved in this, why the Section is involved."

"Go on. You do too. Devereaux."

130

"Why didn't he stay in New York where he belonged?"

"Would that have made it better?"

"I don't know. I just know it couldn't be worse than it is."

It *had* been bad. Yackley, the New Man (to distinguish him from the Old Man, Admiral P. G. Galloway), had called Hanley in at ten. He had a probe from the National Security Advisor. Was R Section poaching on NSA turf? And what about this agent, November? Had he slipped the traces? Yackley gave it to Hanley and Hanley, with no alternative, lied. The lies satisfied Yackley for the moment; they would satisfy the Advisor temporarily. But the Advisor had only asked his questions at the urging of NSA. The Puzzle Factory was doing a move on R Section, covering up for screwing up the Devereaux reprocessing. So Hanley believed. And he would be caught in the middle again.

"After you," Hanley said.

They pushed into the bar. It was dark and dirty as always. They edged behind the people who sat on the bar stools, hunched over their luncheon drunks. Strangers, Hanley thought. And what am I? I've come here for thirty years and I don't know anyone in the place.

Mrs. Neumann was ahead of him. They pushed through the bar to the back room where Hanley always ate. The Greek owner, in white shirt, black tie, and perpetual smile, looked up at him. "Good to see you, sir."

"Yes, uh, hello." He always felt embarrassed. Not that Sianis greeted him every day. Just some days when he least expected human contact.

Devereaux and Rita Macklin were at the table he usually occupied. He sat down and Mrs. Neumann, a bit startled, sat opposite. She stared at Devereaux and then smiled. "Nice to see you," she said in her raspy half-whisper. Then to Rita, "We've never met, but I know you."

Rita nodded, grinned, looked at Hanley. She had spoken to him once, on a phone line from Paris, where Devereaux had sent her during the Helsinki business. Devereaux's control, his master's voice. She watched him with naked curiosity while he removed his hat and coat. His face was pinched, pale, his nose waxen, his blue eyes watery from the cold. His hair was almost gone. She had met bureaucrats like him all her life.

"I didn't . . . expect Miss Macklin to be here," Hanley said.

"Life is full of surprises. Did you bring everything?"

"I'm not in the habit of taking a briefcase to my lunch on normal occasions."

"Rita?"

She handed him a check. She had withdrawn $2,000 from a savings account and $643 from her checking account.

"Get her money, send it to the drop," Devereaux said.

"I didn't know she was going. With you."

"It's always best not to give too much away," Devereaux said. "Melvina had a visitor last night. A Russian."

Damn, Hanley thought.

"You want menus?" The waitress smiled at them. Nice little office group, divide the check, did you have the spinach salad, who had the second soup?

"Martini, perfect, straight—" Hanley began.

"Oh, we know, Mr. H. After all this time. One check or—"

"One check," Devereaux said and smiled. "Mr. H. is paying."

The waitress smiled wider. "What d'you want, hon?"

"Draft beer," he said. As did Rita. Mrs. Neumann ordered a Coke.

"The Russian," Hanley said.

"Identification with the embassy. My . . . friend removed him."

"We could have provided—"

"No. You couldn't have. Not without making this more complicated for the Section."

"Your concern for the Section seems late," Hanley said.

"I don't give a goddam about the Section. Just about you,

132

right now, Hanley. Just about keeping you from getting too rattled."

Mrs. Neumann looked from one man to the other. "You know everything, every name you gave us, is flagged in the NSA computer? I can't get it out without revealing myself. I may have given myself away just by probing." She smiled. "I said I was with State Department special intelligence. That'll give those Harvard boys fits."

Devereaux returned the smile. "Only for a little while. Until they figure out we're the only other game in town."

"Tell me something." It was Hanley, staring hard, his face fixed in a frown. "Why am I doing this for you?"

"You aren't. I wouldn't have put it on that thin a line. I tumbled to this Opposition network. And it turns out that NSA knows all about it. And wants to mess you around for even knowing that they know. And me. And Rita. And it makes you a little mad, a little defensive. All the true instincts of the bureaucratic infighter."

"Why?"

"You told me once you're all pigs eating out of the same trough. The Puzzle Factory wants a bigger portion of slops. Maybe that, maybe something else. This is a domestic operation, it ought to be under the G-men, right?"

"Right."

"Is it?" Devereaux turned to Mrs. Neumann.

"No," she said. "I went to the cupboard and it was bare. They don't have a clue in Hooverville."

"This is empire building in its primal stages," Devereaux said. "NSA is stretching its legs."

"That's crazy."

"The FBI is still shaky from the seventies. You know it and so do I. A nice domestic operation and why is the Puzzle Factory not doing a cooperative act with the G-men?"

"You never used slang—"

It was true. Devereaux said, "I've slipped into bad habits. I'm trying to communicate with you. You're a bureaucrat. I'm selling you a product. A new weapons system, direct dial,

133

a new way to scramble eggs in your microwave. I find I need you right now, Hanley."

The martini arrived. Hanley drank half of it and it didn't taste good to him.

"Lunch?" said the waitress.

"Cheeseburger," Hanley said.

"Cheeseburger," Rita said.

"Nothing," said Devereaux.

"Do you have a salad?" asked Mrs. Neumann.

"No," the waitress said.

"Chili," Mrs. Neumann said.

She went away.

Hanley put the briefcase on the table. Devereaux took it and slipped it under the table, next to his chair. "The money? Passports? Addresses."

"Levy Solomon picked Teresa Kolaki up this morning in Los Angeles. The black fellow is going back."

"You didn't use your own phone."

"No."

"How does Levy feel about this?"

"He likes it. The payment for him is in a separate envelope."

"I thought he'd like it."

"I didn't even know you were aware of him."

"We worked together once in Germany. How long's he retired now?"

"Three years."

"And the other address?"

"Yes. I got everything. They're going to trace this sometime."

"By then, it shouldn't mean anything. I just need time."

"And then you come back in."

"No. Then I . . ." Devereaux paused. "Well, we'll see what the Opposition has in mind."

Rita Macklin said, "Are you going to let them kill him?" To Hanley.

Mrs. Neumann stared at Hanley.

"Do I have a choice?"

"No," Devereaux said.

"The New Man. He's come down on me," Hanley said. "NSA knows something's up. You know you're putting Miss Macklin at risk."

Devereaux frowned, did not look at her. "She was dead," he said. "Maybe there's some way to keep her alive. Other than trusting to your good intentions."

"Damn you."

"Yes. Damn me and you and everyone but it's still the way it is. Hanley, the fucking KGB has an open contract. I'm tagged. And all the king's horses and all the king's men are not going to stop them. I've stopped putting my faith in governments. Or the Section."

"Who did you . . . put in Chicago?"

"A friend."

"I didn't know you had so many friends."

"He was someone I knew. A long time ago."

"A friend," Hanley repeated, turning the foreign word over in his mind.

"Yes," Devereaux said. "Who would have thought it?"

18 ___
Zurich

He was tired of trains.

Felix Krueger folded his copy of the *Neue Zuricher Zeitung* and placed it on his lap and closed his eyes. In a moment, they were open again. He couldn't sleep sitting up, in the middle of the day.

The train rattled along on the edge of a mountain pass, beneath the snowy peaks of the range that contained the Jungfrau. Spiez to Brig in a little over an hour, a perfectly isolated train journey from nowhere to nowhere, just this side of the Italian border.

He had been on many trains in the past two weeks, to Prague and then to various points in East Germany, through to Warsaw, back to Zurich again.

He could not describe his fear of flying, even to himself. Now, in the empty compartment, a thousand feet above the floor of the snow-covered valley, he could look down at the hamlets with perfect, godlike calm. But in the coffin of an airplane, the walls pressed against him, the smell of other people around him, hurtling against the sky . . .

He closed his eyes again to erase the vision.

When he opened them, Morgan was across from him.

"Mr. K." Morgan smiled.

"How do you do again?" Stiffly. "Was this necessary?"

"My favorite meeting place. Just you and me."

"What do you want?"

"Troubles, Mr. K. We got troubles in River City."

"I don't understand you."

"Our arrangement, Mr. K." The voice soft, the bright blue eyes glistening, the black hair pushed straight back from a low crown. "Once is an accident, twice is bad business practices."

"What do you mean?"

"Four days ago Mrs. Krakowski was killed. Might have been suicide, maybe not. She had enough drugs and booze in her to open an all-night liquor store in Harlem."

"I didn't know this."

Morgan smiled. "I figured that. That's what bothers us. You ought to know these things. You're dealing with some very yahoo-type people over there, you know that?"

"Did they kill her?"

"What does it matter? One of her sisters in the house has bolted. We have hysterical women on our hands, Mr. K. Bad for morale, first a kid getting himself killed, then his mom. People stop believing in our religion. We need an evangelist."

Thickly. "Will you please stop this American talk? I can't understand half of what you say to me."

"Understand this, Mr. K. You are making a lot of bread keeping this network alive. A tear in the fabric on their side reflects on us. Mirror to mirror, you might say."

Krueger blinked, stared. "What do you propose?"

"Talk to them. Find out what's going on in their little paranoid minds."

"What do you suppose is going on? In their minds?"

"Christ, if I knew that, I'd be Henry Kissinger, wouldn't I? I'm just a poor dumb American who does what he's told. I'm told that the cost of the network is getting too high."

"The money is justified," Krueger said, missing the point.

"No. I mean if the thing is going to be blown because their side can't handle it, then maybe we should blow it up ourselves before someone else does it for us. We're not the only baseball team in the league."

"Baseball," Krueger said, not understanding again.

"I mean that if we get more accidents, more defections, if the Opposition gets careless, we might just have to shut down the Numbers. Now do you see?"

Krueger saw. Self-interest demanded he see it.

➤ ➤ ➤

THE FOLLOWING MORNING, shortly before noon, the housekeeper ushered the group into the large dining room on the first floor of the house on Frohburgstrasse. This group was Czech, mostly from Prague, a couple from Pilsen. There were four women and two men. Rimsky was there as well, and the Czech translator. All spoke English to some extent, but not always as successfully as Felix Krueger needed.

He had asked Rimsky, carefully, about the return of Mary Krakowski to Poland.

There had been no problem, Rimsky said.

She was all right? Krueger asked.

Still in mourning, Rimsky said.

Would Rimsky convey the bond money to her, the guarantee of 500,000 Swiss francs?

Of course, Rimsky said.

He was certain there was no problem?

None at all, Rimsky said.

Krueger had smiled oddly. He said he would have the money in a few days from the interest-bearing account in his bank.

The refugees had all signed the bonds. They wore their best clothes and appeared, at best, bewildered. One of the women kept looking around as though she had entered the great room of an art museum. True, Krueger had a few treasures on his wall but her awe was greater than that. Outside, it was snowing. A fire crackled in the marble-manteled fireplace.

Felix Krueger took his place at the head of the dining table in the octagonal room.

A French clock on the mantel above the fireplace struck noon with tinny chimes: bim-bam, bim-bam, bim-bam . . .

"My name is Felix Krueger. We will have lunch together."

The refugees had rooms in a small hotel halfway up the hill from the Bahnhof. They had straggled up to Felix Krueger's house in double file with the interpreter at the front, Rimsky at the rear. A double line of children on a class outing.

"It is more beautiful to see Praha," one of the Czechs had said to another as they climbed.

"But the noise of this city is more beautiful," the other had said.

The interpreter sat next to Felix Krueger. Rimsky sat at the foot of the table. He was staring at Krueger. He had forgotten the money, the bond guarantee. He began to figure the worth of 500,000 Swiss francs in rubles. Even at the official rate . . .

The room was intimidating to someone not accustomed

to it. The interpreter, who was new this trip, looked around with the others. The room, immense and spare, spoke of elegance in the muted whisper that is elegance itself. The table was cherrywood. It was bare save white linen place napkins and pewter cutlery and crystal glasses that caught the light of the chandelier.

"I wish you all to have a glass of my Riesling," Felix Krueger said in German. They reached for their glasses, following the lead of the two who spoke German.

A maid brought soup in a tureen, and Krueger, the host, stood at the head of the table and filled each bowl passed to him as a father does for his children. The soup was hot and creamy, filled with puréed potatoes and green chives floating on the cream.

"Do you like this?" he asked one of the refugees near him, a small-boned woman with delicate cheekbones and a wide mouth. She had been at the University of Prague Hospital. She was unmarried. She had a child, four. She now waited on tables in the café of the Intercontinental Hotel in Prague.

"It is very good," she said in English. "Why do you serve us this food?"

"Because you are my guests," he said.

"That seems an odd thing to call us," she said precisely.

"You speak English very well. You'll do well."

"I never thought I would ever leave Prague." Sadly. Spooning the soup thoughtfully.

"Is it difficult?" Krueger asked, smiling.

"Do you always live here? In Zurich?"

"Yes."

"From the time you are a child?"

"My father. And his father. And his father. For six generations. Before that, our people came from Zug, which is not far from here."

"So you go on the streets of the city, you know it so well. You know the people, the cafés—"

Krueger stared at her. "Yes. I see now what you mean. It must be very compelling for you to do this."

"I have no choice," she said.

After the soup came a form of sole meunière, the filets cut at the sideboard, the spines removed, the whole drenched in butter and wine sauce.

"This is excellent. In Prague, at the Intercontinental Hotel, they serve this in the roof restaurant," the pretty woman said to Krueger.

"I know. I've been there many times."

She blushed. "Of course."

"I hope it compares—"

"It is better, I would think. I don't know. I never ate there."

She cut at the flesh, put it in her mouth. Such a lovely mouth, he thought. He thought he would like her.

He glanced down to the foot of the table and saw Rimsky smiling at him.

Krueger frowned and resumed eating.

Course followed course, until coffee and cheese at the end of the meal. During the long, surrealistic luncheon, the refugees had not spoken to each other. Only the pretty young woman had spoken, and only in response to Felix Krueger.

There was no need to tap his spoon against his water glass. He had their attention.

"I hope you have enjoyed this little repast."

The interpreter followed in Czech.

"The contracts are signed, you are delivered on the first part of your journey."

He paused; the interpreter followed again.

"So far, it is as it was explained to you in Prague. All is guaranteed. But now I will tell you something that will not set very well with that gentleman at the end of the table."

Rimsky sighed. It was an old show and his part in it was small.

Krueger pointed a sausage finger at·him. "You wonder about him? KGB, just as you thought. But now you are all

KGB in a sense. You wonder if the agreement will be kept? What are the guarantees but bits of words on paper?

"And why should they trust you? KGB? In America, you will be far from their grip.

"Trust, my friends. The network works on trust. And I guarantee the trust. To you. To that man at the end of the table."

Rimsky scowled on cue. He was calculating the amount of interest 500,000 Swiss francs could earn in a Zurich bank over the next two years.

"You have been studied. All of you. Not everyone can be eligible for this opportunity. For a new life. Each of you has someone you desperately love in Czechoslovakia. And you would not emigrate without that loved one. That guarantees the government's trust in you. You will obey, simply because it is the only way you will see your loved one again. Because if you do not, *you will never see your loved one again on this earth.*"

Krueger paused, looked from face to face. They understood. They always equated the power of this opulent room with the power of his words.

"But your guarantee—that's more subtle, isn't it? The government promises your loved one will be free at the end of your indenture. What is your guarantee of that?

"Me. I am the guarantee of good intentions."

They stared at him while the interpreter rattled on.

"I have taken five hundred thousand swiss francs of my own money and placed it in interest-bearing accounts, in each of your names, in the Schweizerische Kreditanstalt here in Zurich. This is a considerable amount of money—to you and to me. You have the credit letters, the account numbers. At the end of your . . . service to the state, you will sign over the credit letters back to me in exchange for your loved one joining you in America. It is that simple. If, on the other hand, you run away, or if anything happens to your loved one"—he looked up at Rimsky—"then I will lose five hundred thousand Swiss francs. I cannot remain in business if this happens to me. It is based on trust, this network, but it is also based on guarantees." Felix Krueger pounded his fist on the cherry-wood table top in front of him; the glasses tinkled. "You see? Business. To me, you are numbers, nothing more."

The pretty woman stared up at him and believed him. His face, so charming and open during the luncheon, was now completely closed from them, from everyone in the room. He had not altered his appearance but he had changed from within.

"Accounts. I am a man of accounts. You are my accounts, my little numbers. For my service, there is a fee collected from the state. It is worth my while to do these things, believe me. There are others like me, I can tell, in other parts of the world—a man in Hong Kong, one in Caracas, another in Mexico City—but I am your gate here, in Europe, to America. You pass through me. The gate is narrow but it is wide enough." He laughed then and the interpreter struggled, but the joke, if it was that, could not be translated. The six smiled politely.

He looked down at the pretty woman. "Do you have a question?"

She stared at him. There were tears in her eyes. She dabbed at them with a napkin. "No."

"Why do you weep?"

"Because it is final. Because it is two years away from my child."

"Two years is nothing."

"You say it easily."

"Because I do not live your life. But it will be over. For you as it has for many. And then you will be free."

"I don't believe it is that much freer in America. It is just a new life for me."

"You are mistaken," Felix Krueger said to her gently. "America is the freest country on earth. Safe. Free."

19

Santa Barbara, California

Denisov walked along the beach, on the hard, wet sand left in the wake of the retreat of high tide. He walked for miles. He did this most mornings.

Three years in this place.

He had been KGB. This was the place they had brought him to and freed him—the Relocation Division of R Section—after a "defection" that had been nothing more than an abduction by force. The bitterness still filled his heart as he walked along the beach. This was the end of the West. The East was over there, beyond the gray ocean. He would never see it again.

Dmitri Ilyich Denisov was thinner now and looked more than three years older. He was tanned—it was inevitable in this climate—and there was gray at his temples and gray streaking his once jet-black hair. He still wore rimless spectacles. He paused, stared at the horizon. A rare gray day. The seamless ocean was torn only once by the skeleton of a hideous oil rig several miles off shore.

Yes, he would admit to himself, he felt fitter. He walked everywhere. California meals were so light that, gradually, his heavy body had yielded to diet.

Three years before, he had been in Florida, against the American agent who had dogged his steps around the world for twenty years. They knew each other like brothers. Cain and Abel. But which was Cain?

The agent was November. The trap was brutal, direct. "Welcome to America," he had said at the point of a gun.

But, Denisov had thought many times in these solitary

walks along the beach, he had seen the trap as well. Had he wished to walk into it? Had he wanted endgame?

A mental puzzle without solution.

Had KGB believed the lie? Perhaps. It didn't matter. He was dead to them, dead to himself. He was the pawn removed from the board early in the game, sitting on the side, while queen and knight and rook maneuvered still. He waited at the edge of the West for the second death, the one that would be sleep.

He wore a heavy black coat and his hands were folded behind his back. He bowed to the wet Pacific wind slapping along the shore. His glasses were flecked with foam from the sea. He walked on, feeling the cold, thinking the old thoughts.

Devereaux had visited him once after springing the trap. In Washington. In the briefing section, where he was gradually unburdening himself of secrets. He brought Denisov a complete collection of the D'Oyly Carte Company's versions of Gilbert and Sullivan. It was a prize worth more than Devereaux knew; it was strange he had known that, that Denisov's passion for years had been the Savoy operas.

Denisov accepted the gift stiffly. They said nothing of consequence to each other.

He had the collection still and a few other recordings. He played Gilbert and Sullivan sparingly, afraid he might grow tired of the operas one day and then would have little left.

When a felon's not engaged in his employment, his employment
Or hatching out his felonious little plans, little plans
His capacity for innocent enjoyment, his enjoyment
Is just as great as any honest man's, honest man's.

He had a three-room apartment in an anonymous building with a stucco front and red-tile roof in a quiet neighborhood in back of the old mission church at the top of the hill. Denisov received an allowance from the government every month, a green cardboard check that he took to the bank on the first of the month (or second or third, whenever it arrived). Every six weeks or so, he received a visitor from Washington who came to talk to him about old colleagues, old

144

masters, old controls, old operations. They covered the same ground many times. He welcomed the visits; it broke the routine. They would always end up eating lunch on the oceanfront. Denisov knew a place . . .

Once, he had said, "Why is this worth it to you? You ask the same questions someone asked a year ago. The answers are the same. But we keep asking and answering as before."

"Do you think you have the only fucked-up country in the world?" the man from Washington had said. "Hell, I don't know what they do with my reports any more than you do."

They had gotten along better after that.

There were things to do. Even friends. He had acquired his driver's license but did not have money for a car. Occasionally, he rented a car and drove up and down the coast. He had gone to San Francisco once. A year ago, he had seduced a middle-aged widow who thought he was a professor from Switzerland. She had money and gave him some from time to time. It was pleasant to sleep with her—her imagination exceeded her physical presence—but he did not like her family very much. Her daughter reminded him of his younger sister in Moscow. He rarely thought of his family in Moscow. They were better off without him in any case. That's what he told himself when thinking of them so far away made evenings painful to him.

He was forty-six years old. He could live another twenty years or thirty years.

Like this? Walking on this beach? Watching television in the evenings? Going to movies and concerts? Reading books. Playing chess with the old men in the park? What was so bad about this life except that it might go on too long?

DENISOV TURNED THE KEY IN THE LOCK of his apartment door and pushed it open. The shades were drawn. The sun had come out in early afternoon. The rooms were dark. He reached for a lamp switch next to the door and turned it on and closed the door behind him. He dropped his mail on the table next to the wall—a catalog from something called *The Sharper Image*, an account from the electric company, a copy of *The Economist*.

Devereaux sat at a table in the little alcove the Americans called a kitchenette. The word was absurd, Denisov had thought once: it implied there might be larger kitchens. And then he had seen the kitchen in the house of the middle-aged woman he slept with and realized the truth.

Denisov stared at the American agent for a moment with patient, saintly eyes that blinked behind his rimless glasses. He slowly removed his coat, took it to the closet, removed a hanger and carefully hung it. He came back to the middle of the living room and put his hands in his pocket and stared at Devereaux.

Once, in Asia, they had been spy versus spy. They had drunk together, once, at the press club in Hong Kong, a neutral territory. Years later, they had faced each other in Ireland in the plot to kill an English lord. And the game had ended in Florida three years ago. Devereaux had won, not by checkmate but by overturning the board.

"You didn't have any beer in your refrigerator," Devereaux said.

"I thought you drank vodka."

"Not much. I'm getting older. Or my liver is."

Denisov stood very still. He realized how much he hated Devereaux. But the hatred only made his large, blue eyes appear more forgiving, saintly. It was useful to look like a church icon in a business where deception counted for everything.

"Do you want to know why I came here?"

Denisov said nothing. He waited for the other man. He realized he could not trust his voice. He thought about killing him. Would Devereaux be armed? How quickly could he remove his pistol from under his jacket? Denisov was very strong. He could push him back, out of the chair, pin him, break his neck with a well-placed blow. He had done these things.

"You still have a scar. On your neck," Denisov said.

"You saved my life that time. I told you that makes you responsible for me."

"I didn't understand it when you told me. I read a book. Here. About the Indians who believe this. It has to do with interfering with fate."

"Yes," Devereaux said. "Maybe I was fated to die that night in Belfast. You mocked fate."

"And fate? It put me here."

"Is it a bad prison?"

"Are there good prisons?"

"I don't know." Devereaux stared. A single lamp pierced the afternoon darkness but it was not enough. Denisov was framed in the light but his features appeared dark to Devereaux. Devereaux waited in shadows.

"Your English has improved."

"That was inevitable, my friend. If I put you in Lubiyanka prison for three years, I think you would speak Russian very well."

"I would not have been alive for three years."

"Oh, no. You're wrong. Some live forever. Some have been there for thirty or forty years."

"I would not have been alive," Devereaux said.

"Perhaps it is true," Denisov replied.

Neither man moved.

"They gave you a good hiding place."

"Not good enough if you found me."

"I had the address, Denisov."

"What do you want?"

"What do you want is more the question."

"To never see you again."

"What about the money in Switzerland?"

"What money?"

"You have money in Zurich."

"What are you talking about?"

"The money you took. Over the years."

"How do you know this?"

"Are we going to waltz all night? I know you, Denisov. I knew you for nearly twenty years. You're a thief."

"Like you."

"Yes. Like me. The difference between us is that I can get my money. And you can't."

"You came to tell me this."

"Sit down."

"I will stand in my own rooms."

Devereaux smiled, a lazy smile without warmth or mirth. "California dreaming, Russian. Wouldn't you like a car? How much did you put away over the years? When you were in Geneva, for instance. When was that? Early seventies."

"I cannot get my money. There is no way. I buried it too deeply in the account. I have to withdraw in person—"

"I know. At least, I figured it."

"So what do you want with me?"

"Gilbert and Sullivan, walks on the beach. You have anyone to provide companionship? Yes. I'll bet you do by now. Great life."

"It is a life."

"And you have me to thank for it."

The hatred burned in the eyes of the saint; the hatred made the eyes seem wide and full of pity and mercy, qualities not contained in Denisov.

"Should I thank you?"

"Yes. Because you won't get out of here to get your money without me."

Denisov waited.

"You're declawed, Russian. An indoor cat. You'd get torn apart out there. I'll take you in to get your money. And take you out again."

Denisov slowly walked into the kitchenette, pulled out a kitchen chair, and sat down at the yellow plastic-topped table across from Devereaux. His large hands rested on the table. He stared, unblinking, at the American agent.

"When was the Washington man here last?"

"Three days ago."

"So he won't be back for five or six weeks."

"That will be Christmas. He won't be back until January. No one works at Christmas."

"You've learned our secret of survival," Devereaux said.

"Unless he comes early."

"No. They never do that."

"He is from the Section?"

"Yes."

"But so are you—"

"This does not involve the Section, Russian. Just you and me and a couple of other people. A very private matter. Understand?"

"What do you want me to do?"

"Some of the old business. I've got a piece for you, a couple of other things of interest."

"This is a trick."

"No. We can't start off on that basis. You've got to trust me just enough to do what I want you to do."

"And why do you need me?"

"Because I don't have anyone else."

"What's happened?"

"Let's say, I'm expendable. And you've become invisible."

"Expendable by which side?"

"Maybe both of them. Certainly by KGB."

"Why should I help you then?"

"Watch my lips, Denisov, it isn't so hard. California is nice, isn't it? Nicer than Moscow in winter. You can't go home again anyway. You're dirty, marked money, they'd tear you apart. I need a reliable backup man, outside the game. And someone who might still have contacts left in Geneva. I want to get a line on a KGB—"

"Be a traitor?"

"Of course. What do you think I was talking about? Doesn't it get easier every time you do it? Like the two-dollar whore?"

"You are a bastard." Denisov jumped up and grabbed him and the two men crashed to the floor in the kitchen.

Denisov kicked Devereaux in the side and fell on him, pressing down on his neck with large hands, the thumbs on each side of the Adam's apple. In a moment, he would be dead.

A terrible pain between his legs.

Denisov fell back, his head hit the chair. He scrambled up as Devereaux pushed himself against the counter for leverage. Devereaux had blood on his lips. He had a black pistol in his hand.

The two men stood, gasping for breath, for a long moment.

"Sit the fuck down," Devereaux said.

Denisov, slowly, took the same seat.

Devereaux sat down opposite. The revolver was cocked. Devereaux stared at him as though deciding something. "I guess I would hate you as well. But I wouldn't hate myself enough not to see where my self-interest lay. I am talking about the money you have in Switzerland. And ten thousand American dollars that I have waiting for you in Los Angeles after the business is finished. Do you think the amounts would supplement your income from Uncle?"

Denisov said nothing.

"Oh, the hell with it," Devereaux said. He put the pistol on the table with the barrel pointed at himself, the grip close to Denisov's hand. "Pick it up."

Denisov picked it up.

"You want to kill me so fucking bad, shoot me. But remember, I can get you out and get you back in before anyone knows you're gone."

It was a lot of money, Denisov thought.

He stared at Devereaux hard.

Perhaps it was not enough, though.

He pulled the trigger.

Click.

Devereaux smiled.

Click. Click.

Denisov stared at the pistol, then at Devereaux. Suddenly, he smiled at the other man.

"You see?" Devereaux said. "We don't have to trust each other as long as it works."

"It is a lot of money," Denisov said. "In Zurich, I mean."

"Good. I hoped it was. I couldn't get ten grand to tempt you otherwise."

"Are you legal?"

"No. Not at the moment."

"What do you want to know?"

"Everything about Felix Krueger. About an operation."

"How long will it take?"

"A couple of days I hope."

"There is some risk."

Devereaux smiled. "Of course. Don't worry, Russian. The next piece I give you will be loaded."

Denisov shook his head slowly, the smile lingering. He put the piece on the table, butt end toward Devereaux.

"At least we know where we stand," Denisov said.

"And mine will be loaded too," Devereaux replied.

20 _____

Los Angeles

Devereaux walked into the apartment. Levy Solomon closed the door behind him. He locked it by turning a deadbolt twice with a key.

"Safe," Devereaux said.

"Listen. Nothing is safe."

"Tell me."

"The woman is getting antsy. You know something?"

Levy Solomon stared at him with large, protruding eyes. "I think she's anti-Semitic."

"If she wasn't, she'd be the first goy Pole who wasn't."

"I feel sorry for her. She's afraid. She even talks to Jews."

"Everyone has a cross to bear," Devereaux said.

Solomon grinned. "I put it down in notes. You can take it with you."

"Where's Rita?"

"With her. In the bedroom."

Devereaux opened the door of the second bedroom. It was a high-rise near Century City in the heart of west L.A. An ugly building with a beautiful view. Devereaux figured Levy Solomon had stolen a bit too, to supplement his pension. He had had enough opportunities in nineteen years in Central Europe.

Teresa Kolaki sat on the edge of the bed, still in the same sweater and skirt. She looked ill, old.

"You got news, mister?"

"Everything is going along well," Devereaux said. "I'm going to Europe. We made a contact. Inside." Most of it was a lie. He felt she knew it. Her expression stayed sour, down.

"When?"

"Tonight." He looked at Rita and she understood.

Rita got up. "I'll be right back, Teresa."

"Sure," the woman said. She stared out the window at the setting sun. Her face was old, drawn by tiredness. She hadn't slept through for five nights, from the horror of the moment when Mary learned her child was dead. Then the black, Peter, had taken her on the long flight to Los Angeles. She felt afraid of them all. Jews. Blacks. Now the interrogation, careful, insistent. She told them everything. She didn't care if she was dead. She should have stayed with John Stolmac. She was as dead as Mary.

Outside the bedroom door, Devereaux took Rita's arm. He led her to the room that Levy Solomon used as an office. He had no business, he was retired, but he had an office. Books lined shelves neatly, floor to ceiling, on one wall. There was a desk with no papers on it, only clippings from the editorial pages of the *Wall Street Journal* and the New York *Times* and half a dozen other publications. Levy Solomon confessed he wrote letters to the editor on important issues. Sharing his experiences, he called it.

Devereaux closed the door behind them. He thought to lock it. He sat down on the chair in front of Solomon's oak desk. She sat on the leather couch.

"I hate leather couches. They remind me of press rooms," Rita Macklin said.

Devereaux filled his eyes with her. He stared, tried to see everything. He wanted to carry it with him. He tried to frame her like a photograph.

"Denisov is at the airport. He takes Swissair to Zurich tonight at seven."

"You?"

"A few more loose ends. I'll be in Zurich by Wednesday afternoon."

"I'm a loose end."

She wore a blouse, cream-colored silk. Earrings. He couldn't remember her wearing earrings before. Her eyes were green crystals.

"Yes."

"What do you want to tell me?"

"Oddly enough, there's a will."

"Come on."

"I know. Mundane, middle class. But it's a will. Levy has it. I have a lot of money."

"From your family?"

"A trust in part. From Melvina. And other money." Vague, his gray eyes shifting in the dying light of afternoon. "In banks in Zurich. Two banks, in fact."

"How did you make so much money?"

"The old-fashioned way. I earned it."

"Why are you doing this? This grand good-by?"

"Because it probably is good-by. And I love you."

Quiet. She wouldn't accept this. Her hands were crossed

153

on her lap. She looked at them, looked up, her green eyes a little angry. "What am I going to do with money if you get killed? Who's going to save my life?"

"Getting killed is what I got paid for."

"Stop being a smart ass with me."

"All right. What do you want me to say?"

"I want you to say where you're going to meet me."

"I'm trying to put this the right way. They want to kill you. They will probably kill me. Nobody will be on your case."

"You said that last winter. I just hide for two years, is that it? You thought I'd be safe. It didn't work out that way."

"Yes." He bit the tip of his thumbnail. "It should have. I think it's all mixed up with this business with Teresa. And the others. The closer I get, the more they don't want me around. Not just KGB. They were looking for me before. Now they're dragging the lake for me."

"Hanley. Why can't he help you?"

"He has. But Hanley can only stick out his neck so far. He has to survive. What interests him is that the Puzzle Factory is fucking everyone around. Moving on the Section. Hanley lives and eats and breathes the Section. It was my leverage with him."

"I must have six hours of tape with Teresa. She's worn out. Her son. Are you going to get him out?"

"No," Devereaux said.

"Jesus Christ."

"They won't hurt him, I think."

"You keep making up theories that don't turn out right."

"No reason to hurt him. But there's plenty of reason to hurt Teresa Kolaki. There was a guarantee—five hundred thousand Swiss francs. About two hundred and thirty-five thousand dollars. Not all the money in the world, but Felix Krueger could use it. Who couldn't? The guarantee is a legal document, an insurance policy. I think that I might be able to use it to play with Krueger. If he wants to play. In any case, it gives Teresa a start if nothing turns out right."

"What deal could you make?"

He seemed surprised. "Me. For Teresa. And Stefan. It depends if they want to play."

"What the hell are you telling me?"

"What I told you in Washington. What I tried to make you understand. They want me, Rita. Nothing else matters right now. So what do they lose if they terminate Teresa's contract right away, give her the kid, get Krueger's guarantee back? And get me in return?"

"How can you give up like that?"

"I'm not sure I can. But I know I can't go into Poland and find Stefan and bring him out. This isn't a movie. They have to want to let him go."

She stared at him. Her eyes were damp. "You bastard. You're going to let them kill you. You don't even care what I want."

"On my terms. If I can arrange it that way," he said. "I told you that in Washington."

"Why are you doing this for her? She's nothing to you. What about me?"

"You're the other part. I want to see why they want you. If they don't care that much, you're free. And you've got all of Teresa's tapes about the network. You can use the tapes as leverage. Against them. Against the Section if the Section comes down on you. Mainly, I think, against NSA."

"Loose ends. You were talking about loose ends."

Devereaux ran his hand over his chin. He felt tired. His mouth was sore from the blow Denisov had given him. "Trust is limited, Rita. I think you've learned that. But I'm not trying to fool you."

For the first time, he looked vulnerable. He stared at her, his hands open, his legs apart. "I used you twice. It's my turn to pick up the check."

"I didn't care. I love you."

"I love you. So what does it mean? I mean, if we can't survive?"

"What about Melvina?"

"She's all right. My friend Rocca took out the Russian. Peter is back. He'll watch out for her. You can tell her what happened after this is over if it fulfills your familial sense of duty."

"You arrogant son of a bitch."

"Exactly," he said. Paused. Slowly. "Son of a bitch." His gray eyes glowed in the light of the red setting sun. He looked away from her. "My father worked in high steel. He was killed. Fell thirty-six floors. My mother was a drunk. I saw Mary Krakowski that first morning in Melvina's kitchen, I knew her." His face was savage. "I knew that bitch. I knew she was going for the vodka. I was only interested at first. Fascinated with her. Then the kid was killed. And then Teresa happened. No. I don't know Teresa and I don't want to know her. She's just another poor soul in life who thinks she has to be happy. I never told you those things because they weren't important."

Rita touched her cheek. "Your mother—"

"Melvina was right. My mother was a drunk, worthless. Even before the old man was killed. I was two or three, I barely knew him. I remember the way he smelled. Sometimes I think I can smell him. It's forty years later and I remember his smell. He never drank, never swore. I didn't know about the swearing but Melvina told me that. I knew about drinking. I knew my mother's breath." Devereaux glanced out the window; the sun was down, the sky was red. "She drank gin at the table in the morning. The way Mary drank vodka that morning. I couldn't save her. But Teresa. Well, who says that people can't delude themselves?"

"Me. My happiness counts."

"You'd never find it with me, babe."

"You never gave it a try."

"I ran around," he said after a long pause. "Killed a kid. I was eleven."

"You killed a kid?"

"He had some territory, it turned out. It was pointless. You had to run a gauntlet to school. Through his territory. I

156

went to the dime store on Forty-third Street one afternoon—
we lived down there—and bought a yellow-handled switch-
blade knife. A buck ninety-eight. Money I stole."

She stared at him. His gray eyes were shining with memory; his voice, still flat, was edged with a funeral pace.

"I knew what I was going to do. He came up and gave me
his shit and I just pulled the knife and stuck him. In the tit.
Right into his heart."

"Jesus."

"He couldn't believe it. He held my shirt. A big kid.
Stupid fucking bully." Devereaux smiled. "I pushed him back
and he went down." He looked at her. "You see? Killers are
born, not made."

She said nothing.

"The cops got me. I went down to family court, over to
the Audy Home. And Melvina bailed me out. Went to court,
had my mother declared incompetent. Melvina had her pull.
Hell, my mother was incompetent. But that didn't make me
want to kill someone. I just wasn't going to put up with
that shit."

"What happened to your mother?"

"She drank herself to death a bit faster than she was supposed to do it. She died two years later. I saw her twice. At
my first communion and at my confirmation. Melvina was
churchy. She made it clear to my mother that it was a special
treat for her. Melvina is a bitch. Was. Is. I don't know. She
made me what I am." He paused. "No, I don't mean that. I
made myself what I am." He smiled. "Sordid, huh?"

They sat for a moment, frozen in their places like actors
in a mime company, waiting for lights, for the magic of some
music or spoken command to unfreeze them.

"Why are you going to kill yourself?"

"Because you are the only thing I ever wanted," Devereaux said. He altered his voice. "And if I can't have you,
there's no point to anything."

She giggled. He stared at her. Smiled.

Still in a changed voice: "Maybe I won't kill myself if you promise to be mine ever more." Then, softly, "Rita."

She began to unbutton her blouse.

He watched her.

She took her blouse off and unfastened the front clasp of her brassiere. Her breasts were freckled, her nipples red, large. She stood up. "Do you want to feel me?"

He touched her. Her bare breasts pressed against his jacket.

"At least take your gun out," she said.

He unzipped his trousers.

"Not that one," she said.

He grinned and removed his jacket and the pistol clipped to his trousers. He took off his trousers.

"You locked the door."

"I thought of everything," he said.

"My God, I love you," she said and she was crying. He felt her tears on his bare shoulder. He held her too tightly but she didn't care. He kissed her eyes and tasted her tears.

They lay naked on the leather couch. For a long time, he kissed her, softly, insistently, his tongue on her breasts, nipples, between her breasts, on her neck, her mouth, her eyes, to kiss the wetness away from them. Her body arched toward him, her belly pressed against his belly. She groaned and took his neck with her hands and pulled his face to her and licked his lips with her tongue. She took his hand and placed it between her legs. She was open for him. "See," she said. "See?"

He moved over her, pressed into her deeply, kissed her, arched his body down to meet her body rising. He lay in her lap. He moved. She moaned, dug her nails into his back; at climax, her head rocked back and forth like a child's head, listening to secret music, her eyes closed to feel the music. He pressed still in her. He closed his eyes. He saw her in his mind as she was, naked beneath him, and saw her another time, when he first took her in the house on the mountain, before the fire, her body glowing in the reflection of the flames. He saw green eyes like prisms bending the spectrum until she was all colors. He opened his eyes. Her eyes were open, watching him. She moaned again and he could feel her convulsions, and this time he was lost in her. It never ended. When it ended, he kissed her, very gently, on her lips and slipped out of her lap, beside her, holding her.

They lay huddled, side by side, on the leather couch for several minutes.

"No more crying," he said.

"Big girl," Rita said.

"Everything will be all right," he said. He held her naked against him.

"Don't tell me lies. Not now," she said.

"Maybe it'll work out."

"No. You don't believe that."

"No."

More silence. It was night. The room was dark.

"There's no way out of this," she said.

"No. If we don't do anything, we've done something. Might as well go down swinging."

"I want you to save yourself for me. No more good-bys, no more facing facts. Fuck facts," she said. "I want you. There must be desert islands still or slow boats to China. KGB isn't God, is it?"

"No."

"Then save yourself. I'm going back tomorrow. I'm not afraid of them. I'm going back home and if they start leaning on me, I'm going to tell them about their goddam Numbers and tell them to lay off."

"Tough guy."

"Yeah. I'm a helluva lot tougher than they are."

"Don't leave yet. It isn't safe."

"When will it be safe?"

"When I call you. From there. In a little while."

"You're not coming back. You bastard. I see you going away right now. You're lying here and you hold me but you're already taking off. You bastard."

Another silence.

159

"I'd go anywhere for you," she said finally.

"I'll remember it. Can you keep house?"

"Is that going to be necessary? You want somebody to keep house, get a housekeeper. This is all I'm good for."

He kissed her on the cheek; he licked her ear.

"Levy is going to suspect we're up to no good in here," she said.

"Yes. He's a good agent."

"Look." She leaned on one elbow and stared at him. "I don't want you to die." Her eyes were shining clear, without tears, glittering though there was no light. "I don't care about your mother or father or your great-aunt or whether you believe in God or root for the Cubs or brush your teeth after meals. Am I getting through to you?"

He waited, smiling slightly.

"If you get killed, I'll feel terrible. But if you just die, just walk in and lay down and play dead, I'll never forgive you. Just once put aside all your reservations and your little secrets and your 'perhapses' and tell me you won't just lay down and play dead. Not for them."

He kissed her.

"Tell me," she said. She hadn't moved.

"I won't die," he said. "If I get killed, I want you to feel terrible. But I promise. No reservations, no secrets, everything open." He kissed her again. "I won't just die."

21

Washington, D.C.

"What about November?" asked Yackley, the New Man, head of the Section. His eyes were in shadows. A single lamp on his desk and nothing else to light the room. Hanley sat across from him. Beyond the window, the red-eyed aircraft warning lights in the Washington Monument blinked on and off. Winking.

"Stripped. We were crossed by the Puzzle Factory."

"Why?"

"Too big a job? I don't know. KGB is going at this full tilt. There's more."

"Do I want to know about it?" Softly.

"Not now. I gave him what he wanted. He said he'd be back to us. It's a matter of days now." Hanley was so tired; his voice seemed slow to his own ear. "He needed an independent contractor. Two, actually. I gave him names. Some money out of the special fund. Passports. Identification."

"Why?"

"Why is up? Why is down? Why did he go back to Chicago in the first place? He's found the tip of something. It looks small but it just might be the tail of the dragon. Somehow, the Puzzle Factory is involved and they've got a hard-on. For November, for the Section. I did what I did for the Section."

"You could have told me this before."

"No. You would have found some reason to stop it."

"I can still stop it."

"No. He's beyond us."

"Where is he?"

"I don't know," Hanley lied.

161

"What did he want?"

"He said if it worked out, he'd give us a present. To take care of his girlfriend. He said he's finished."

"They can't do that to one of our—"

"He isn't our agent now. They know that. We stripped him clean too when we turned him over to NSA for repro work. *He's arranging his own funeral.*"

"Shit," said Yackley.

22

Fort Meade, Maryland

Craypool took one of the pens out of his shirt pocket and marked a note in the margin of the yellow legal pad in front of him.

O'Brien made a face and lit a cigarette. "Why do you have so many pens?"

"What?"

"Why—forget it."

"Pens?"

"Forget it."

Craypool stared at the sheet. It had been a rebuke; he was sure of it. "We could upset the Numbers ourselves. Turn it over to National Security Council at the next meeting."

"Give it to the Hooverville crowd."

"Yes," Craypool said.

"I'd rather try to contain it. If it's still possible."

"Item: Macklin is gone. Item: Devereaux is gone. Item: Teresa Kolaki is gone. Gone where? We ran an airline credit check. Do you suppose they paid cash? If they got cash, who did they get it from?"

"What about the shine?"

"He's back in his cage in Chicago. Something happened there."

"Tell me something happened there. We get signals out of the Opposition camp you wouldn't believe. They don't even know where Malenkov is."

"But the shine wasn't there when it happened. Whatever happened."

"So what happens now?"

"The shine took Kolaki somewhere."

"Flights at that time?"

"Early in the morning. Not overseas but anywhere else. New York, D.C., L.A., Frisco. Anywhere."

"Shit. Doubleshit."

"I think November has to probe Krueger in Zurich. I told Morgan to stay there."

"And Krueger?"

"He's as pissed off as we are. This Rimsky tried to hold him up about the guarantee money. Said Krakowski was back in Poland."

"Everyone is working a con. We point the finger at November, they can't waste him. He's moving. I can feel it. He's doing something out there and we don't know what it is."

"He's got Kolaki. We have to figure that. But what does that mean to us? Or him? It's a matter of time for him. Even for his broad."

O'Brien blinked at Craypool's sudden vehemence. It was the hour, he decided. Nearly midnight. The days were too long. He'd have to talk to the Director in the morning. What could O'Brien tell him?

"I really don't want to blow this."

"Neither do I," said Craypool. "But how long until the Section tumbles to what's going on?"

"That depends on November," O'Brien said. He stubbed out the cigarette. He lit another. "We alerted Morgan, in the clear. KGB has to pick it up. Let's just wait on it."

"How long?"

"Forty-eight hours, tops. Then we have to go one way or the other. If they haven't taken care of our problem."

23

Warsaw

Matron woke him at 4:00 A.M.

"Stefan. Stefan."

He opened his eyes. She put her finger on her lips.

"Wake up and get dressed."

Obediently, he sat up, put his feet on the cold floor. Stefan Kolaki, age nine, resident of State Children's Asylum Number 3, in a suburb of Warsaw, occupied bed 34 in a dormitory for boys between the ages of seven and ten. The younger children were in another asylum. The older ones were on the top floor. The girls were in another wing.

Stefan Kolaki rubbed sleep from his eyes.

The dormitories were long but not wide. The ceilings were painted gray and the walls green; the windows were small because heat was a precious commodity. His personal things—clothing, a photograph of his mother, pencils for school, books and papers—were arranged in a wooden footlocker at the head of his bed. He stood up and picked up his glasses and put them on. He looked at Matron, who stood waiting for him. He removed his nightshirt and put it under his pillow and shivered naked in the cold. He slipped on underpants and then his jeans. He reached for his shirt, put it on, buttoned it.

"Sweater, too," Matron said. "Hurry along. And bring your coat."

"Where are we going?"

"Put your clothes in a bag. Everything."

"Has my mother come? Is she here?"

"Be quiet. Don't talk foolishness. Hurry or you'll wake the others. Hurry, you'll miss breakfast."

Socks and leather shoes. He opened the footlocker and put the photograph of his mother, wrapped in a shirt, wrapped in a sweater, in the bag.

"You won't need your schoolbooks."

"This is my notebook."

"All right. Take it."

The dining hall was in the basement; the food was prepared in large pots. There wasn't much meat but there never was, for anyone. No one in the place was particularly unkind to the children; some were very loving.

He felt giddy. Maybe it would be a surprise. She would be waiting for him at the train station.

Stefan Kolaki was not tall for his age. He was puny and had little energy. He had vision problems and wore glasses nearly all the time. His hair was blond and his eyes were bright blue. If he had known it, he resembled his father at that age. His father was dead. He remembered, in a dream, his father bending over his crib one night, kissing him on his forehead. His friend Jozef said Stefan couldn't remember what happened to him as a baby; he must have dreamed it.

He followed behind Matron, who carried his bag, down the sleeping dormitory corridor, through the double doors, down the concrete steps to the basement. The lights were on already; the cooks were preparing hot cereal for breakfast, baking bread. Milk in steel containers sat on a wooden counter. He pulled out a bench and sat down in front of a cup of milky tea and a bowl of hot cereal. He sipped the tea, which tasted sweet, and scalded the tip of his tongue.

A man in overcoat, glasses, and black hat came up to him. He sat down on the bench opposite. Matron left the dining hall.

He spooned cereal and put it in his mouth. He didn't look at the man.

"Are you shy, Stefan?"

What a dumb thing to ask, he thought.

165

"Are you shy?"

"No."

"How do you feel?"

"Fine."

The man did not remove his hat. He smiled at Stefan. Jozef said men in hats are secret police. They don't have any rules in secret police, Jozef said. They even wear hats in church, during mass, Jozef said.

"Stefan, did you ever see the circus?"

"Yes." Spoon. "Once when it came to Warsaw. We were all allowed to go except Jozef, because Jozef had written on the walls in the lavatory."

"That was a bad thing to do."

"He was caught," defended Stefan.

"So. You are a lucky boy to see the circus. Now you have more luck." The smile again. "You are going to have a chance to work for a while in the circus. Would you like that?"

Stefan said nothing. He was waiting for his mother, didn't this man know that? He couldn't be secret police if he didn't know that. It was better for Stefan to stay here. But he had his bag packed. Matron was gone.

"My mother," he began.

The smile was frozen. "What about her?"

"She won't know where to reach me."

"I think she will."

"Will she know I'm in the circus?"

"Yes. I think she will. In time."

"But doesn't the circus go to different places? Where will she write to me?"

"She may come to see you. That would be nice. Would you like that?"

"Come here? Back to Warsaw?"

"Maybe you would go to her." He patted the boy's hand awkwardly. "Would you like that?"

Stefan didn't smile. The man talked to him as though he were a baby.

"Maybe the circus would go to America. Would you like that?"

"America?"

"Your mother is there. In America."

"You mean you are going to take me to my mother?" He stared at the man in the hat with new interest.

"Yes. In a way."

"When will I go?"

"This morning. We have a journey to make, you and me."

He put down his spoon.

"Are you finished?"

Stefan stood up. "Yes." He picked up his bag. "I can go now," he said.

24 ___
Zurich

Denisov, in black overcoat, black homburg, and rimless glasses that framed saintly blue eyes, stood on the east side of the Rathausbrucke, the bridge that crossed the Limmat almost exactly halfway between the Hauptbahnhof and the entrance to the Zurichsee. Across the river, the immense clockface of St. Peter's church tower read precisely one. The weak afternoon sun, obscured by frequent raids of low-flying clouds, painted the bricks of the Rathaus in shades of orange.

He waited five minutes for contact. He was only supposed to wait five minutes. He had been in Zurich two days.

He started to cross the river back to the west side when he saw the other man emerge from a candy shop and cross busy Limmatquai against the light. Denisov slapped his gloved hands against his arm and waited. He had grown unaccustomed to the cold in three years in California.

When the Swissair flight had touched down at Zurich International, he had felt a leap of nostalgia to see snow again, to feel the cold sting his cheeks. The nostalgia faded quickly. He caught cold on the second morning. His nose was red and runny and he took aspirin.

Devereaux did not greet him.

He fell in beside him and the two men walked across the Rathausbrucke together, their shoulders slumped, Denisov's gloved hands clasped behind his back, Devereaux's bare hands jammed into the side pockets of his overcoat. He wore a black turtleneck and was bareheaded. His face was reddened by the cold, damp wind. They were brother oxen, dragging the same burden along the same familiar trail.

"Felix Krueger definitely exists for one thing," Denisov thought to say in the middle of the bridge.

"His name is in the phone book. I didn't need you for that."

"Everything is true as Teresa Kolaki remembered it. This is a city with many secrets and all of them can be purchased."

"Did you get your money?"

"Yes."

"You want expenses too?"

"Secrets are expensive, as I said. It wasn't that difficult. I knew men here from ten years ago, when I was a diplomat. In Geneva."

"At the permanent UNESCO conference."

"Felix Krueger travels in Comecon extensively. Prague and Warsaw primarily, but also Sofia and Budapest."

"And he brings out people."

"No. KGB does that. But he has luncheons for them at his house."

"How do you find out all this in two days?"

"That is the problem."

Devereaux waited. They crossed in silence through the

tangle of little streets around St. Peter's, on to the Paradeplatz, where the streetcars converged before spreading west, south, and north through the city. The shops of the Bahnhofstrasse were dressed for Christmas. The glittering store windows were filled with expensive things. West of the Paradeplatz were the offices of airlines and banks. The banks were housed in squat, substantial buildings.

"Let me buy you a beer," said Devereaux.

"That does not cover the expense," Denisov said.

Devereaux smiled. He pushed into a bierstube off the Paradeplatz. The place was noisy in a good-natured way, full of smoke and people leaning over steins of beer. They sat at a table and a middle-aged women in a peasant blouse and apron came over. They ordered two steins.

"What is the problem?" Devereaux said.

"I found a man named Glosser," Denisov began, sipping the beer. He removed his handkerchief and blew his nose. His glasses were steamed but he did not remove them. Gradually, they cleared. He sipped his beer again.

"Glosser was useful in the old days. He still is. A Swiss. Which means he will do anything for money. He didn't know I wasn't still KGB. We had a nice talk and he knew about Mr. Krueger. I had to be careful. After all, I am KGB; I should know about Krueger too. I was doing a double-back, I told Glosser."

"So what does he tell you?"

"Krueger was in Berlin in the late sixties. He made a lot of money getting people out of East Berlin. After the Wall. He had connections, very small, he bribed people on both sides. Checkpoint Charlie was Highway one oh one to him."

"You're turning California on me," Devereaux said.

"The problem, my friend, is that Glosser tells me so much about Krueger that I am embarrassed. How can Krueger be so open in this matter? What he does is bond people. That is slavery, is it not?"

"The way they are bonded it is."

"And so open. The Swiss? Well, I know the Swiss a little

169

bit. They don't want problems from anyone." Denisov finally removed his gloves. "It is cold here."

"You're a Russian, you're used to it."

"Not anymore. Damned cold. I had to buy a hat."

"It looks good on you."

"But Americans are here. In Geneva, Bern, here in Zurich. Agents. They must know these things after a while. He does not bother to hide himself enough. Why?"

Devereaux waited.

Denisov stared at the other man and then nodded.

"He's dealing both sides," Devereaux said.

"It has to be." Denisov blew his nose into a handkerchief.

"But which side is he selling out?" Denisov continued after a pause. "Soviet side? Or the Americans?"

"We don't have a side, you and me. Not now. Don't forget it, Dmitri Ilych."

A silence fell between them like a sudden shadow.

"So damned cold," Denisov said, rubbing his hands. "Don't you feel it? You don't even have a hat."

"I always feel it. You get used to it."

"No," Denisov said. "I had family in Moscow. Not much of a family. They were always fighting with each other. I couldn't think. Sometimes I was thankful I was assigned. Anywhere. But I had a warm place if I wanted it. I don't think you get used to the cold. Ever."

"Thankful for the Geneva assignment?"

"It had its advantages."

"Are you a wealthy man?"

"What is money for us? Just a way to avoid being unhappy."

"The melancholy Slav strikes again."

Silence.

"There's another possibility," Denisov said.

Devereaux waited.

"KGB is getting rid of people it doesn't want anyway. Krueger makes a small percentage on them. They work for KGB. Maybe it is worthwhile, maybe it is not—"

170

"How many? Does Glosser know?"

"Hundreds in a year. He doesn't know exactly. Half of what Glosser knows is rumor. A lot is based on the various accounts that Krueger holds in the banks."

"The accounts are secret."

"There are no secrets. Even in a Swiss bank. Interest accounts in different names."

"Like Teresa Kolaki's?"

"Yes."

"So if there are hundreds in a year, where do they all go?"

"Mostly to the United States. Some to Western Europe. Some to Canada."

"All right," Devereaux said. "Go on with your scenario."

"But if they work for KGB and the Americans know, perhaps they control the information that is passed along."

"That's a remote possibility. It's too scattershot. If an agent is working in one place, on one assignment, it's possible. But hundreds of half-educated immigrants working all over the country? It's not realistic to think we could control the information flow."

Denisov chewed his lip for a moment. "All right. Maybe the Americans know about the operation and want it to go on because . . ." He faltered.

"Because why?"

"I don't know."

"Continue it."

"Because . . ."

"Because they are turning them. Some of them. Not all, just some. Using them."

"But for what?"

"What is the hold KGB has over these people?"

"Their children, their kin, still inside."

Devereaux nodded. "And what is the hold we could have over them?"

"Nothing."

Devereaux waited. If Denisov could see it, then it was possible. No matter how impossible it seemed.

Denisov stared at the American, tried to see what the man with gray eyes wanted him to see.

"Teresa. Her child. She wanted him out, she gets him out."

"Of course," Denisov said.

"It works for them, it works for us."

"But if the Americans hold the children as hostage—"

"Not literally. They just let the immigrants know that we know. After their contract is up—"

"But what use could they be? I mean, KGB tainted them in the first place."

"I don't know. I need to know that. And now I want you to find a KGB for me."

"Why?"

"So I can give myself up." Devereaux smiled.

Denisov waited.

"The deal is simple. You find a KGB, you cut a deal. You give him me, he gives Teresa the child."

"They want you that bad?"

"It seems so."

"What about my money?"

"Greedy Russian bastard," Devereaux said. He opened his coat and took out an envelope. "Ten thousand."

"I had expenses."

"Fuck your expenses. You kited your account for years but I'm not the KGB paymaster."

"I could take the money—"

"And run? Run where? You've got it made in California. Relax. Buy yourself a car and you'll be Sporting Life on Sunset Strip."

"I don't understand that."

"Find a KGB. The country is lousy with them. Go down to Geneva and make a deal."

"I could make a deal for myself."

"I thought of that. If you cross me, the deal's off and I'll kill you. You know I will. Or if you think you might be able to beat me, you'll still be worried that I might get you before you get me. You cross me and I'll survive the cross and I'll kill you. Not just bang-bang either, Russian. I'll cut your fingers off and your toes and your goddam big red nose and let you bleed to death."

"And I am a barbarian, is that it?"

"No. You're not. You're a choirboy. You never did wrong in your life, officer. The deal is for Stefan Kolaki and not for anyone else."

"And why would they trust you?"

"Because they want me so fucking bad they've been falling all over themselves for a year trying to find me."

"And when I make the deal?"

"We do the trade here. I see the kid, they see me. Just like that."

"I can use Glosser to find someone for me," Denisov said thoughtfully. "But how is the child brought out?"

"Once the kid is definitely coming out, once we have a date, I'll have somebody here to pick him up."

"I don't believe you. I don't believe you will give up. Always survive. You always survive."

"Not this time. I'm too damned tired to survive."

"Your friend. The lady—"

"My friend is out of it."

"You're not telling me the truth."

Devereaux smiled then. "All right, Russian. Which part is a lie?"

"Why do I do this for you?"

"Not for me. For ten thousand more. The minute the kid is standing in front of the train station. Or at the airport. Or wherever we do the trade."

"And if KGB . . . if this can be arranged?"

"Then it will be guaranteed."

173

Denisov smiled then. "By Herr Krueger."

"Exactly," Devereaux said.

> > >

GLOSSER COULD NOT BELIEVE THE PAIN. They had taken a shard of glass from a broken bottle, a large piece, placed it in his mouth and forced his lips and his cheeks together and the glass had slashed the soft inner lining of his mouth. He had been crying but nothing moved them.

Rimsky said, "Spit it out."

Glosser spit. Blood foamed on his lips.

"Now tell me about the KGB man."

"He was Denisov. I knew him. Ten years ago. I told him some things about Felix Krueger. He knew about Krueger."

"Denisov is not KGB."

"He was. I knew him in Geneva." As he spoke, he bled.

"He is working for the Americans."

"Mein Gott."

Rimsky held the Uzi next to the small man's eye. Glosser could see the barrel blocking part of his vision.

"You die, Glosser. In pain or easy. But you die. Now tell me about Denisov."

"He said he wanted to trade. An American agent. He said he was working private. He said the agent was called November. He said that name I told you."

"Stefan Kolaki."

"Yes."

"Where was the American?"

"He did not tell me this."

"Are you sure? You want more glass."

"Please, please, please. I want to tell you everything. He said to meet him tomorrow. At 4:00 P.M. At the zoo."

"Where?"

"He just said to walk around, that he would find me."

"Where?"

"I tell you the truth."

Rimsky said, "I believe you now, Glosser. You made it

174

very bad for yourself that you didn't tell me everything at first."

"Please let me go."

"No. That would not be wise. You aren't useful anymore."

Glosser, in the straight chair, in the rented room where he lived, his head filled with pain, began to speak.

He never uttered another word.

$$\succ \quad \succ \quad \succ$$

MORGAN CALLED AFTER MIDNIGHT, ZURICH TIME. When O'Brien got on the line, he turned the lock on the portable scrambler. The machine emitted a barely perceptible hum that had the desired effect on possible taps. Not that Morgan thought he was tapped.

"Zoo. Tomorrow."

"Terrific."

"Rimsky took out Glosser. I heard the whole thing. Glosser set a meet with the R Section stooge. It's going to be tricky. I don't want Rimsky to take him out before I find out where our target is."

"Neither does Rimsky. Just keep your distance and let him handle it. Anything on where Kolaki is? Or this Macklin broad?"

"Nothing. I haven't even seen November yet. But tapping Glosser was a good shot. You got a name on the stooge?"

"Yeah. We tapped into the computer at the Section. Denisov. He was KGB, picked up three years ago in Florida and reeducated. November again. The guy is a one-man band in that rinky-dink outfit. Another thing. We traced a couple of computer inquiries we got the other day. They stopped just short of triggering the alarm. All flagged files. Guess who?"

"Krueger for one."

"You got it. And Mary Krakowski. And Teresa Kolaki. And John Stolmac."

"So Teresa—or Mary—spilled her guts."

"The Chicago cell is through. They're going to have to

scatter it. Meantime, we were going to blow the whistle on the Numbers network, turn it over to the boys in Hooverville—"

"Until I got the line on November," Morgan said. He was in his hotel room, sitting on the bedside, sipping a glass of scotch. He'd earned it.

"That's it, kiddo. You stay on the stooge's ass, make sure Rimsky gets all the help he can get. When he takes out November, we can concentrate on more important things."

"Macklin. Kolaki."

"A couple of civilian casualties by the time KGB takes care of them. Knowing that November has Denisov helps a lot. He was stashed in California so we're going over agent lists. When November and the Macklin woman did their duck, they didn't have a big choice of places. Same for Kolaki. It must have been California, close to Denisov. Close to a nice pool of ex-agents. Retired agents. We've got about two dozen in the San Diego area alone."

"You think he used someone off the payroll?"

"Sure. This is all set up by that clown Hanley." O'Brien's voice spit contempt, for R Section, for its personnel. In the next congressional budget he was going to turn R Section into a paper army, shuffling divisions of spies who counted crop yields in Upper Volta. The time for NSA to move on was at hand, and R Section was going to be blown out of the water.

"Hanley must have pulled a fast one out of his slush fund. He's a jag."

"It means they're onto the network."

"Not if November had to go to Zurich to find out what's going on. KGB can waste him and the stooge there and we take care of the girls at this end."

"Kill them?"

"No, Morgan. We're not barbarians." O'Brien paused. "KGB has been on Macklin's case. Now they want Teresa Kolaki. All they need is an address. Something laying around on a matchbook."

176

"How long is it going to take? To find them?"

"A couple of days. This is all going to be wrapped up in a couple of days."

25

Washington, D.C.

Mrs. Neumann slapped a thick sheaf of computer printout sheets on Hanley's desk.

He looked up, mildly. Mrs. Neumann's face was set, her eyes were glittering. Hanley sighed, felt his stomach rebelling already at the coming unpleasantness.

"What you have here are names, backgrounds. On our agents. Retired agents."

Hanley placed the tips of his fingers together. "Is there some reason you're showing them to me? Are we taking up a collection?"

"Dammit, man, we were raided."

"By whom?"

"NSA."

"When?"

"This morning."

"Are you certain?"

"I'm your goddam computer expert," Mrs. Neumann bellowed in her raspy voice. "Yes, I'm certain. They leave fingerprints. They broke through the computer's defenses, picked up our names, and left the same way they came in. The whole thing took less than ten minutes because they knew what they were looking for. Why do you suppose they knew what they were looking for?"

"Tell me."

"The probe I did. On your orders. Remember the names? Kolaki, Krakowski, Krueger? They finally found my footprints in their file. So they decided to do the same thing to us."

"Levy Solomon," Hanley said slowly.

"That's one of the names they picked up. All of them in California. Why?"

"They're after Teresa Kolaki. And maybe Rita Macklin." Hanley shook his head. "They finger Devereaux in Chicago, now this. Why would this involve NSA? We're on the same side, aren't we?"

"Everyone's on his own side," Mrs. Neumann said.

"What could they possibly want with information like this?" But he knew the answer. He knew Levy Solomon's name would be on the list of retired agents scanned by computer probers from the Puzzle Factory. Nothing was secret for long; you just hoped you kept things secret long enough to get a head start.

"Are you certain it was NSA?" Hanley said.

"Pretty sure," she said. "They left tracks, I told you."

"Could it be . . . the Opposition?"

"Anything is possible," Mrs. Neumann said. "We live in miraculous times."

Hanley made a face and decided. "How long have they had this information?"

"Nine hours at least."

He reached for the red scrambler phone and punched in ten numbers. The phone rang five times. Then he heard Levy Solomon's cautious voice ask, "Hello?"

"Abort," Hanley said. He replaced the receiver.

Mrs. Neumann said, "The women?"

"If it was the Puzzle Factory, they're doing dirty work for someone. They fingered Devereaux in Chicago. Fingered him for the Opposition." Hanley spoke bitterly. "Maybe that's what they're going to do with the women."

"Where can they hide?"

"It's not a matter of hiding now," Hanley said. "They're just going to have to run. Teresa Kolaki had a brother-in-law in Chicago. It was the fallback in case . . . in case what has just happened happened. But it's pretty thin and there's nothing we can do. Until . . . until he gets back from Zurich. If he gets back from Zurich."

26

Chicago

The second man opened the door of the Schwaben Stube restaurant and tavern, on a corner of Lincoln Avenue in the still-German section of the North Side. For a moment he stood in the door frame, holding the door, looking from table to bar to the dining room beyond. The walls were decorated with wood paneling and faded murals of the Germany that had vanished in the blood-soaked fields of Europe after August 1914. Fat maidens with breasts spilling from their blouses cavorted with fat men in lederhosen and Bavarian caps. *Gemütlichkeit*.

"Is cold," a small woman near the piano said. Alexander Vishinsky frowned a moment and then realized the open door was chilling the inside of the bright tavern. He smiled an apology, closed the door firmly behind him, and walked to the bar and took a stool.

Vishinsky was an accredited journalist with the Soviet news agency, Tass. He had an apartment in Georgetown in which he sometimes gave parties and slept with beautiful women. He was a charming man of middle height who spoke excellent English, particularly when he defended the Soviet international position to Ted Koppel on "Nightline." His eyes were cobalt, his firm chin line suggested purpose and an ordered existence. Vishinsky had been the target of at least four investigations by the FBI in the past three years. He was, of course, an agent of the KGB. The FBI knew it and the Soviets knew they knew it; but no one could do anything with the knowledge except to watch Vishinsky carefully. This had made it difficult for Vishinsky to slip his traces for the matter in Chicago.

Vishinsky ordered a dry martini at the copperplated bar. When the drink arrived, he said something to the barmaid and pushed a five-dollar bill across to her. She made change and he pushed the change in the trough of the bar and the woman rewarded him again with a smile. And a blush.

The first man, the one who had been waiting for Vishinsky, got up from his table in the corner and went to the bar. Mikhail Korsoff, one of the permanent stationmasters in Chicago, had dreaded the visit.

Korsoff was a thick man with dark complexion and gray, bristle-thick hair that grew in clumps on his round head. He smoked Parliament cigarettes and the index and second fingers of his right hand were yellow from nicotine.

At the piano, a melancholy man of middle years in a shiny blue suit played softly, his fingers remembering Mozart until someone reminded him that "Edelweiss" had been ordered up again.

"Hello," Mikhail Korsoff said.

He slipped onto the stool next to Vishinsky and tried a tentative smile. Vishinsky did not look at him, but sipped the first icy breath of the martini. His face took on color. "What bitter cold," he said. "Moscow."

"You get used to it."

"I couldn't. Not anymore. But you, you're built for it. Do you eat here often?"

"Sometimes. Are you hungry?"

"No. Rather, not for the food here. Couldn't you have chosen a French restaurant? I suppose they have them in this city." His voice matched the temperature of the drink.

Korsoff raised a finger to the barmaid and ordered a glass of DAB beer. She filled a stein and placed it in front of him.

"So. She has come home."

Korsoff saluted with his glass and took a swallow. "Yes.

The information was good. NSA was useful. They put enough pressure on them, wherever they were hiding, that they had to come out. That and the pressure we applied. Teresa Kolaki is with her brother-in-law. The complication is the Macklin woman. She's there as well."

"There are other complications." Vishinsky still would not look at the other man. His eyes were fixed on the change in the trough. His voice was clipped, cool, as though he were reciting something so obvious that it should not have needed saying. "Kolaki had a guarantee. If she can't get the money, sign it over—five hundred thousand Swiss francs—we have to reimburse our middleman in Zurich. The same thing happened with Mary Krakowski. A million Swiss francs in less than two weeks, in addition to the usual middleman fee."

"Refuse to pay—"

"Are you a fool?" Vishinsky turned for the first time to face Korsoff. His eyes made judgments. "The man in Zurich would refuse to bargain with us again. He's the best in Europe; he could do it. A lot of cells are involved, a lot is based on the trust these wretched people have in him."

Vishinsky turned away again. His voice was brittle. "You've been out of the active game too long. If you had been more persuasive with that old woman in the beginning, we would have located this . . . November. Now we have to close down our cell and start a new one. And mollify the middleman in Zurich. And we have to get Teresa Kolaki back inside."

"Besides the money—"

"Besides? This is hard currency, my friend, not rubles, not dreams. Teresa Kolaki needs reeducation. She needs to be reunited with her son. She needs to promulgate . . . the cause."

"How?"

"Guarantees," said Vishinsky, surprised that something so obvious escaped Korsoff. "In time, she'll work for the government. She will help our middleman and our agents to convince these . . . traitors who choose exile that we will keep our word. She is a proof, a bit of living proof. As Mary Krakowski would have been."

"What does the Directorate want?" Mikhail Korsoff said with sudden humility. He sighed, picked up his stein, and tasted the beer. He felt very tired, even a little afraid.

He worked as a printing company executive in Chicago and had access to a number of people in high-tech industries developing along the mini-Silicon Valley strip in the western suburbs. His life had become low key, comfortable. At fifty-seven he hoped to end his years with KGB at this assignment in Chicago, where he had been for five years. He had a daughter who devoted herself to the Cubs just as his wife devoted herself to Marshall Field's department store. He had not expected such trouble from a routine assignment to question an old woman about her nephew.

He had misjudged his assignment badly, from the first; he should have forced the matter with the old woman. Now he was being blamed for some of what happened afterward.

"The Warsaw Circus," Vishinsky said softly.

Mikhail Korsoff just stared at him.

"The Directorate assumed that it would be impossible to find Teresa Kolaki in time to keep her . . . silent," he began slowly. He held up his glass to the barmaid, dazzled her with a television smile, and resumed when he had his second drink.

"Malenkov went to see the old woman about Devereaux. He has not been seen since. In our surveillance, we discover the house is practically under guard. There is a Rocca person who has vague underworld ties. Also a blackie who lives with the woman."

"Peter," Mikhail began.

"Yes. The Directorate said the two matters had become entangled. November is one matter; protecting the network is another. We are no longer concerned with Macklin or November. They will be taken care of by others. We are concerned only with Teresa Kolaki and her return to Poland as quickly and as quietly as possible. Which means there must be a certain . . . willingness to her actions. We have stirred up enough trouble—"

"Why will she return willingly?"

"The Warsaw Circus," Vishinsky said again and smiled oddly at Korsoff. "It arrives tonight, after midnight. It opens tomorrow for one week. After the Chicago engagement, the circus and its personnel return directly to Poland, a special arrangement with LOT for this single engagement."

"You are confusing me."

"Not a difficult thing, I think," Vishinsky said. "How do we make contact with Teresa Kolaki?"

"We—"

"No. I tell you. We knew about her brother-in-law, of course. It was all part of the . . . research on her before she was permitted to leave Poland. After she disappeared, after our troubles started, we placed John Stolmac in charge of surveying the brother-in-law. You understand?"

"Why wasn't I told?"

"Because it did not concern you," Vishinsky said. "Another." He held up his glass and the barmaid came down to refill it.

Korsoff still nurtured his single beer. He glanced slyly at Vishinsky. Except for a certain puffiness around the eyes and broken blood vessels at the base of his nose, Vishinsky didn't have the face of a drinker. Did the Directorate know this?

"Teresa Kolaki called her brother-in-law two nights ago, when our friends at NSA put pressure on her. It was enough. We had to be cautious, in case NSA was putting together a trap for us. But it wasn't that. They fingered the Macklin woman and, apparently, accidentally flushed Kolaki out of her hiding place."

"What about the telephone call?"

Vishinsky smiled at the third martini. Or perhaps at the question. He enjoyed centering attention on himself. One of the members of the Directorate in New York had praised him

183

for presenting the Soviet position so "charmingly and forthrightly" on "Nightline" during a debate over cruise missiles.

"Stolmac had a portable monitor. Her brother-in-law told her about the advertisement in the local Polish daily paper—"

"The *Zgoda*," Korsoff said.

"For the Warsaw Circus. You see, we took her son out of Poland six days ago to join the circus, after she disappeared."

Mikhail Korsoff laughed. Out loud.

Vishinsky turned to look at him.

"I don't believe it. It's ludicrous."

"Tell that to the Directorate, Mikhail Vladimir," Vishinsky said slowly. "This is a vast country. There was not much time. We needed to contact Teresa and we did not need to involve ourselves in further, clumsy actions such as you and Malenkov—I am certain, the late Georgi Malenkov—used. Used to obtain exactly nothing."

"It was not me, citizen. It was the Bulgarian. He insisted on carrying a pistol."

"Recriminations. He is already back in Sofia. The Bulgarians failed twice in the business of November. A simple matter of elimination and they have failed, you have failed."

Korsoff bit his lip. He must say nothing.

"It is a vast country but we knew that Stefan Kolaki, Teresa's brother-in-law, was in Chicago. And she knew he was here. At first, we thought she had gone to him, which would have made the matter somewhat easier. Now she is definitely with him but too many agents from America have been stirred up over this matter. We do not wish to attract any more attention. So when Stefan Kolaki purchased the *Zgoda* three days ago, as he always does, every day, he could not miss this advertisement for the Warsaw Circus." Vishinsky took a copy of the advertisement from his pocket and unfolded it.

The advertisement, in Polish, featured the usual circus pictures of clowns and acrobats and high-wire performers.

Korsoff could see nothing in the ad that indicated the boy was with the circus.

"Is it a code?"

"No," Alexander Vishinsky said coyly. He was smiling.

"I don't understand."

"The star is Wojo the Clown. There. He is an interesting case," Vishinsky said. "He is forty inches tall—or perhaps I should say short. This makes him too tall to be unique as a midget, and yet that is what he is. So he has become a clown. This is the first time we have permitted him in America. You see, there are problems with him—"

Mikhail Korsoff frowned. He stared at the photograph of the clown reprinted in the Polish-language paper. What was he supposed to see in this?

"He is an alcoholic for one thing," Vishinsky said.

Korsoff waited.

"And he is a sexual pervert. This is well known in Poland. In certain circles."

"Why do you make this a mystery?"

"There is no mystery. Who stands next to Wojo? In the photograph where he wears a wedding suit and stands atop a wedding cake?"

Korsoff was tired; his eyes were tired. He squinted and stared.

"Another clown," he said.

"A midget?"

"Yes. By her size."

"Not her, Mikhail Vladimir," Vishinsky said.

God. He understood in that moment. He could not look at the photograph. He turned away. And then, fascinated, turned back to it.

"Stefan. The boy," he said in a dull voice.

Vishinsky smiled.

Mikhail Korsoff's hands shook.

Wojo was dressed in top hat and morning suit. The boy named Stefan Kolaki, whom Korsoff had mistaken for a woman, was not smiling. He was dressed as a bride, in wedding gown and veil and bouquet.

Teresa Kolaki knew now; knew there was something so terrible that she would have to agree to any terms they offered to her.

> ➤ ➤ ➤

JOHN STOLMAC HAD WATCHED THE HOUSE ON Ellis Avenue for two hours. He had a 9-mm. pistol in his coat. He stood in the entry of an apartment building across the street and stamped his feet to stay warm. It had been light when he began his vigil but the gray afternoon had long faded to black.

John Stolmac was frightened.

He was blamed for the death of Mary Krakowski and the disappearance of Teresa Kolaki. He was told he should have known that Teresa Kolaki would disappear when she learned that Mary was dead. Stolmac argued at first but they were relentless, and he saw, finally, that there was no point in resisting. They had to have someone to blame; it was part of the bureaucratic housecleaning. All files had to be closed finally, all blame apportioned, all cases finished neatly. He was part of the solution.

He had tapped the telephone line at Stefan Kolaki's apartment. His luck turned when Teresa called her brother-in-law and then got better when Teresa and the journalist came to the apartment two days ago. They—the bureaucrats from the embassy in Washington—had merely grunted when he offered his information. It was not enough. The cell in Chicago had been broken, the whole network had been put in danger. Stolmac knew he was not forgiven. Not yet.

He was going to kill the black in the house. That would be the first thing.

The old woman would see the body, understand that Stolmac was capable of killing; then she would tell him where November was, this agent who had upset the cell, who had pierced the network, who had escaped a contract against him for nearly a year.

That would be information worth giving to the embassy.

He had been cautious. He knew that Malenkov had disappeared. A man named Rocca, a gangster, had taken the house under his protection. The people from the embassy had turned down Stolmac's suggestion to question the old woman. It was—what had they said?—"not productive" to question her while they were still involved in the operation to get Teresa Kolaki back. Bureaucrats.

She was only an old woman. With a blackie to guard her. And a cheap gangster to watch the house.

He had taken care of the gangster first. Two shots through the side window of the gangster's car, both hollow-point, Teflon-coated 9-mm. shells. The Italian's head had exploded, as though someone had put a bomb in his brain and set it off. The body of the Italian was still in the car, parked in the alley behind the house on Ellis Avenue.

And still Stolmac had waited, to see if there were others. But no one had ventured out; the house was dimly lit and still. It was time.

John Stolmac emerged from the entryway and crossed the street, down a gangway separating the old woman's house from a three-story apartment building that faced 46th Street. He went around, through the alley, to the bare back entry. He climbed the stairs to the back door. He fumbled with a dozen keys on a chain, found one, pushed it into the lock and turned. The back door did not budge. He shoved and felt the door give slightly. He pushed again and burst the second lock. The woodwork splintered. He was in the kitchen.

Stolmac removed the pistol from his coat and unlocked the automatic safety.

He took a second step into the room. It was dark. A thin light came from the front hall.

He took a third step.

"Stand there," she said. He saw the old woman framed in the light suddenly. She held a pistol in her hand.

Stolmac turned, hesitated. He hadn't come to kill the old woman. Not at first.

"Where's the black man?"

"Who are you?"

"Put down that gun. That's dangerous."

"Who are you?"

He took a step toward her. The old hand trembled. He reached for the pistol.

She fired.

John Stolmac could not quite believe it. He stood still, staring at the old woman. It was absurd to think he would be frightened of an old woman, waving a pistol.

"Give me the gun," he said. And then he felt the sudden rush of pain in his belly. His own pistol felt too heavy for his hand. He dropped the gun, felt a rush of nausea; was he going to be sick?

When he fell, his head struck the side of the kitchen table, but he was beyond feeling.

➣ ➣ ➣

WHEN PETER RETURNED, SHE DIDN'T ASK HIM what he had done with the body.

Peter was amazed at her. She wasn't even shaking. Tough old bitch blew that dude away just like nothing. Tough like the other dude, the nephew or whatever he was.

She had a suitcase and some papers in a small box.

"We finally going?" Peter said.

"Yes. I never thought it would come to it."

"Shoulda gone before this."

"He brought this—when he came to the house."

"You was the one wrote him."

"I didn't want him to involve me. I told him that."

Peter said nothing. She was jiving him now, the way she'd go on about something that happened only she'd suddenly decide to remember it differently. When he first met her, Peter thought she was crazy. Old. But then he saw through her, saw right through those gray eyes, saw she knew exactly what was going on, what had gone down, but wanted to jive. Jive herself or someone else, just try out a different version, see if anyone would believe it. See if she would believe it.

"Where we going?"

"It doesn't matter. It should be someplace warm."

"California."

"No. I think it rains there this time of the year. Or something. It should be someplace warm."

Peter waited. She already knew where she wanted to go; she was just jiving again.

"Well, it doesn't matter." Said lightly, as though it really didn't. "I suppose we're going to have to wait until morning," she said.

"Ain't no planes at 3:00 A.M."

"We'll find someplace," she said. "Then I'll have Monsignor O'Neill get my mail, send it along. And I'll sell the house. I've got all the papers here."

He waited as though she was leading up to something.

"You're taken care of, Peter." She glanced at him sharply. "If you don't want to go, I can make a settlement. Or there's a will."

He stared at her blankly before he spoke. "I got no particular place to go. It don't matter that much."

"All right."

"'Sides, the hawk is biting, cold goes right through me. I ain't young neither. Got old waiting to get outta the place."

"All right," she said again. "In the morning."

"That all you gonna take? One suitcase, that box?"

"Papers. The lawyer can take care of the house, not that it will sell for much. But it suited me."

"They ain't necessarily coming again. You might give it time," Peter said.

"No. I killed a man here."

"He was gonna kill you."

"But I killed him." She looked through him. "That's what Red brought me to."

"But when he comes back—"

"No. He won't be back. They . . . they're hunting him.

189

And they'll find him and kill him. I knew it when I looked at him, before he left, before . . ." She blinked. Her eyes were wet. She frowned and turned. She wouldn't cry. Tough old bitch.

27 ____
Zurich

Denisov stepped off the number 6 tram from Paradeplatz and waited for it to go on. The streetcar clanged farther up the street, turned a corner, disappeared. Denisov pulled his black homburg firmly down until it rested above his ears. He put his bare hands in his pocket and felt for the piece Devereaux had given him. It was a Walther PPK, reliable at close range but without high impact over distance.

Devereaux had said, "If you want distance, buy a rifle."

Denisov crossed to the entrance of the zoo and shoved coins across the counter to an old woman. She stripped off a single ticket from a roll and pushed it over the counter. Denisov took the ticket to a gate, paid, and entered the enclosed zoo grounds.

The afternoon was lost in fog on the Zurichberg. The mountain was full of trees and old homes and sports facilities and a cemetery where James Joyce was buried. And the zoo.

He started along the paths.

The zoo was halfway up the mountain. It seemed remote, distanced from the world by fog and an eerie quiet broken only by the restless roar of caged animals and the cry of caged birds.

Denisov walked slowly, stopping now and then to peer at an animal peering back at him in the gloomy light. He smiled slightly, sadly, at the brown bears sitting patiently on rocks, waiting for sleep or darkness or a feeding.

Denisov thought: Why is he arranging this elaborate farce?

Denisov did not believe Devereaux would surrender himself for the release of a Polish child, or for the release of anyone, even the American journalist. Devereaux had not survived so long to surrender so easily.

What other reason existed for this charade? To trap Denisov? Trap him in what? If Devereaux wanted him dead, he would have killed him long ago, at his convenience. Instead, he released Denisov, gave him a passport, money, even the Walther PPK he fingered in the pocket of his coat. In the gloom, somewhere ahead, a tiger growled.

Perhaps Devereaux intended to trade Denisov to KGB for the Polish child. That thought had come more easily to Denisov. KGB would like the return of a defector, even a reluctant defector. Trade a spy's life for the life of a child.

Denisov had decided this must be the truth. Denisov had decided to meet with Glosser, keep the game alive, arrange a meeting with Devereaux. And kill Devereaux. This time without words between them, this time without any subtlety.

He would not go back to California, of course. That path would be closed. And he would not go back to Moscow.

Denisov had nearly 350,000 Swiss francs. They were at the Hauptbahnhof, in a Swissair travel bag. A case full of neat hundred-franc notes in Locker B112. Enough to begin a new life. Perhaps in Marseilles. He had once had connections there when the heroin trade was flourishing between France and the United States. It would be a warm place, away from KGB if they were to look for him. Away from the Americans.

He would meet Glosser in the zoo, arrange the matter of trading Devereaux. He would report to Devereaux, a second meeting would be arranged. And then he would kill both of them—Glosser, who knew him and could betray him, and Devereaux, who had betrayed him before.

Perhaps having Devereaux's body in Zurich would satisfy KGB. At least until Denisov made good his escape. A train to Geneva, a transfer to the fast train to Lyon, always

191

watching his trail, giving himself time. A car from there down to the Côte d'Azur. There was money to be made still in the drug trade in Marseilles; not enough to become greedy but enough to live comfortably.

For a moment, he stood in the swirling fog, lost in thoughts of his escape. Then he saw movement in front of him. He smelled sweat, the stench of foul breath. He wrapped his hand around the pistol in his pocket. The shadow in the gloom shifted.

Denisov took a step forward. The fog shifted again in the strange, yellowish light.

A tiger. It was a tiger crossing from rock to rock carelessly in the cageless preserve surrounded by a deep, rocky trench which defined its prison. Denisov smiled then.

He turned, read the sign in French that said this carnivore was among the endangered species in the world.

So were we all, he thought.

Another step. His hand relaxed its grip. Then he saw the other man.

Rimsky held a pistol pointed straight at Denisov's chest.

"Where is your master?" began the other man in harsh Russian.

Denisov's saintly eyes blinked in surprise. His hand tightened around the pistol in his coat pocket but the distance was too far to be certain, even if he could remove the pistol in time. A fine line of sweat formed on his face, above the black eyebrows.

"Where is your master?" the other man repeated.

"Who are you?"

"My name is Rimsky. I understand from Glosser that you wanted to meet me."

Ten feet. The two men could see each other clearly, as though a space in the fog around them had been cleared for this little drama.

"Where is Glosser?"

"As dead as you will be, Dmitri Ilyich Denisov. It was

Major Denisov before you became a traitor to your section, to the Directorate, to our—"

"Yes," Denisov said calmly. "And you are a politician then, making a speech?"

It was absurd, he thought. He heard his own flat voice as though hearing the voice of a stranger. The flat tone was a matter of training, of having learned never to reveal himself. The complete secret agent. Yet it was an illusion, like everything else. He was afraid. Terribly afraid.

"I was not a traitor," Denisov lied softly. "I bring you November."

"Your master."

"I led him here. I was going to kill him."

"Well, that's no concern for you anymore, Dmitri Ilyich."

"He wanted to arrange a trade—"

Rimsky smiled. "For what?"

"A child. In Poland."

"Teresa Kolaki's child," Rimsky said. His voice was almost eerie, catching its tone from the flatness of the fog, from the flat, fading yellow light of a still afternoon.

"You know this; then you know I tell you the truth—"

"We have Teresa Kolaki's child taken care of."

He waited. The pistol in Rimsky's thin hand did not waver. Someone would come along in a moment, someone would intrude on the melodrama. I beg your pardon, is that a pistol? What is going on here between you? I'll call the police.

"He is dead," Denisov said.

"We do not kill children," Rimsky said. "He is safe, in America, with his mother."

Denisov blinked again. His clothes felt damp beneath the layer of heavy coat, and the homburg held the dampness of his scalp.

"Then why arrange this . . . absurd thing?" Denisov asked the question not of Rimsky but of himself. He was an innocent extra in an opera of the absurd who had been pushed onstage with a spear and costume and who had no idea what was going on.

"Where is November?" the Russian asked suddenly, sharply.

"Here," Devereaux said, standing behind him. Rimsky felt the black barrel of the .357 Colt Python revolver pressed against his right ear. He did not turn.

"Pistol," Devereaux said.

Rimsky opened his hand and the weapon clattered to the pavement.

Denisov stood stock still for a moment, his mouth open, sweating freely now, adrenaline surging through him, his heart racing, his hands trembling. All control in his body was loosed. He felt like retching.

Devereaux pushed Rimsky down on a wooden bench behind them. He slapped the Russian across the bridge of the nose with the barrel of his pistol. It was a gesture so casual it seemed an afterthought. Blood dripped from both nostrils, spreading across Rimsky's upper lip, dripping onto his coat.

Denisov took two steps forward and bent down for the pistol. He put it in his pocket. He walked to the men.

"You wanted me, Russian, and now here I am," Devereaux said in English, in a flat, calm voice lazy with intended violence, the purring voice of a great cat pacing in the foggy half-light of a winter afternoon.

"You're dead," Rimsky said. As simply as a child stating a lesson. "And you, Dmitri Ilyich—" He switched to Russian. "Death to spies."

"Beginning with you," Devereaux said. "I hit you to get your attention. This is a pistol and I have a question: Where is Stefan Kolaki?"

"You are a dead man," Rimsky said.

"No. That's not the answer," Devereaux said thoughtfully. His back was to Denisov. He was very close to Rimsky's face. He hit him very hard across the nose again. This time a bone cracked and Rimsky blinked with pain. He did not cry out.

194

"Not hard enough," Devereaux said with the same concern. He hit Rimsky a third time. Even Denisov winced at the casual infliction of pain. He understood pain; he knew it was necessary; he had used it as a surgeon uses a scalpel to cut open the belly of a patient. An instrument only. But he winced anyway.

This time, Rimsky groaned. He wept, not in sorrow and not in repentance, but in reaction to bodily pain.

"You understand now?"

"I'm not afraid to die," said Rimsky. That was a lie, Denisov thought; that is training.

"It's not a question of that. Not yet," Devereaux said. "There is death as easy as going to sleep and death that's hard. You know the difference, don't you?"

Rimsky said nothing for a moment. Then he groaned again. His face was soaked with blood.

The single shot was muffled in the fog. It might have been a stick rapped sharply against a log, it might have been anything but what it really was.

Rimsky's head exploded. Brains splattered Devereaux's coat, blood streaked Devereaux's face. He was not aware of it. He was down already, beneath the bench, and Denisov was flat on the ground beside it.

"There," Denisov said. He pointed across the cages to a hilly walk near the section where they kept the bears.

Devereaux rolled once onto the walk, his pistol cocked, got to one knee and waved with his hand to the Russian.

Denisov was already running along the fence.

Devereaux disappeared up a second walk. It circled an oasis of cages and outdoor exercise areas for the animals, rose through a gardenlike setting toward the other path.

Two old men stood ruminating, staring into the sad eyes of a water buffalo. Devereaux brushed past them. Later—when he got home—one of the old men would notice that grayish matter had fastened to his coat. And the next day, in the *Zeitung*, he would read about the man found shot to death in the zoo, near the outdoor cages of the great cats.

195

Devereaux, in the half-light, saw the man running up the path. A thin man without a hat, holding a pistol.

Devereaux fired low, his own pistol cracking sharply against the muffling fog. The figure seemed to stumble, then fell. The pistol clattered away. The man reached for it. Denisov hit him then like a fast train slamming through a country crossing.

Devereaux was out of breath when he reached them. He picked up the pistol. Smith and Wesson .45. Welcome to America.

"Who are you?"

"You're in trouble, shithead," Morgan said, clenching his teeth. "That was a Soviet agent you were dealing with. Selling out to—"

"We've got to get this asshole out of here," Devereaux said. "Pick him up on that side."

Denisov and Devereaux raised the man between them.

"You shot me, you son of a bitch," Morgan said. "You shot a goddam agent of the government, you son of a bitch."

➤   ➤   ➤

"I WANT TO KNOW ABOUT ZURICH, about Krueger," Devereaux began.

"I don't have to tell you. You have to tell me what a goddam R Section agent that we're supposed to be reprocessing and—"

"You're NSA," Devereaux said.

"And you? What have you become? A KGB stooge?"

"Why did NSA know about Krueger? And about Rimsky—"

"We are talking secrets, asshole," Morgan said. "You don't seem to appreciate the seriousness of the situation any more than your girlfriend did."

Devereaux stared at him. "You talked to her."

"We talked to her."

"He's just getting off the subject," Denisov said gently.

"I think his leg is broken. He's probably in shock. That's why he doesn't feel the pain. We can wait until the pain comes but that might be too long. I suppose he might die."

"Yes," Devereaux said, almost in a trance.

Three men in a car, parked on a quiet street on the Zurichberg, in a neighborhood of old homes and large estates high over a city obscured by the fog. It was night, just that suddenly. The wet thaw made everything seem sticky, even the inside of the Mercedes.

Morgan's face was quite chalky now, almost transparent. There was some pain but not as much as there would be later.

"Who is Felix Krueger to you?" began Devereaux.

"I don't know what the fuck you're talking about—"

"Then I'll kill you," Devereaux said.

He sat next to Morgan. Denisov sat in the front seat, behind the wheel. Denisov eyed them through the rear-view mirror, like a driver watching his passengers during a long ride. Little dramas in the backseat of a cab.

Devereaux waited.

"Not me. We're the same side, Jack. You don't gimme a lot of shit. My people know I'm here, don't forget—"

"And that I'm here," Devereaux said. His lazy gray eyes never left the other's face. "What should I do about that?"

"Kill me and they know it's you."

"But you were willing to let Rimsky kill me."

Morgan's silence said yes.

"Why is this Russian operation important to NSA?" Devereaux said.

Denisov grunted.

"I don't know what you're talking about," Morgan said.

Devereaux shot him then, in the fleshy part of the thigh. The other leg. The air of the car was suddenly acrid with smoke from the pistol. The three were temporarily deafened by the sound of the shot in the small space. Even Denisov jumped at the sudden explosion. Because of the ringing in their ears, they did not hear Morgan scream at the moment he was shot. They heard only the sobs after.

"You sadistic bastard—"

"Then your right hand," Devereaux said. "Do you think I'm playing, you bastard? Is this a game to you? You wanted me killed and you've been on my case for weeks. You want me dead, you push Rita Macklin around. Do you suppose I'm going to let you do it?"

"Son of a bitch," Morgan muttered through the pain that was enveloping both legs, rising through his body. He felt sick. He vomited soundlessly on himself.

Devereaux waited.

"This makes the car smell," Denisov said.

"Krueger," Morgan said. "He works for us. Now do you see?"

"There's more," Devereaux said. "If it were that simple, there wouldn't have been all these games. Back in Chicago. Putting the finger on me, on Rita, forcing us to get away. Those two clowns in Chicago, what were they supposed to be? Highway signs for the Opposition? This is Devereaux, this guy right here, shoot him, please."

"You were interfering, you bastard, in an operation of the United States government—"

"And him." Devereaux pointed the pistol at the back of Denisov's head. He had removed the homburg because it was too tall for the interior of the car. "They know about him?"

"By now—"

"All right."

Silence a moment. Three men breathe. One man groaning softly. The car still, the night still, the black fog over everything.

Devereaux waited a moment, watching the face twisted in pain before him, but not really seeing it. Seeing, for the first time, the possibility he had given up on. Just possible, he thought.

"Drive," Devereaux said.

➤ ➤ ➤

CRAYPOOL RECEIVED A MESSAGE IN NSA CODE ULTRA, from Zurich. He ran it through the code computer, read the clear message twice, then hurried up the hall to the corner office and entered without knocking. O'Brien was alone. Craypool put the message on O'Brien's desk. "From our man in Zurich," Craypool said. O'Brien read it three times.

"Done then," O'Brien said.

It was just after three in the afternoon. Washington was waiting for its first winter storm. The inch of snow that was predicted would, of course, shut down most of the functions of government for a day. The president was at his ranch in California. The vice-president was in Beaumont, Texas, speaking of morality to a group of born-again Christians. The National Security Advisor was in Palm Springs, California, at the home of a friend who owned 200,000 shares in the world's largest computer company, a company that was trying to re-structure the computer systems used by NSA.

"We'll inform . . . our friends at the Section, certainly. In proper voices of respect," O'Brien said with a smile.

"Everything has turned out satisfactorily," Craypool agreed, nodding his fishlike head, his cheeks sunk in, his eyes large and colorless.

"We've got a couple of things to do now. Clean up California, interview the retired agent, try to get a line on what Macklin knows and where she's put her information. There have got to be tapes, transcripts, something. I put my money on the Jewboy . . . what's his name, Levy Solomon. She didn't take them back to Chicago with her—"

"What then?"

"We let things happen the way they're supposed to happen," O'Brien said smiling. "We let things take their course. We let Teresa Kolaki go back where she belongs, we go back to our old relationship with Krueger."

"The Macklin woman?"

"Let that smart-ass broad look out for herself. Her boy-friend gave Gleason three thousand dollars in dental work,

199

she's fucked us around. If the Opposition is still on her case, fine. If she wants to recall what Teresa Kolaki told her from memory, fine. It's bullshit anyway without tapes, without Teresa Kolaki. No one is going to touch it except the *National Examiner* or something. Rita Macklin is finished as far as I'm concerned. I got the boy I wanted. I got his ass."

"What about Morgan?"

"If he's so goddam jumpy right now, let him come home for a little while. Send him the message; tell him there's a circus we want him to go to. In Chicago. Tell him we'll even buy the ticket so he can watch the last act go off."

Craypool managed a watery sort of smile. "He'd like that. Be in on it. I mean, buttoning it all up."

"Yeah," O'Brien said. "Yeah, and he deserves it. He's done the job for us."

28
Washington, D.C.

An hour later, as the first of the snow began falling over the capital, a message came over the safe phone, and for a long moment Hanley held the receiver in his hand after the connection was broken. A phone call. The bastards didn't even come to tell him in person.

Hanley put down the receiver at last and then picked it up again. This time, he punched an unfamiliar number, one he had written down when Rita Macklin called him from California. Damn it, he thought. He had put his neck out for Devereaux, for the woman. And they had just chopped it off and now there was blood all over everything.

He didn't owe her this.

"Yes?" A male voice. A thick accent.

Hanley said her name. It was stupid, all of it had been wasted. Hanley realized his hand was shaking.

Rita's voice on the line.

"What is it?"

"Devereaux," he said, using the real name; it didn't matter anymore.

Rita could hear the trembling in Hanley's voice. It was going to be as bad as she had dreamed. It was going to be that bad awake. Rita Macklin stood in a dark hall in a dark apartment in Chicago, in a flat full of religious icons and photographs. Teresa Kolaki's refuge, her immigrant kin. And now the horror of waiting was going to be over and the horror of action was going to begin.

"The Opposition finally caught up with him. In Zurich."

"God damn it," she said. Three distinct words, harsh and flat.

"They dumped their bodies in the Zurichsee. According to our . . . source. There's been a sudden thaw in Switzerland, the lake ice is breaking up."

"Damn," she said, softly.

"Both of them," Hanley said. "You have to tell Teresa Kolaki."

"Yes."

"It's over. You realize that?"

"Yes."

"When . . . when you come back—I mean, when you come back to Washington—I can . . ." He hesitated; why was he saying this to her? For his sake? He saw Devereaux in his mind's eye, sitting across from him that night in New York long ago, at a table outside the hotel, on the sidewalk, drinking vodka, explaining about the mission in Teheran. Before he met this woman.

"I can watch you," Hanley said. "For a while. I don't know if they're satisfied. The Opposition, I mean. With one death. I mean, they weren't interested in you except you led to him."

"I suppose," Rita Macklin said. The softness had become dulled.

"Teresa has no protection," he said. "It was an NSA operation. You understand? He was wrong. NSA had it buttoned from the beginning. Everything he thought about it was wrong."

"Wrong?"

"It was legitimate," Hanley said. "I shouldn't even tell you this. But it was legitimate. A nice deep probe. And he screwed it up."

"I don't believe that," she said. Just as flatly, without tone or color to her voice. "But it doesn't matter, does it? I mean, what happens now doesn't matter."

"No," Hanley agreed.

The worst thing had already happened. Devereaux was dead.

29 ___
Zurich

Felix Krueger walked up the damp sidewalk, brushing against the college kids marching down toward the old city on the east side of the Limmat, for a night of drinking. Children, he smiled. He was a benign man, at peace with the small world he inhabited.

The streets were clear and shining in the darkness, full of traffic, headlights glittering, stars above the mountains of the city in the clear, cold night. The fog was lifting, it would be clean winter again. Trams ground up the hill surely and slowly, as Krueger walked up the hill just as surely and inevitably.

"*Guten Tag*," said a man who had not been there a moment before but who was now walking beside him.

Felix Krueger turned, his hands in coat pocket, his large head protected from the cold by a black beret. He smiled in friendly puzzlement. Many greeted him in his native city; people knew him because he had spent his life here. He could not possibly know them all, or their faces.

But he was certain he had never seen this man before.

"Good evening, sir," he replied in simple German, uninflected, off guard, a German that called up the faces on the frescoes of Bavarian beer halls, all glowing and overfed and laughing.

"I have come to audit the books, Herr Krueger," the man said, the German uninflected.

Almost said pleasantly.

"Do I know you, sir?" Felix Krueger said. He stopped on the slanting walkway and turned to the other man.

"No. But I'm the auditor."

"Are you English?"

"No. Would you prefer to speak in English?"

"I can speak in many languages. It is—" He smiled broadly but too quickly. "It is the necessary gift of the Swiss to know many languages well."

"Good," said the American in his native tongue. "I put off seeing you for a long time."

"Should I know you? Or who sent you?" Still a bit of a smile at the corner of his lips. He had felt so pleasant in the sudden thaw of the past two days. He had just eaten that night in the Kronenhalle on Ramistrasse, near the opera. The taste of sausages lingered on his breath with the smell of beer.

"Yes. You should. But we have not met before."

The smile faded, slowly, to nothing. The evening was becoming colder, the brief thaw was chilling. Rivulets of sweat coated Krueger's back beneath his heavy brown overcoat.

"Are we talking in riddles?" Felix Krueger said, annoyed, his voice rumbling slowly.

"No. It's time to speak plainly," Devereaux said. "I met a man named Morgan."

Felix Krueger waited.

"And a man named Rimsky," Devereaux said.

"And who are you? Who are these men you talk to me of?" His syntax was suddenly shaky. He felt his hand tremble.

"People who know you," Devereaux said.

"And you are an agent?"

"Perhaps."

"What is 'perhaps'?"

"It means I may be what you think. Or I may not be."

"Do you have an identity?"

Devereaux smiled. "Let's go to your house, it's just up the street. We can talk inside."

"I prefer not to talk to you. I might call a policeman."

"No."

"What do you mean? This is my city."

"And this is my gun."

Felix Krueger clearly saw the pistol, clipped to the other's belt, when Devereaux opened his coat.

"You understand?"

"Yes," Felix Krueger said.

"Let's go in. By the back door, I think."

The two men entered the house as cautiously as burglars. The housekeeper was gone for the night. Felix Krueger, a man of solitary ways and solitary pleasures, kept a lonely house because he preferred it.

He led the other man to the library. The room, like the dining room opposite, was octagonal. The walls were stacked with shelves and thousands of books in several languages. An immense fireplace held a flickering wood fire. Krueger opened the glass screen and placed a new log on the fire. The birch crackled in the flames, filling the room with wavering light.

"The housekeeper always leaves me a fire before she goes," Felix Krueger said. His eyes were wide with a child's delight. He stared at the flames, saw stories in them. "I like a fire at night, especially a wet night," he said. And he turned to the American.

"Would you like a drink? Schnapps?"

"Vodka."

"Of course." He smiled again. Why wouldn't this other man smile at all? "Only the Russians like schnapps." His little joke but the other man waited for the glass of vodka.

Krueger made the drinks, passed one over, led him to chairs set before a chessboard. A game was in progress. Krueger played with a man who lived in Bern and called him nearly every night with his next move.

"So, mister. Why have you come?"

"I came to audit the books," Devereaux said.

"You are not serious, are you?"

"We pay you," Devereaux said.

"We? I work for myself. I am paid commissions."

"Fees for people. Rather, for slaves."

"I do not believe in slavery," Krueger said stiffly. "You are in my house and you insult me."

"You are a slavemaster. You buy human beings and you sell them. How many times do you sell them?"

"What?"

"You buy them from the Soviets. You sell them their freedom. You collect from the Soviets, you collect from the slaves. Then you sell the slaves again. This time to Uncle. But is that the last time you squeeze a profit out of them?"

Said so reasonably. Said almost gently.

"What are you talking about?"

"The Zurich Numbers. Morgan told me that. At the end. At the end, he told me everything. About you and about Rimsky."

"What do you—"

"Morgan is dead. Rimsky is dead. Do you want to be alive?"

"You cannot threaten me."

"I did. Now. Tell me about the Zurich Numbers and tell me how far they go. And tell me what happened to Stefan Kolaki. You know, don't you?"

"I know nothing, I—"

"Tell me." Gently. Insistently. The voice of a lover. "Tell me."

How frightened he was. In his city. In his own house. In this library with the familiar books waiting for him like old, welcoming friends. Before the fire, sitting in this chair, listening to the stories of the crackling logs.

"I know nothing."

"Where do you keep the books?"

Krueger got up suddenly, with a little angry burst, and went to the wall. He pulled down a red leather book, similar to the other red leather books on the same shelf. He turned, smiling viciously for the first time.

"You are an auditor? An accountant? Then audit my books, friend without a name. Here. Here is the information you want. Here, take it, it won't bite you. Open it up and see all of Felix Krueger's secrets and then tell me what you will do with them."

Devereaux stood up slowly, walked across the room, took the red book. He glanced at Krueger a moment before he opened it. In the light of the fire, he turned to the first page. He thought: *I am born.*

Numbers.

Endless numbers. Some in rows, some in columns. Columns from the top of the page to the bottom. No signs of currency, no dollar symbol or pound symbol. Just numbers.

Numbers that stood for names, lives, terms of slavery, terms of bondage, whatever terms were set. Set by this man. By the Soviets. By American agencies.

The numbers ran into each other without spacing. No lines underscored any numbers. No totals were final. Some numbers were clearly symbols for units of money. Others might be for names, for years to be spent in bondage.

In the end, Morgan had told him they were called Numbers because that is all they were; that's what the network was called within NSA. Morgan had not been afraid, not at first. He had been as brave as his masters would have expected him to be. Morgan had endured a great deal before he spoke of the Zurich Numbers.

Devereaux turned the pages slowly. What could he do to Krueger? Kill him? Threaten him with pain? There was plenty of that. Morgan only understood pain, even as Devereaux would only have understood pain.

He glanced at Krueger. He would tell him so much and it might be all there was. Or there might be more. He had to be certain. He did not want Krueger to lie to him. And Krueger might lie if it was only pain.

Devereaux tore the first page from the book.

Felix Krueger stared at him, transfixed by horror.

Devereaux crumpled the page in his hand. The paper was expensive, thick and stiff under his touch. He threw the crumpled ball into the fire.

The flames leaped to the paper like devils greeting one of their own. Devereaux stared at the paper as it turned black beneath the flames, as parts of it broke off and floated up the chimney flue, light as angels.

He glanced at Krueger.

"Mein Gott in Himmel," Krueger said slowly.

"Yes," Devereaux said and tore a second page along the binding. Again he crumpled the paper. Again he flung it into the fire. Another rush of flames, a burst of light.

Krueger stood on unsteady legs. "That is valuable only to me. What do you do to me?" The accent had thickened, the syntax collapsed under the weight of stress.

"When it's done, it won't be valuable to anyone," Devereaux said and tore a third page quickly.

"No." Krueger charged blindly, his fists doubled, throwing his large body against Devereaux. The American took the weight of the charge, turned his body into it, felt a fist against his face. He pushed Krueger over, slamming his bulk against the bookcase, sending him crashing to the carpet. A splash of blood appeared on Krueger's forehead.

For a moment, the two men were fixed in a tableau be-

fore the footlights of the flames. Then Devereaux dropped the
torn page into the fire.

Tears welled in Felix Krueger's eyes.

"What do you want?" he said. A child's tearful question.

"Information." Softly again but without gentleness now.
"I want to know everything."

"I cannot. It is everything I—"

"It is nothing now," Devereaux said and tore a fourth
page from the red book.

"*Bitte,*" Krueger pleaded, stretching out his hand.

"No. No tears, Herr Krueger, no pleas for mercy. They
mean nothing. No more than Teresa Kolaki's tears would
move you."

"I meant her no harm."

"No, perhaps not. But she is harmed. And Mary Krakowski."

"It was an accident. The child. It was a stupid accident, and everything that has happened happened because of
that—"

"Act of fate."

"Yes. Stupid and senseless. *Mein Gott.*"

"Tell me," Devereaux said.

"I meant them no harm."

"The gentle master. You only took away their years,
their loved ones, gave them dreams that weren't going to
come true."

"Not all," Krueger said.

Silence. Then, "Tell me."

"Who are you? I must know this."

"The auditor," Devereaux said.

"If you destroy all those books, you harm your own side.
Where does the accounting for one side end and another side
begin? Tell me that." Krueger rose, slowly and painfully,
from the carpet.

"There are no more sides," Devereaux said.

"Is this true?"

"Yes. Now. Tonight. The sides are down."

Krueger stared at him a moment, turned, walked to the window, looked down on the darkened street. A man in an absurd homburg waited on the walk across the way. A stupid hat, a stupid senseless accident in Vienna and . . .

He stared at the glass, stared at the clear night in Zurich, nestled in the ring of mountains that stretched all the way to Italy and France.

"The Zurich Numbers," he began as flatly as though he were reciting a poem again as a child. "The Numbers are the people inside who wish to be outside. I am the guarantor. I am neutral. I am a functionary, an insurance broker. I am the honest dealer. After they serve their old masters, they are free. Most of them. Some just acquire new masters."

Devereaux waited, holding the book tightly in his large fingers.

"The new masters are you. The Americans. Who use them again against the old masters. Some even serve willingly."

"And others?"

"Others must do as they are told. There are slaves in this world, yes. But you do not seem to understand that there are people who are not unwilling slaves. You do not seem to understand that. Take the dog without a leash who stays at the heel of its master. The horse who responds to the slightest touch of the reins. They are animals, they are trained to do this. And then there are people who long for the shackles, who long for the master's reins on them. Slaves. All slavery exists only because slaves permit it."

"But that's not everything."

Felix Krueger turned, a little drunk, a little insane in that moment. His head throbbed with pain. "You wish to be God? Only God can know everything."

Devereaux waited, poised as delicately as a cat on a branch, waiting, not willing to upset the prey.

"Of course they know everything."

Felix Krueger blinked. "Who knows everything?"

"The Opposition," Devereaux said.

"Is that what they are to you? The Opposition? How amusing. They send spies to your country and you turn these spies into your own agents. They steal trash and send it back and sometimes you make certain the trash is exactly what you wish to have stolen. And then, when the time comes, when the slave is let out of his slavery, you lock the manacle on him again. You, Mr. American. You do this. And you come to me, Felix Krueger, and you ask me: How can I use this slave again inside? How can I place my own slaves inside the enemy? You have your slaves as well, Mr. American, if you didn't know that. Criminals. Those whom you blackmail. They work for you unwillingly as Teresa Kolaki works unwillingly. All are slaves."

"We turn people and we create new slaves too."

"Yes. Let us call it what it is. A slave trade. All right. I accept this." Krueger walked around the room suddenly in a manic burst of energy. "I have numbers. Three young men from California who sold computer secrets to the Soviets. Arrested and tried and convicted. And after the horrors of life in prison, after only one year, they are willing to risk everything to be spies for your side as well. And I am the guarantor. I give them a written guarantee. I am the honest broker. Are you going to reveal this? To whom? This is for the good of your country."

Devereaux studied the large man for a moment and then put the book down, carefully, on the mantel. He had been telling the truth. All of it.

Felix stopped and stared at him. "Now, who are you?"

"It doesn't matter," Devereaux said. "What matters is the child."

"Stefan Kolaki? One child balanced against all of this?" Felix Krueger shook his head. "I am amazed."

"Where is he?"

"Look at me. What is dirty in this business is you and people like you, not me. It is Morgan and Rimsky and their masters, not me. I am Swiss. I choose to be a free man, not a slave. Let others do as they wish. I have nothing to be

210

ashamed of. I give you honest counting, each side. In the Middle Ages the Jews were despised because they were money lenders, but why did they lend money at all? Because they were needed, because even men in Christendom needed a loan broker and because the Christians were forbidden to practice usury."

"This is not usury. This is slavery."

"You, Mr. American. Do you act for your own sake? Do you do as your own will commands or as others command?"

"I make the choice."

"No. You are not free, I can see it in your eyes. You are nothing more than Teresa Kolaki with a different name. You have something to lose too, eh? You have a hostage, eh?"

Devereaux did not speak for a moment because his voice could not be trusted. He saw Rita Macklin clearly in his mind's eye and the words of Felix Krueger seemed to frame her.

Krueger grinned. "I am right, American."

"Perhaps," Devereaux said. "Perhaps the reason I ask you about Stefan Kolaki is that our plans have changed."

"I know nothing of your schemes. Cross and double-cross each other, that is not my concern."

"It is now," Devereaux said. "You told me nearly everything. Except about Stefan. Perhaps you don't know, perhaps you are forbidden to tell me. In that case, it isn't everything. So I'm going to end your life." Gently, almost sadly.

"You are insane."

Devereaux removed the pistol as effortlessly as a man glancing at his watch, one fluid movement of his wrist.

Felix Krueger took a step back. He held out his hands. "They need Teresa back in Poland, they won't harm her. They need her to keep the arrangements going—"

"To recruit more numbers for your red accounting books," Devereaux said.

"Some of the numbers belong to your side."

"And you sell them, don't you? Our side? You sell them to the Soviets after a while."

211

Krueger's eyes widened in horror. It was the last answer, Devereaux thought. Krueger sold out both sides, again and again, until the slave had no more use to anyone. The honest broker, the guarantor. The trader in human beings.

"Let me live," Krueger said.

"On my terms," Devereaux replied.

"Yes."

"Tell me about Stefan. And the Numbers, all of it."

For a minute—no less than that—neither man spoke. They both could hear the logs crackling stories. Only one man listened, though. In the end, he began his own story, above the words of the burning logs.

"He is in America," Felix Krueger said.

30 _____

Los Angeles

It was raining. Frankfurter's face was swollen so Gleason did most of the talking.

Levy Solomon sat as calmly as a plaster buddha in the only comfortable chair in the living room of his condo in the Century City complex in Beverly Hills. Gleason and Frankfurter were on the sofa, which was too soft to support their weight. Solomon smiled because he knew the sofa was too soft.

Frankfurter spread his hands in a gesture of openness so patently false that even Gleason winced, not with pain, but with embarrassment. Rain in L.A. Just their luck. Nothing was going right on this whole rotten assignment.

"We'll make it fast," Frankfurter said. There was a nasty snarl to his voice. He was tired, tired of the job, tired of chasing that fucking broad and then pulling back to clean up behind her. He'd fix Rita Macklin. Someday, somewhere, on his own time. He'd fix that little tit good.

"You're Solomon, worked in Poland, retired. You stashed Teresa Kolaki and Rita Macklin here for a few days. Now, where's the tapes?"

Levy Solomon blinked, smiled, and said, "Where's the beef?"

"Jesus Christ, you think this is a fucking joke?" Gleason said.

"You have oral surgery?" Solomon asked.

"Yeah."

"I feel for you, I really do. It's the worst."

"The guy caused it has it worse. Your buddy."

"Who's my buddy?"

"Devereaux."

"Never heard of him."

"Cut the shit. We got a plane to catch at midnight back to Chicago."

"You live in Chicago?"

"No."

"I had a brother lived there once, ran a haberdashery. On the South Side. I—"

"Cut it, will you? We're all pros."

"Is that right?" asked Levy Solomon.

"Look. What I like to do and what I'm gonna do is two different things. Personally, what I'd like to do is dangle you by your ankles out the window and maybe forget myself and let go."

"Is that right?" Levy Solomon stared at Frankfurter.

"What I'm gonna do is tell you to call your special number."

"My special number?"

"What is this guy, an echo chamber?"

"What number is that?"

Gleason spoke the number. It was right. Levy Solomon sighed, staring from face to face. "What's it about?"

213

"Devereaux is blown away by KGB. In Zurich. We want the tapes that Little Miss Reporter made with Teresa Kolaki."

"You can search the place. You got a search warrant?"

"You're tiring me out, you know that? Fuck search warrants. I can give you dozens. What I want is no more shit. I want you to call up that special number which I know that you know and I want you to talk to your main man and he's going to tell you to do just what I told you to do."

Levy Solomon shrugged. It was amusing, playing with these two. Even if they were a bit slow. He stood up. "I'll call in the other room."

He went to the kitchen, dialed the number of the house in Arlington that patched through to the special number.

Hanley said, "Hello."

"All right, it's me," Solomon said.

"Go ahead. Give it to them."

"Is he really dead?"

"Yes."

"All right."

That was all. He replaced the receiver. Too bad. He had known Devereaux in Berlin—a little business ten or twelve years before. Devereaux had been a cold fish, all right, but he knew his stuff. He had let Levy Solomon direct the operation; he had held up his end with the East Germans. Too bad.

He walked into the living room again. "Locker at the airport."

"We figured that."

"Should be five tapes. Nothing was transcribed. No time. A few documents. Teresa gave Devereaux some stuff."

"I don't know about that," Frankfurter said. "He can keep it now." He laughed.

"Give it to the fishes," Gleason said. "Dirty prick."

"Devereaux was a good man," Levy Solomon said as though he should say something like that. He didn't like these guys.

"He was a prick," Gleason snarled.

Levy studied him. "He hurt your mouth, huh?"

"Fuck you too."

"Son, it's amazing the riffraff they let in NSA these days."

"We didn't tell you we were in—"

"You didn't have to," said Solomon. "You smelled up the room the minute you walked in." He took a keychain from his pocket and walked to the wall switch and opened it with a screwdriver on the chain.

"Simple stuff," said Frankfurter.

Levy Solomon turned, gave a vague smile again. "Okay, Einstein, find it yourself."

Frankfurter pulled off the plate, turned it over, found nothing. He looked in the electrical box and found nothing.

Solomon stared at the pair of them. "I ought to make you sweat your flight some more but I can't stand to have the apartment fumigated with the stink from you guys."

Frankfurter said nothing.

Solomon took the plate and pried it apart. It was really two parts, sealed so tight that it appeared one. The key fit in a shallow hollow between the two plates. He gave it to them and turned his back to replace the wall plate. He spoke very softly.

"When I turn around I don't want to see you guys here. Or you'll both be picking teeth out of your palates."

He screwed in the wall plate, humming to himself.

When he turned, they were gone.

31____

Chicago

A reporter from the Chicago *Tribune* was told that he could not interview Wojo the Clown because the star of the Warsaw Circus was a bit ill and needed rest for the performance that night. In fact, Wojo was blind drunk.

In two days, they would all return to Poland.

The circus cars were on a siding in northwest suburban Rosemont, near O'Hare International. The railroad siding was next to the Rosemont Horizon, a stadium that attracted basketball games, circuses, and rock shows.

The strange little European circus had not been as successful as the American entrepreneurs who imported it had hoped. Poland, however, had been pleased. The money for the circus had been paid at the beginning of the tour. In hard Western dollars.

"Too European" the promoters had been told after disappointing box offices in half a dozen cities across the United States.

Most disappointing of all had been Wojo, the midget clown with the largest following in Europe. Or so the Polish government had claimed. Wojo had been drunk for most of the tour, even during performances, despite the best efforts of three Polish Security Police agents to keep him sober.

The reason was simple. He had been frustrated at the beginning of the tour because of his separation from Monika, the midget woman clown who was quite beautiful and quite afraid of Wojo and who had run away from the circus in Poland before the tour began.

He had been frustrated in the last few days of the tour because of Stefan Kolaki.

Wojo wanted the boy. He wanted to dress him and pet him. He wanted to play with his mouth. To give him lipstick. To humiliate him and make him pretty.

Jan Tomczek, a member of the Polish Security Police, had decided Wojo was insane. Jan, by his own lights, was a decent man. He had reddish hair and hazel eyes and a blunt manner. The circus—the world it made on this train, in this strange country—seemed like a nightmare to him. And then two days ago he had been told of the plan to seduce Teresa Kolaki, to force her to return to Poland. He had been told by Korsoff, a Soviet agent in Chicago, and by Vishinsky, a KGB from Washington.

"Guard him well," Vishinsky had said, not understanding about Wojo.

Jan Tomczek was a part of the atheist state but a man of strong convictions, a man of innate conservatism, a man who understood the rightness of things. And what was wrong.

"The boy is a boy. A child. Regardless if you are a homosexual." So he had begun one night to explain to Wojo when the midget clown had not been drinking too heavily.

"You bet I'm a man." The voice was raspy, deep, from beneath the throat, even the diaphragm; a voice that expressed far more contempt and hatred than Jan thought could pour from such a small vessel. "More of a man than you are, you state stooge. I'm not afraid of you. I can get it up all day long if I want. You ever done that? I fucked ten women one night and one of them almost died because it was so big in her. I was too big for Monika, that's why she ran away. Made her bleed, the little cunt—"

Jan Tomczek endured this, did not speak, felt the burden of the state. In another time or place, he would gladly have killed the midget.

"He is a child," Jan Tomczek said patiently.

"He's beautiful."

The midget clown Wojo was drunk. Jan Tomczek, who had searched for bottles to smash them, could smell liquor in the small compartment in the middle of the train. Wojo's home in America.

Wojo had not shaved for two days. He had performed badly in Minneapolis, missed his stunt fall, endangered the lives of two other clowns when he playfully put too much powder in the mock explosive detonated at the climax of the midget auto race. As it was, Miki the Clown had been burned and hospitalized in Minneapolis. The circus had received bad publicity because of that. Which did not bother Wojo.

He was small, in perfect proportion, a little man with tiny, raisin eyes and brown hair and a sharp face. His parents had been normal size. He was born in a suburb of Gdansk.

His brother and sister were normal size. Only he, Wojo would think from time to time, bore the curse.

Wojo pitied himself, had done so all his life. The circus rescued him from the taunts of children, turned jeer into laughter to his profit. His success even enabled him to escape the regimentation of the state and attain a certain status; despite the conservatism of the Polish government, he could indulge an increasingly bizarre sexual appetite.

Nearly forty, a performer for twenty years, Wojo was sick of life and himself. He was consumed with the thought of sex. In his sexual encounters, there was always the matter of dominance, no matter what partner or sex, no matter what other fantasy was played out. Everyone in the circus was afraid of Wojo, and drawn to him.

Jan Tomczek locked the boy in his room on the train. It was the only way to protect him. Even Jan Tomczek could not be everywhere. A week ago, when the boy joined the circus train, reluctant and bewildered, Tomczek left him alone in the communal dining car in the middle of an afternoon. Wojo had found the boy, talked to him briefly, and then kissed him, held him, touched him. Until the child began to scream hysterically.

Tomczek had returned in time, had slapped the clown away, and the midget had refused to perform that night.

That same night, Tomczek had been warned by his superior in a message from Washington: Never touch the clown, he is important. And protect the boy.

Impossible.

The impossible was accomplished by imprisoning the child. Jan Tomczek felt miserable, felt haunted. And he felt fear for the first time in his life: the clown, Wojo, incarnated evil for him.

It was Wojo who arranged to have the child replace Miki after Minneapolis. Stefan, dressed as a bride, stood perched atop a twelve-foot wedding cake made of wooden braces and plywood sheeting painted crudely to resemble frosting.

Wojo, dressed as a groom, clambered up the tiers of the

cake—with much slipping and pratfalling—until he reached the top of the cake to embrace his "bride." They were married then by a clown at the bottom of the cake dressed as a priest. At the climax Wojo picked up the "bride" and, hidden from the audience, tumbled down a wooden slide in the cake into a pile at the bottom, falling on top of the priest and "witnesses" as the cake suddenly exploded with fireworks and roman candles.

"Where is my mother?" Stefan Kolaki had asked Jan Tomczek after he was attacked in the dining car by Wojo.

"Soon, little one," the agent said.

It was the last question Stefan would ask him. The last thing Stefan would say to him.

Afterward Stefan, mild eyes peering weakly out of his glasses, would sit in the locked compartment and stare out the window at nothing at all. He was a child and accustomed to the sudden madnesses of adults who controlled the world. Like his mother, running away to America without him. Like this grotesque clown. Like Jan, who promised him lies.

Stefan would not speak of Wojo. Would not speak of the moments when, hidden in the darkness of the wedding cake as it was wheeled to the center ring, Wojo grabbed him and held him and forced kisses on him, his foul vodka stench suffocating the boy, his arms squeezing the boy, his fingers probing the boy. Wojo had killed one of the aerialists three years ago, the circus people said. It was true that the aerialist, a woman, had spurned his sexual advances; it was true she had ridiculed the midget once in the dining tent for his sexual pretensions. It is true, further, the aerialist missed an easy turn in practice one morning, fell thirty-five feet, and broke her neck and died. All true and all proving nothing. Except the superstition of people in the circus.

Wojo contented himself with a Hungarian boy of seventeen, an apprentice in the tumbling act. The boy—who made fun of Wojo to the others but had no great moral pretense—slept with the clown for the money that Wojo gave him. It was substantial. Wojo was a rich man.

219

The circus manager once told Jan Tomczek: "The human mind is incapable of seeing beauty unless it is to destroy it." He was a middle-aged man and cynical.

A strange thing to say to a member of the Polish Security Police. But he said it about Wojo, about his lusts, his foul tongue, his rages, his abandons; Jan Tomczek understood perfectly. The midget did not love the little boy; he merely wished to destroy him.

"You are afraid of the midget," the manager had said to Jan Tomczek. "Yes. Don't lie. I know you are secret police, but it is true. The child fears Wojo; you fear him, you smell evil from him. I smell it as well. You are right. He is a devil."

"A very small devil."

"See? Everything is his size. You ridicule him. But quietly. He cannot bully you but you can still fear him. He knows he is a freak, always has known it. He is too insignificant in his own eyes so he must be larger than life. For good, for evil. He chose one." The manager paused. "Perhaps it chose him."

And through the nightmare days and nightmare nights, the child named Stefan Kolaki, hostage on a circus train in a strange land, slept alone, locked in a train compartment so that demons would not destroy him.

32

Zurich

Devereaux slipped into the car and turned to Denisov behind the wheel.

"Can you find the airport?"

"Is it over?"

"Yes."

"What are you going to do?"

"I don't know."

"You are dead. To KGB, even to your own people."

"Yes."

"You have money. Why are you going back?"

"I didn't say I was. It doesn't concern you."

Denisov took the pistol out of his pocket and looked mildly at the American agent. "You see, it does. I was going to finish you."

Devereaux said nothing. He stared straight ahead through the windshield at the silent length of street. Below, Zurich was beginning a night on the town.

"The message you sent to NSA in Morgan's code. It will be picked up by KGB; they will write your name off the books. And mine. I don't need American protection anymore."

"Fine. I didn't ask you to go with me."

"You are going back."

"I didn't say that."

"If you are dead, I am revenged. If you are dead, there is no possibility that my file will be reopened. By anyone. No more visits from Washington every six weeks."

Devereaux smiled in the thin light of the street lamps that illuminated the interior of the car. "Was that prison so hard?"

"No. It was not Lubyanka. But it was a prison."

"Well, I won't tell anyone. If you don't."

"What about my revenge?"

Devereaux turned and stared at the Russian for a long moment.

"Don't talk me to death," Devereaux said.

"The man. Krueger. You took care of him?"

"Why do you want to know?"

"Killing isn't very much." Denisov spoke softly. "Two men killed today. Maybe three. It could have been me in the zoo. It could have been you."

"It wasn't. Do you suppose we have a divine purpose?"

"Why do you mock God?"

"Why do you even ask?"

221

Silence again.

"The airport," Devereaux said.

"I thought and thought about you. About this child, this Stefan Kolaki. You don't even know him, have never seen him. I think I understand you. I had your file in Moscow once. All of it. When you were a child, you were taken from your mother and put in a house with your aunt. Is this true?"

Devereaux said nothing.

"Very touching," Denisov said.

"Yes, isn't it?" Devereaux turned. "I'm going to the airport. Now. Or you're going to shoot me."

"An ironic place," Denisov continued.

"What?"

"I thought about Zurich. Did you know Lenin lived here before the revolution? He plotted in the cafés here. The social revolution came from Zurich. And it is such a city of capital. That is ironic, isn't it?"

Devereaux said nothing.

"You and me. Twenty years from Asia and we are both dead men now."

"No. We died a long time ago," Devereaux said.

"Yes. So it won't matter too much. To you. What I do now."

Devereaux thought about it. In a voice of exquisite weariness he agreed it probably didn't matter. It was all a lie.

Denisov put the black muzzle of the Walther against Devereaux's left temple. The metal felt cold.

Devereaux closed his eyes. He never heard the explosion.

33

Washington, D.C.

At that moment, Hanley stood in front of Yackley's desk. Yackley had just finished. Hanley took the pen, bent slightly at the waist, signed the resignation.

Yackley, head of R Section, a man in his late thirties, almost boyish, had been quite willing to let Hanley run operations, until yesterday.

The National Security Advisor and the Director of Central Intelligence had gotten a complete fill on R Section's abortive attempt to short-circuit a sensitive counterespionage operation conducted by the National Security Agency. The operation involved the detection of a vast espionage network in the United States run by KGB. They had heard about the illegal and dangerous use of an agent of the old KGB who had been held in California. They had been informed about the assaulting of NSA officers by a dangerous R Section agent code-named November.

Hanley accepted responsibility for botching the operation. He knew that NSA had told only a small part of the truth of the matter, but Hanley couldn't prove them liars.

So Hanley was being forced to resign, and R Section was in extreme danger of fulfilling O'Brien's promise to make it "a paper agency with paper networks and paper armies." NSA, in a bureaucratic sweep, was about to swallow R Section whole in the next federal budget.

And Hanley had let it happen.

"I never wanted to hurt the Section," he said after putting his name on the line.

Yackley almost felt sorry for him. "Yes. But you did. You and November."

"Well, he's paid for it, hasn't he?"

"I suppose. He didn't have to take the risk. And using that Russian defector—Hanley, what were you thinking of?"

Yes, Hanley thought. What was he thinking of? He had let the agent control him instead of the other way around. He had believed Devereaux. Perhaps Devereaux had believed himself, right up to the moment he was dispatched, dropped like a parcel in the icy waters of the lake in Switzerland.

He walked out of the office, still in a daze. Fired. The place looked different to him. He blinked and realized he was in something like a state of shock. This could not be happening. But it was.

➤　➤　➤

WHEN RITA MACKLIN left Teresa Kolaki in Chicago, she had felt she was running away. But Teresa, bitter and harsh, had made it plain that Rita was not welcome. Not in her brother-in-law's home, not with her anymore.

Rita had argued with Teresa, fighting off her own grief, not quite believing she could still care about anything else. She had fought ever since the telephone call from Hanley. There had to be a way, there still had to be a way.

But there was no way to resist anymore. They both knew it. Only Teresa had admitted it.

"He told me he could do this thing. He lied to me. I'm not sorry he's dead. I don't care about him, about you. Both of you used me, used my son."

Words as bitter as poison, spit out one by one, made to cause pain. For Rita, for herself.

And Rita had finally left a few hours after the call from Hanley, after the second call from Levy Solomon that even the tapes were gone.

The plane dipped now, preparing for the descent to National Airport. It was just after midnight, the last plane of the day.

Rita Macklin stared at the clouds. The moon was full, the clouds were ghostly meadows and mountain peaks under the light of the moon. They extended all the way from Chicago.

She closed her eyes now as she felt the plane fall down through the clouds.

Rita Macklin had not felt tears. She had felt rage, an unspeakable frustration, a sudden rush of emptiness inside her that scraped her like a knife. Everything had been lost. Most of all, he was lost.

She tried, with her eyes closed, to remember him that last time, in Levy Solomon's apartment in Los Angeles; to remember him watching her open her blouse, remember his touch on her, remember the smell of him, his weight on her, the way he felt inside her. She would remember little bits of it—she almost felt she could smell him next to her—but it was too incomplete. And in a while she would remember less and less. As she remembered so little of her dead brother, or of her father. At least she had photographs of them.

When she opened her eyes, the plane was on its final approach. She wished it would crash. Pain, death.

The wheels struck the ground, bounced, the brakes screeched, the flaps caught the wind and held it. The plane slowed, taxied to the terminal.

In a moment, like a sleepwalker, she was outside, automatically going through motions she was not aware of. She hailed a cab, gave her address on Old Georgetown Road, and sank into the backseat.

Teresa Kolaki had shown her a photograph of her child, Stefan. Teresa had talked about her husband and about life in Poland. In three days she told Rita everything. And now she was going back.

Everything was starting over, as though Devereaux had never existed. It had only been a week; it seemed like years had passed from the moment those two men surprised her in her apartment.

She entered the apartment still sleepwalking, threw her

bag on the chair, shrugged out of her coat, and walked into the bedroom. She fell on the bed without undressing.

Once, in the middle of a night of dreams in which Devereaux was alternately alive and dead, floating face down in a lake, she woke enough to roll into a blanket. She was cold. She had cried during the nightmares, called out, sweated her clothing damp. But she was too tired to get up, to change, even to crawl under the covers. Grief had finally, mercifully, drugged her.

So much so that she did not hear the phone ringing at first. Then she thought it was part of a dream. Then she opened her eyes. It was morning and the phone did not stop ringing. She lay in bed, waiting for it to stop. It kept ringing. "Godammit," she said. She got up, staggered, lurched into the living room.

She picked up the phone and didn't speak.

"I have to see you." It was Hanley.

34

Chicago

"Ladiessssss and gentlemen! And childrennnnn of all ages!"

The spotlights played on the man in black tie and tails who waved a top hat in his left hand and held the microphone next to his lips with his right hand.

His accent was pure American, bred for television; he had been hired for the circus tour to give attendance a boost and reduce the "foreignness" of the show. In fact, he seemed the most exotic thing about it.

"Now, for your pleasure, an aerial act of prestidigious proportions, the death-defyingggggg Grabonow-skissssssssssss!"

Floor spots were extinguished. Ceiling spots suddenly revealed two empty trapezes while another spot followed two sequined figures in tights scrambling up a twisting rope ladder. At the top platform, one reached for the empty trapeze, pulled it, leaped forward, and grasped the bar, followed by the other. They sailed across the roof of Rosemont Horizon from trapeze to trapeze, dancing on air, while a small band below played a frantic melody of impending danger.

Cymbals and drums and roars of the crowd.

A too-small crowd for the matinee. Clusters of schoolchildren, sectioned off by ushers and teachers; families with children, children's coats, children's caps, gloves held and gloves about to be lost, popcorn kernels over everything; and, strangely, groups of adults sitting alone or in pairs, come to see the circus not for the sake of any children but for their own childlike selves.

Alexander Vishinsky stood at the gate closest to the north entrance of the auditorium. He put the pocket field glasses to his eyes, scanned the crowd. He was—if anyone asked him, if anyone detained him—a correspondent for Tass. He had come to write a story about the triumphal tour of the Warsaw Circus, which served to further cement the friendship of the Polish government and the United States.

At the far end of the east boxes, Mikhail Korsoff, without benefit of field glasses, saw her first.

As instructed, Teresa Kolaki sat alone in a section of empty seats. If she had not appeared alone, the child would not have been permitted to perform. They had contacted her, quite openly, by telephone after Rita Macklin was seen to leave the Kolaki apartment.

She looked frail, Mikhail Korsoff thought. And very young. He felt uncomfortable about the business, about the interference from Washington in the form of Vishinsky, about being chided for his "failures" in not finding November right away.

An hour before, Vishinsky had actually smiled at Korsoff. "Good news for you, comrade. November is killed. In Zurich. You are off the hook."

Patronizing bastard. Yet Korsoff would not feel comfortable until the woman and the child were on the special plane back to Poland and Vishinsky was back in Washington where he belonged.

Vishinsky had instructed her carefully. Come alone. The child will be shown to you. And when the performance is over, you will go to O'Hare International, Terminal C, and wait. You will then be given fresh instructions. No, the child will not be harmed. Yes, you will have him returned when you are safely on the plane.

But, she almost sobbed, why can I trust you?

Because, Vishinsky replied coldly, you have absolutely no other choice.

So she had come as instructed.

"A mother's love," Vishinsky said softly to himself as he spotted her through the pocket field glasses. Alone and no one around her.

➤　➤　➤

STEFAN, HUMILIATED, BLUSHING BENEATH THE MAKEUP, stumbled toward the giant wooden cake near the entrance to the arena floor. He wore the white wedding dress and veil and his glasses had been taken from him. He could not see very well without them.

He knew that Wojo was already in the cake, waiting for him. The routine was simple. When the lights went out, the cake was pushed on a wheeled cart to the center ring and Stefan climbed a ladder inside to the opening at the top tier. He would stand on top of the cake while Wojo came out the door of the bottom tier, comically climbed to the top tiers, and "married" the boy before a clown priest on the arena floor.

Inside the wooden cake, during those few minutes, Jan Tomczek could not protect him.

It was always horrible. Brief seconds in the darkness, with the stench of the midget overwhelming the closed space. He had wanted to speak of it to Jan Tomczek, but Jan lied to him as all of them lied to him. He would never see his mother again; this nightmare would go on and on.

"If you tell anyone, if you tell that goon from the secret police, I'll cut your little cock off, right there, and you'll be a real little girl for the rest of your life, you understand me?" And Wojo, his breath reeking of the smell of fierce liquor, his reddened eyes wide and mad with a kind of lust, would grab him in the darkness as the clowns wheeled the cake to center ring. Only a matter of seconds to be endured.

"It will be all right. In a little while." It was Jan Tomczek talking to him as he tottered toward the cake. Liar.

The hidden door opened.

He heard the hoarse whisper from the darkness like the voice of the devil: "Come on, my precious baby, follow me. Follow me—"

Jan touched the boy's hand. He turned, looked at the man. Jan had pain in his eyes. There was nothing to be done.

"Little one."

Into the darkness. He felt the hands touch him. He pushed away. He could smell the animal presence of the other, crouched in the hiding place.

"Little one," rasped Wojo. Stefan closed his eyes.

➤   ➤   ➤

A BLUE, UNIFORMED USHER crossed the empty section and bent over and whispered to the woman sitting alone. Teresa looked up, turned chalk white, nodded, and got up.

Vishinsky saw this through the field glasses.

What was happening?

A sudden panic clutched his throat. He glanced at Mikhail at the other end of the arena, but Mikhail had his eyes on the wedding cake being wheeled to the center ring.

Vishinsky looked back to see Teresa disappearing through an exit ramp.

What was happening?

Vishinsky shoved the glasses into his coat pocket and ran down the concrete steps to the concourse behind the stands.

The concourse was filled with circus workers preparing to peddle their souvenirs and drinks and sandwiches during the intermission scheduled after the clown wedding sequence.

She was supposed to wait for it. To see Stefan. What had impelled her to leave?

Alexander Vishinsky ran along the concourse, slipping past the workers crowding the aisle. From the auditorium, the band struck up strains of Lohengrin's "Wedding March." In a moment the lights would go on and Stefan Kolaki, dressed as a bride, would be perched atop the smallest tier of the cake.

Something was going wrong.

Vishinsky reached in his pocket for the pistol, drew it out.

The backup instruction: in the event that all blandishments fail, if she refuses to return despite your efforts, kill her. Simply and directly. The order could not have been more specific.

It was the final option. Not that Vishinsky had suspected it would come to this. It would be an admission of failure.

He reached the end of the corridor. Mikhail was running down the steps and nearly bumped into him.

"Where has she gone? Where?"

Mikhail Korsoff was frightened: "I noticed she was gone, I—"

"You've lost her!"

Mikhail shrank in horror. This too would be his fault then.

"There!" he cried. It was her, in dress and coat and scarf, walking quickly on high heels toward the exit door.

"She's gone mad," Vishinsky shouted in Russian. He was going to be ruined because of this; this was not his fault.

Both men ran along the concrete corridor, away from the main concourse, toward a side exit door.

That is when Mikhail saw the pistol.

"We are not going to kill her," he said.

"Yes. That is what I will do," Vishinsky said.

"Teresa!" Mikhail cried.

Mikhail reached her first, pulled her around, tore the scarf from her head.

Vishinsky stopped, pistol drawn, stared.

Rita Macklin.

"What the fuck is going on?"

In that second, Vishinsky turned, saw the policeman pounding down the concrete walk toward them.

The policeman reached for his holster as Vishinsky fired. The force of the impact knocked the policeman backward. He hit the cement block wall, smeared it with blood, slid to the floor.

Vishinsky turned, squeezing the trigger already.

Rita Macklin smiled at him. Bitch.

The bullet broke Vishinsky's spine. His skull shattered when he hit the cement—a doctor at the Cook County Morgue later marveled that someone with such a fragile skull had survived without injury for so many years. The pistol clattered from his hand.

Mikhail Korsoff stood frozen, without a pistol, waiting for the next shot.

Denisov stepped from the alcove that led to the men's room. He smiled and shrugged. "I'm sorry, comrade." It was an apology, Mikhail understood that, the apology of the executioner in medieval times. Denisov turned the pistol toward him and fired directly into Mikhail Korsoff's face.

"Now, Miss Macklin," Denisov said slowly.

She stood very still.

He took her arm. "We will leave them."

➤   ➤   ➤

"I LOVE YOUR PRETTY LIPS," the midget crooned, touching them. The boy reached for the ladder. He felt he might scream. He had screamed the first night but no one heard him except the clown wheeling the cake to center ring.

The midget kissed the child in the darkness; his fingers probed Stefan's body beneath the layers of wedding dress.

God, Stefan prayed, kill me. Let me die now, this moment. Hot tears stained his powdered cheeks. He reached for the ladder, through the opening, reached for the floor of the top tier. Wojo's hands lingered on him from below. Escape.

He clambered to his feet, stood braced with one hand against the wedding canopy support. In a second, the lights flicked on, hot and bright. They always blinded him. He stood perfectly still, blinking, staring straight ahead.

At the bottom of the cake, the little door opened and Wojo tumbled out. Children laughed.

Stefan blinked, felt the tears on his face, wiped at them. He heard the laughter. He hated the laughter, he hated Jan Tomczek, he hated the clowns, all of them so afraid. He hated his mother, who had left him to this terrible end.

Stefan was twelve feet off the ground. The platform was narrow. Wojo would roughhouse at times, push the child until he thought he would fall. But Wojo would grab him at the last moment and that was part of the act, part of what made the children laugh, even as he screamed. Above the roar of laughter, they could not hear his screams.

Wojo was beside him now, pushing him playfully. This time, Stefan let go because he wanted to fall. Perhaps he would die then. Perhaps they would let him go back to the asylum. Perhaps—

"Oh, nononono, little one," Wojo cackled and grabbed him with strong arms and drew him back.

Stefan felt dizzy from the lights, the insane laughter, the loud, booming music of the "Wedding March" dressed up in a jazz tempo. He wanted to fall, to die, and he could not.

Mother, he thought in that moment. *I don't hate you. You would not permit this. You don't know.*

The preacher was blessing them, Wojo was doing a mock exaggerated bow. Wojo pushed him again, the slide appeared magically, and they tumbled down it, one atop the other, landing in a pile at the bottom while the cake suddenly exploded with roman candles and pops of firecrackers and brightly colored puffs of smoke.

Applause rolled over them from the stands and then Wojo jumped up to take a bow and another pratfall.

Stefan ran, half blind in the lights and smoke, for the exit to the work tunnel off the main arena floor. Wojo did a mock bow, kicked the preacher in the pants. The applause and laughter did not stop.

Inside the work ramp. Safe for another few hours. But where was Jan? There. Leaning against the wall. He ran up to retrieve his glasses.

Jan stared at him. His eyes were wide, his face puffed. His tongue was protruding from his lips. His face was red and his lips were blue. Dead.

Now Stefan screamed.

A hand reached for him. A man in a black coat with strong hands tore him away from Jan Tomczek's propped body. He was pushed toward the ramp leading to the work tunnel. "Who are you? Who are—"

Suddenly, behind them, the midget screamed in Polish. "What the hell is going on?"

The man who held Stefan's arm turned. Wojo ran up to him. The stranger pushed him, almost lightly, casually, away. The clown slammed against a cement block wall, fell down, got up, cursed, produced the knife.

"Don't," said the stranger. Once, distinctly.

Wojo smiled, his rotted teeth glistening under the yellowish lights in the entry tunnel. Frightened. They were all frightened. Terrified of this demon. This man saw the devil in Wojo.

The midget rushed forward with the knife, screaming in Polish, "Mine. My property, she is mine—"

The tall man stepped aside and simply tripped the clown. He fell gracefully, a pratfall really.

Except the knife was wrong. The knife was not supposed to be there. It slid into his chest just beneath the throat, chipping the sternum, pushing through all the way, out his back, and Wojo lay dying, cursing.

The stranger stepped over his body.

Wojo cried then, a deep wailing cry from a pit beneath the surface of the earth, a primal cry of rage and terror and hatred that echoed back and forth down the cement block walls, amplified, distorted. Stefan heard, turned back once, and saw the blood-soaked floor and the midget clown thrashing out the remains of his life, trying to pull the knife from his chest.

Through the crowds, through the aerialists, through the high-wire performers, past the cages full of beasts, roaring and pacing behind their bars, a great cat reaching at them, not touching them.

No one moved toward them. The others fell away from them.

Stefan felt the nightmare was ending, that perhaps he was dead. Or dying. That he was going to float away in a moment like gossamer on the breath of a spring morning.

They reached the door to the parking lot that led to the train on the siding. Stefan looked up once at the wintry-faced man who held him. The stranger shoved open the door, held it, pointed with his free hand.

Stefan saw a black car in the parking lot, the motor running, plumes of exhaust blowing up from the tail pipe into the cold, bright air of winter afternoon.

The boy hesitated. He could not see clearly without his glasses. He saw the outline of someone beckoning to him. He stood, unsure. The stranger glanced down at him and nodded and pointed again.

"Stop the kid, stop that fucking kid!"

Two men, pistols drawn, running through the obstacle course of people crowding the work tunnel, past the caged beasts, running at them.

The stranger shoved him then. Stefan stumbled outside. It was cold, so cold the air numbed him almost at once. He shivered.

The stranger slammed shut the exit door behind him.

"Stefan!"

234

It was her voice, distorted by memories, nightmares. From far away—

He blinked, felt tears again.

"Stefan!"

And the vague figure by the car was a woman, holding out her arms.

The nightmare broke like glass shattered by stone.

"Mother!"

He ran, tripping on the absurd white dress, veil torn from his head by the wind, hair blowing wildly. "Mother!"

➤   ➤   ➤

"SHOOT! SHOOT THE SON OF A BITCH! Shoot him, he's got the kid!"

Gleason raised his piece but the man at the door fired first. In the half-light of the work tunnel, they could barely see him in outline at the door. But they both saw the flash of gunfire.

Gleason felt his side burn. He took another step, then sank to one knee. He groaned, reached for his side, felt the warm wetness of blood.

Frankfurter fired, the shot slamming into the steel door, embedded in the insulation.

Both men fired a second time. Gleason lay prone on the floor.

Frankfurter hit the door of the electrical closet between him and the shooter at the door. He shouted, "Federal officers, throw it down!"

The man at the door, without any cover, took a step to the side as though to better see Frankfurter. He raised his piece slowly.

Thinks this is a fucking contest, fucking asshole, Frankfurter thought and fired twice.

The first bullet went wide; the second hit him in the right arm, below the elbow, bit off a chunk of flesh and sinew, and kept on into the cement block wall behind.

Then Frankfurter saw him clearly.

"Son of a bitch, son of a fucking bitch!" he shouted and fired again.

The man at the door fired, the bullet chipping at the wall. Then he turned, pushed open the door, and slammed it shut.

"Jesus, help me!"

Gleason was moaning. Frankfurter ran out of his hiding spot and knelt beside the wounded man. "Gleason, Gleason, you know who that was?"

But Gleason had passed out.

"Son of a bitch," Frankfurter said, thinking that the assignment was all fucked now, that it was going to be blamed on them, that—

"Freeze! Freeze right there!"

Frankfurter turned, frowning, thinking of something else, intending to say, very annoyed, "I'm a fucking federal officer."

Instead, as he turned, the two Rosemont policemen who had a total of seven months' experience between them saw only the gun. Had seen only horror of dead bodies in the past two minutes, including the body of a fellow officer. And here was a man with a pistol, turning it toward them, the man who had killed these people.

That was what they would explain later. The policemen, Officers Daggart and Rourke, were exonerated at the hearing that followed. For firing simultaneously, in error, at a federal officer with the National Security Agency named Leo Frankfurter. The first bullet split Frankfurter's nose, the second severed the carotid artery in his neck. He was dead as he fell on Gleason's unconscious body.

236

35 _____
Washington, D.C.

Summary transcript of meeting of the National Security
Council, briefing 35/FY1985. To be filed at Archive 13, avail-
able only to Ultra clearance personnel (Secty. rank) and
downhold until AD2090.

National Security Advisor: Zurich Numbers was an
espionage network operated by KGB in cooperation with
Warsaw Pact government, principally Poland, German Dem-
ocratic Republic, and People's Republic of Czechoslovakia.
Twelve hundred fifty-six persons were processed into the network in the United States and six NATO countries over
the past ten years. Principal work at the time the network
was destroyed consisted of penetrating Operation Crypto, a
research project for development of a new computer-based
coding program usable by the armed services until the
twenty-first century.

R Section has provided a complete scenario of the penetration of the Numbers network by personnel from Section
G (counterespionage) within Department 21 of NSA. The
penetration was directed by C. J. O'Brien, assisted by H. L.
Craypool. Penetration involved the appearance of a counterespionage system to misdirect information gathered by the
agents of KGB in the United States.

R Section was subverted in its efforts to obtain information on the Numbers network by agents of Section G, Department 21. See attached statements 1, 2, 3, and 21 by NSA,
R Section, the FBI.

See attached statements 4, 5, 6, 13, and 20 by special
agents, FBI, assigned to surveillance of Soviet Embassy headquarters. See attached statements 7, 8, 9, 10 as well as attach-

ments thereto, authorization of wiretap surveillance. See statement 11, summary explanation of NON repeat NON authorized wiretap surveillance of subject, Rita C. Macklin, journalist (see Dossier 1183/2/FY 81, R Section).

See attached statements 12 through 19, particularly summary by C. L. Hanley, chief of operations, R Section.

Recommendations:

1. Deny budget year requests for FY 86 from Section G, Department 21, NSA. Recommend disciplinary action (Label E) on control personnel in G, 21, NSA. Resignation of GS-16 O'Brien is to be accepted, with prejudice. Results to be turned over to the Attorney General for further action. (Action, for the sake of security, is not recommended.)

2. Commendation medal (authorization AA-21/FY 85/12) for C. L. Hanley, chief of operations, R Section; posthumous to special agent P. X. Devereaux (authorization AA-21/FY 85/13).

3. Authorize (DD-879/FY85/475, Special Order 23) appropriation (contingency 39) to R Section ($2.1 million) for further investigation of Numbers network, rehabilitation, recompensation, and damages for those coerced, threatened, or otherwise injured by actions of agency Section G, 21, NSA, in UNLAWFUL repeat UNLAWFUL pursuit of NSA objective (Ultra Code 2154).

4. Authorize (DD-879/FY85/476) compensation ($413,-498.21) to R. C. Macklin, journalist, in exchange for completion of Form 21.44 DD/R.

5. It is affirmed (sworn) that principles embodied in amendments 1,3 14, 15, Constitution, will be enforced vigorously by intelligence agencies operating on the soil of the United States.

➤   ➤   ➤

"WHAT IT MEANS," Hanley said to Mrs. Neumann as they sat in the little bar and grill on Fourteenth Street over a cheeseburger lunch that had spilled into late afternoon, "is that we won't do it again."

"Won't we?" she said, toasting him with her own glass.

"No. At least . . ." He paused, considered the clear liquid. "At least I don't think so."

"Poor Hanley," she said.

"At least I have a job again," he said.

"Poor Devereaux," she said.

"Well." He tasted the liquid. He was quite drunk. The first time in years. "We must expect some casualties when we fight the good fight." And he winked at her.

36 _

Spiez

The man who did not exist trudged along the icy side street until he reached the corner of the alley that led to the back of the apartment building. The building was set in the side of a hill that tumbled down the streets and meadows, all the way to the frozen shore of the Thunersee.

Spiez rested in the cup of a mountain, surrounded by a brother range of mountains brooding white and snowy silent along the stillness of the shoreline. The only sound was the clanging of bells tied to the necks of winter sheep still on the village commons, feeding themselves fat for slaughter in the spring. Soundless otherwise and frozen. Brilliant cold in a brilliant sun resting on bright snow. It was windless at noon. They might have all been at the edge of the earth.

He turned the key in the unneeded lock—this was Switzerland, safe and secure—and opened the door. He clumped up the carpeted stairs, leaving a trail of snowy prints. He turned the key in a second lock on a second door and opened it.

The window opposite the door was large and opened on the mountains.

This was a safe house, Hanley had said, selected by a custodian long ago in R Section on behalf of some forgotten assignment, kept by the Section simply because no one in auditing thought to question the small expense of keeping it and because the custodian who had selected it had gone on to acquire cars with puncture-proof tires and built-in dashboard computer files and machine guns that telescoped into the lining of ordinary briefcases and the other magic things that dazzled the masters of the Section.

Devereaux put down the string bag filled with groceries. He had carried them, on foot, from the market on the main street of the village. There was a car, of course, provided by the European desk of the Section, fitted with Swiss plates of the canton of Bern, marked with the CH international symbol of Switzerland, built with care and caution by a custom-work factory in Lille, France.

But Devereaux preferred to walk down the sloping streets of the hillside town to the center of the village. Preferred to breathe the cold air, to walk in the brilliant sunshine of midday, the only time when the sun poked down shadowless into the hollow of the mountains.

The first night, Rita Macklin, lying naked next to him, had asked:

"Why did you want me to do it?"

"Because you would."

"You're so sure of me."

"Yes."

"Should I be sure of you?"

"Dead men tell no lies," he had said.

"Booga-booga. I don't believe in ghosts."

"Fortunately, no one else does either."

"Hanley knows you're not dead."

"That's one."

"And Denisov."

"My brother."

"Why didn't he kill you?"

"Because I told him about the Zurich Numbers."

"I don't understand."

"Felix Krueger. He's still in business. Under altered circumstances. He has a partner. A nice fat Russian named Denisov. Who is getting fatter all the time, eating the food in Lyon. The Franco-Russian connection. He lives in California, travels to France every month. They should be happy together."

"More of the slave trade."

"No," Devereaux said softly. "Felix Krueger has renounced his former life. He has repented and prayed to God and reformed. No."

"Then what?"

"Espionage, I think. I don't want to know really. Secrets from Silicon Valley, I expect. Denisov is a charming fellow."

"That's not all there is to it."

Silence.

"No. It's more than that," Rita pushed him.

"More? Yes." He paused, stared past her. "Denisov pitied me. I hated that but I let him pity me. He caught me unaware. I never expected him to kill me."

"He would have."

"No. I'm not sure of that. When you play chess, sometimes you know that the other player can't bear to lose his queen. That knowledge can make you tempt him, fool him. Denisov is lost in the world. He needed to know I wasn't dead. Not yet. But I suppose I had to give him some way to save face. So I gave him Felix Krueger. Krueger sells the secrets that we invent for him. Odd computers that are going to work only for our advantage. So Hanley tells me."

"And I'm just a nice little semi-rich free-lance writer. I knew the Irish always get jobs for their relatives but I never knew that included their girlfriends."

"Everyone has died, Rita. You and me. This is heaven."

"I didn't know heaven had mountains."

"Let me lick your nipples."

He tasted her. She held him and there was no tension in

him anymore. He did not awake to dreams anymore. He was well and truly dead.

They felt so curiously free they did not understand the feeling between them. Except that it was fragile; they walked carefully around it.

She was waiting for him now.

"I've got groceries."

"Good. Look at the lake. I see cracks in the ice from here."

"Spring is coming," he said. He slipped his arm around her. "Cracks are everywhere."

"You're insatiable," she said.

"I don't want you to regret living with an older man."

Standing against the window, he pressed against her, lifted her cotton skirt, touched her between her legs. "Naked again," he said. "You might have some shame."

She opened her legs and he slipped into her. Dressed. Pressed against each other.

"Can anyone see us?" she said.

"No."

"Damn," she said.

37____
Chicago

Melvina caught cold in January. Peter cared for her, worried about her, made soup for her. Peter, she thought, was a fussbudget.

"I told you I have cancer. I'm hardly going to die of a cold."

But she insisted on returning to the house on Ellis Avenue in any case. On dying in her own old bed if it came to it.

Monsignor O'Neill gave her the last sacraments twice. She enjoyed the attention.

As she had predicted, she did not die. And one afternoon, in the grayness of a dark January day, she came downstairs.

Peter had accumulated her mail on a sideboard near the front door. She thought there was an awful lot of it. She picked at the mail like a shopper, considering this and rejecting that.

A letter from Florence Callaghan took her interest. She opened it, read it twice. An indomitable old lady was Florence, surrounded by family who scuffed shoes impatiently in her imperious presence and grumbled about her longevity. Florence said in the letter she was as mean as Melvina and intended to die only after Melvina showed the way.

Melvina smiled, put the letter down, decided she would reread it later.

Then she saw the package.

It annoyed her.

She picked it up, shook it, realized she had not ordered anything. It was from Field's. She'd send it back.

But she opened it. And then it was no good. Her eyes swelled with tears, so sudden and unexpected that she forgot to be stern with herself for crying.

She hadn't cried like this since she got the letter from a Mr. Hanley at something called the Government Research Bureau of the Department of Agriculture. A letter regretting to inform her that her great-nephew had died in service of his country. And enclosed for her a medal, awarded posthumously.

She let the tears fall and she let her thin, old body shake with sobs for a moment because no one was in the house and no one would see her weakness.

She opened the box because she knew what it was, who it was from. Blue stationery with her name on it. And matching blue envelopes.